"I'm your surveillance, Cassie."

Disbelief clouded Cassie's expression. "You've got to be kidding… Chief Bradley assigned *you?*"

"Yep."

Her eyes narrowed. "And if I say no?"

"Doesn't matter."

"But I don't want you," she snapped.

"Too bad, baby. You've got me."

Dear Reader,

Happy New Year! Silhouette Intimate Moments is starting the year off with a bang—not to mention six great books. Why not begin with the latest of THE PROTECTORS, Beverly Barton's miniseries about men no woman can resist? In *Murdock's Last Stand,* a well-muscled mercenary meets his match in a woman who suddenly has him thinking of forever.

Alicia Scott returns with *Marrying Mike... Again,* an intense reunion story featuring a couple who are both police officers with old hurts to heal before their happy ending. Try Terese Ramin's *A Drive-By Wedding* when you're in the mood for suspense, an undercover agent hero, an irresistible child and a carjacked heroine who ends up glad to go along for the ride. Already known for her compelling storytelling abilities, Eileen Wilks lives up to her reputation with *Midnight Promises,* a marriage-of-convenience story unlike any other you've ever read. Virginia Kantra brings you the next of the irresistible MacNeills in *The Comeback of Con MacNeill,* and Kate Stevenson returns after a long time away, with *Witness... and Wife?*

All six books live up to Intimate Moments' reputation for excitement and passion mixed together in just the right proportions, so I hope you enjoy them all.

Yours,

Leslie J. Wainger
Executive Senior Editor

Please address questions and book requests to:
Silhouette Reader Service
U.S.: 3010 Walden Ave., P.O. Box 1325, Buffalo, NY 14269
Canadian: P.O. Box 609, Fort Erie, Ont. L2A 5X3

WITNESS... AND WIFE?

KATE STEVENSON

Published by Silhouette Books
America's Publisher of Contemporary Romance

In memory of my father, Aleck Fine
1916-1995

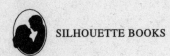

SILHOUETTE BOOKS

ISBN 0-373-07984-2

WITNESS... AND WIFE?

Copyright © 2000 by Kathleen F. Williams

This edition published by arrangement with Harlequin Books S.A.

Visit us at www.romance.net

Printed in U.S.A.

Books by Kate Stevenson

Silhouette Intimate Moments

A Piece of Tomorrow #576
Witness... and Wife? #984

KATE STEVENSON

After more then twenty years in Colorado, author Kate Stevenson considers herself a "near native." Drawing on her knowledge of people and the Rocky Mountain Front Range, she writes stories about strong, risk-taking heroes and heroines who struggle to build lasting relationships in today's challenging world.

Now that her children are grown, Kate spends her time writing and teaching. She shares her home, at the base of the Rocky Mountains, with her husband and their cat, Spike.

Kate always enjoys hearing from her readers, who can write her at P.O. Box 20271, Boulder, CO 80308-3271.

IT'S OUR 20th ANNIVERSARY!
We'll be celebrating all year, starting with these fabulous titles, on sale in January 2000.

Special Edition

#1297 Matt Caldwell: Texas Tycoon
Diana Palmer

#1298 Their Little Princess
Susan Mallery

#1299 The Baby Legacy
Pamela Toth

#1300 Summer Hawk
Peggy Webb

#1301 Daddy by Surprise
Pat Warren

#1302 Lonesome No More
Jean Brashear

Intimate Moments

#979 Murdock's Last Stand
Beverly Barton

#980 Marrying Mike... Again
Alicia Scott

#981 A Drive-By Wedding
Terese Ramin

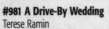

#982 Midnight Promises
Eileen Wilks

#983 The Comeback of Con MacNeill
Virginia Kantra

#984 Witness... and Wife?
Kate Stevenson

Romance

#1420 The Baby Bequest
Susan Meier

#1421 With a Little T.L.C.
Teresa Southwick

#1422 The Sheik's Solution
Barbara McMahon

#1423 Annie and the Prince
Elizabeth Harbison

#1424 A Babe in the Woods
Cara Colter

#1425 Prim, Proper... Pregnant
Alice Sharpe

Desire

#1267 Her Forever Man
Leanne Banks

#1268 The Pregnant Princess
Anne Marie Winston

#1269 Dr. Mommy
Elizabeth Bevarly

#1270 Hard Lovin' Man
Peggy Moreland

#1271 The Cowboy Takes a Bride
Cathleen Galitz

#1272 Skyler Hawk: Lone Brave
Sheri WhiteFeather

Prologue

Cassie Bowers hated being late, even a little. Even when it wasn't her fault.

With an impatient gesture, she shoved back the hood of her khaki raincoat and hurried away from the security checkpoint at the Boulder Justice Center. Water dripped from the hem of her coat, leaving a trail of moisture in her wake, and her shoes made a squishing sound against the marble floor. Without slowing, she nudged aside her wet sleeve and checked the time—6:05. She quickened her pace and angled left into a dimly lit hall.

From behind the closed door of one of the offices she passed, a phone rang unanswered. Except for Cassie and the guard who'd let her through security, the Justice Center seemed empty.

Of course, she knew that wasn't true. Besides the night cleaning crew, at least one other person was here late—Judge Thomas Wainright, the man who'd left the message on her home answering machine. The only man capable of pulling her away from her snug house on a soggy evening after a day of running down leads.

A gust of wind rattled windows high on the wall across from Wainright's office, and as Cassie rapped on the door the lights flickered.

When no one responded to her knock, she tried the knob. The door swung open to reveal a small, shadowed anteroom. In the feeble light cast by the only window, the room's furnishings appeared indistinct and vaguely threatening. Along one wall, file cabinets stood sentry duty, while a secretary's desk in the center of the room guarded the entrance to the judge's chambers.

"Judge Wainright?" Cassie stepped forward, her soggy shoes sinking deep into plush carpet.

"Judge Wainright?"

Behind her the latch clicked softly into place.

"Judge Wainright, it's Cassie Bowers."

Rain splattered against the window like the echo of distant enemy fire. A shiver ran up Cassie's back.

Where is he?

Crossing to the desk, she switched on the brass lamp and examined the appointment book that lay in the pool of light at its base. Strange. Her name wasn't there. Flipping the page, she checked on the next day's calendar. Not there, either.

Puzzled, she glanced toward the judge's chambers. The door stood slightly ajar, but no light showed.

Mentally she reviewed bits of the message she'd heard on her answering machine when she'd returned from Denver. *...something odd... Meet me at six. I'll explain then.*

If it weren't for the note of urgency underlying the words, she'd have postponed their meeting till morning in spite of her curiosity. Instead, she'd thrown her coat back on and raced across town—to find him gone.

Unless he'd just stepped out for a bit.

She hesitated an instant, then shrugged out of her coat,

depositing it across the top of a wing-backed chair. Since she was already here, she would give him the benefit of the doubt. Plopping onto the chair, she crossed one leg over the other and ran her fingers through her damp curls in a hopeless attempt to make herself look presentable. Water trickled down her neck.

A sigh of exasperation escaped from her lips. She hated delays. When she'd taken the job on the *Denver Tattler* a year ago, she'd thought her days of hurry-up-and-wait were at an end. With a weekly publication, she'd believed she could pick and choose her times. Yet, here she was—cold, wet…and waiting. Only one step removed from her years on the local daily newspaper.

Impatience wriggled inside her, betrayed by the soundless tapping of her fingers against the upholstered armrest. Shifting her weight, she tried to calm her irritation by envisioning the public's reaction to the articles taking shape on her computer. Local drug traffic. Money laundering. White-collar crime. The series was certain to stir up a furor, establishing her once and for all as a top-notch investigative reporter. A reporter even Pop would approve of.

Her meetings with Judge Thomas Wainright were going to be instrumental to her success. In today's world, nearly anyone could write a decent piece on drugs. But not everyone had access to Wainright. One of the best-known judges in the state, he was celebrated for hard-nosed justice when dealing with the drug cases that passed through his courtroom.

And he never gave personal interviews.

Cassie, however, held a trump card. Wainright and Pop had sat on the bench together, and even better, they'd remained friends after her father had retired to teach law.

She'd been certain Wainright would assist her in her mission. Though she'd seen him only occasionally in recent years, she still recalled his visits to the family home in Denver. His imposing figure, the air of reserved authority that clung to him, as well as her father's obvious respect for the man's integrity, had all combined to make an indelible impression on her young mind. Wainright was one of the few men Pop truly admired, and given half a chance, he'd expound for hours on some of the judge's more famous cases. "Mark my word," Pop would say. "Some day you'll see Wainright on the Supreme Court."

A crack of thunder split the muffling quiet. At almost the same instant the room brightened with a flash of lightning. Startled from her musings, Cassie checked her watch.

6:15.

In spite of her determination to be patient, she frowned. Where was he? She was positive she hadn't garbled the message, yet it wasn't like Wainright to overlook an appointment, and she'd only been five minutes late.

Maybe she'd misread his tone, mistaken distraction for urgency. Or he could have hoped to fit her in before another meeting, then decided not to wait when she didn't show. After all, he couldn't be sure she'd received his message in time to come.

A glance at the window told her nothing had changed outside. Rain buffeted the building, rippling the clear glass like a fun-house mirror. Unwilling to brave the weather again so soon, she decided to give him more time. Half an hour. If he hadn't come by then, she'd leave a note and call in the morning.

Shadows crept across the carpet until she was finally on the outer fringe of lamplight, the darkness pressing at her back. The air in the room grew heavy and oppressive, a result of excessive humidity, she felt sure. But knowing the cause didn't calm the jittery feeling in her stomach nor make breathing any easier. When she felt an eternity had passed she tilted her wrist.

6:20.

Maybe she should find the guard and ask for help locating the judge. She rose from the chair, then hesitated. What if Wainright showed up while she was gone?

A barely audible scraping sound, like the whisper of cord across metal, emanated from the room on the other side of the desk.

Cassie froze, hairs rising on the nape of her neck. When the sound failed to repeat itself, she let out the stale air locked in her lungs. She paced to the window and peered into the dreary landscape, feeling more sympathetic toward Noah than she ever had during years of Sunday school.

Air shifted against her back. Her heart thudded.

Get a grip, woman! Next, you'll be seeing ghosts.

She smiled nervously. Cassie Bowers *never* let her imagination run away with her. She was too sensible, too down-to-earth. Why, if a ghost had dared rear its head, she would have laughed it back into the grave.

Although she'd checked her watch mere moments ago, she looked again... 6:22. She pressed her lips together and decided her nerves couldn't take eight more minutes.

Her mind made up, she crossed to the desk, intent on scribbling a quick note. Something halted her hand as she reached for the notepad next to the lamp.

A soft, nearly inaudible sound.

A moan?

She held her breath and waited for the sound to repeat itself. It didn't. Narrowing her gaze, she stared at the slit of black that outlined the unsecured door to the judge's chambers.

No way could he be here. All the lights had been turned out, and she'd called loud enough to wake the dead.

Dead?

A sudden vision of the man, lying ill or injured, floated through her mind. She took a hesitant step toward the door. "Judge Wainright?"

With the flat of her hand, she pushed at the unresisting barrier. It swung noiselessly inward. In spite of the prickling along her scalp, she took another step and ran her fingers along the wall in search of a light switch.

A movement within the darkened room caught her attention, drying her mouth and making her pulse flutter.

"Judge Wainright?"

Even as she spoke, she suspected it wasn't the judge. The shape that detached itself from the murky shadows wasn't tall or solid enough.

Unnerved by the apparition's failure to respond, she widened her eyes, trying to adjust her vision to the deep gloom, and groped once more for the elusive light switch.

The figure seemed to sense her purpose. With lightning speed, it leaped forward. In the dim light something glinted in its upraised hand.

Cassie's heart thudded wildly.

Disbelief cramped her stomach.

Fumbling, she found the switch as something crashed against her skull.

Bright light exploded.

The room went dark.

Chapter 1

Straining to open her eyes, Cassie fought the darkness that pressed in from all sides, ominous and threatening like the murky depths of a midnight ocean. An undertow caught her, dragging her deeper and deeper into the abyss. Desperately she snatched at handholds to slow her descent.

Her clutching fingers came up empty. The current grabbed her, sent her tumbling and spinning farther and farther from the surface. A scream welled up inside her. She was trapped. Prisoner in a surreal world of turbulent water and inky despair.

Minutes…hours…went by while she struggled, driven as much by fear of the unknown as by instinct to survive. Seaweed tangled around her legs. Her movements grew sluggish. Warmth drained from her body, like blood from an open wound.

A traitorous voice urged surrender, told her she couldn't win. She refused to listen. Ignoring her aching chest, her cold-numbed limbs, she gathered herself for one final assault.

She called on her last bit of willpower and launched herself.

Forward.

Upward.

Toward freedom.

For long moments she floated, pulling great gulps of air into her burning lungs as the nightmare receded. Gradually her breathing steadied and the world stopped spinning. The gentle rocking of waves solidified into a hard, lumpy surface that poked uncomfortably into her backside. She opened her eyes. Beneath her head, the pillow was damp. A sheet twisted around her legs.

Sounds, muffled and distant, grazed her ears. A low hum. A faint rattle. Her muddled brain registered the whisper of rubber-soled shoes brushing against tile. An antiseptic smell hung in the air.

Groggily she peered around, straining to make sense of the dim shapes. Metal bars hemmed the bed. The outline of a nightstand. And on the other side of the room, the edge of a darkened doorway.

A hospital? What was she doing in a hospital? Alarm spasmed through her.

"Awake?" a voice whispered.

The single word perforated the quiet of the room. Her heart lurched. She jerked toward the source and instantly regretted the movement. Pain stabbed behind her eyes, setting off a jackhammer in her skull. Muscles screamed in protest.

She gasped. What on Earth was the matter with her?

"Take it slow, slugger."

Slugger? No one called her slugger anymore. The only ones who used the nickname she'd earned at age eight were her brothers and...Luke.

No, it couldn't be him.

The metallic taste of despair coated her throat, overriding the throbbing in her head. She closed her eyes in denial, remembering the last time she'd lain in a hospital bed, the last time she'd heard the same gravel-edged voice utter the silly nickname.

The last time.

Or was the last time now?

Her stomach knotted and she clenched a fist against it in an attempt to ward off a rising tide of nausea. Surely she hadn't just...

Fragmented scenes flashed across her mind—bits and pieces of her life that assured her she hadn't imagined the passage of time. Her queasiness eased.

A nightmare, then.

She frowned, wincing as skin tightened over bone.

No nightmare. She felt too awful to be dreaming. Taking care to make no more sudden moves, she shifted her head and peered into the shadows, hoping she was wrong about the speaker's identity.

"Can you stand a little light?"

No. She didn't want to see, didn't want to know who was there. Before she could protest she heard a click, and white pricked the darkness, illuminating the figure next to the bed. She squeezed her eyes shut as her suspicion was confirmed.

It was Luke.

A rush of longing, more potent than anything she'd allowed herself to feel in ages, clogged her throat. What was he doing here? No one had told her he'd returned to Colorado. But then, why should they? No one knew it mattered. No one—not even her family—knew what it had cost her to offer her ex-husband his freedom and then watch him walk out of her life. Without a single protest.

A familiar, aching hollow opened inside her, an emptiness more draining than whatever had landed her in this bed. Wearily she opened her eyes, knowing she had to say something. "What...happened?" Her tongue, suddenly three sizes too big for her mouth, stumbled awkwardly over the words.

"There was an accident." He lifted the water container

from the table beside the bed. "Would you like some water?"

She nodded, then regretted the movement as pain needled down her neck. What did he mean, "an accident"?

Before she could make sense of the statement, he'd slipped an arm beneath her shoulders for support and eased her higher, allowing access to the container's plastic straw. She gulped greedily, trying to ignore the pressure of firm muscles at her back and his palm warm against her arm. When he finally drew away, it was like losing him all over again. Perilously close to tears, she said the first thing that came to mind. "I thought you were in Texas."

Only when his expression tightened did she realize how accusatory she sounded. Helplessness enveloped her. Around Luke, it seemed she never said the right thing.

"I've had enough of Texas. Two years was all I could take." He shrugged, the nonchalant gesture at odds with his bleak tone. "No Rocky Mountains."

Two years? It seemed like yesterday. Through eyes barely open she studied his heavily shadowed jaw and uncompromising mouth. He hadn't changed a bit. Except that now, instead of condemnation, she sensed a flicker of concern in his eyes. Tears prickled against her lids.

Too late. An eternity too late.

Two years ago she'd needed him. Not now. She concentrated on the throbbing in her head in an attempt to blot out the pain in her heart.

It hurt so bad.

When she raised a hand to her forehead, her fingers brushed a padding of gauze. "What—"

"Leave it alone," Luke said. Laying a restraining hand on her arm, he reached across her to press the button on the bed's control panel.

Although Cassie tried to summon resentment at the authority in his tone, her senses overrode her. His touch warmed her chilled skin. His familiar scent filled her nostrils, stirring old memories, old needs, old desires.

The hall door swung open.

"You've finally decided to rejoin us, have you?" said a cheery voice. The nurse touched Cassie's wrist, checking for a pulse Cassie felt sure was elevated, then smoothed the bedclothes. "How do you feel?"

"Like I've been keelhauled."

"That's to be expected. How's the head?"

"Sore. What happened?"

"You had an accident." The nurse shot a glance at Luke. "Hasn't Detective Slater—"

Confused, Cassie saw Luke shake his head, halting the nurse midsentence. A look of consternation crossed the woman's face, but she recovered quickly. "You'll be fine," she assured Cassie with a comforting pat before leaving. "I'll let the doctor know you've regained consciousness. He'll want to see you right away."

Cassie scarcely registered the nurse's departure over the sound of blood rushing in her ears. Every instinct screamed they were hiding something—something worse than the car accident she'd imagined when Luke first spoke. But that was crazy. She wasn't pregnant. Not this time. Dizzy with tension, she fumbled for alternatives. For an instant she envisioned herself paralyzed, but a quick test of her legs beneath the covers assured her everything was in working order.

The fact that she was relatively uninjured did little to stem her rising flood of panic. She *hadn't* imagined the odd exchange between Luke and the nurse, so what else could it be?

A gruesome thought popped into her head. "Did someone die?"

Avoiding her eyes, Luke massaged the back of his neck in an all-too-familiar gesture of reluctance.

My God, that's it. I've killed someone! Her breath caught in her lungs as she waited for the answer.

"Yes."

She recoiled. Around the lump of horror forming in her throat, she managed to croak, "Who?"

Luke turned away, his voice muted. "Judge Wainright."

Judge Wainright? Why would Judge Wainright be in her car?

Cord whispered across metal.

Cassie's gaze leaped to where Luke stood at the window, pushing aside the curtains to look at the predawn sky. She stared in alarm at his slumped shoulders while faint impressions brushed her consciousness.

Rain.

Shifting shadows.

Darkness.

Abruptly, before she lost her nerve, she spoke. "I don't remember the accident. Tell me."

"No accident." Luke let the curtain fall back into place. "Murder."

Light flashed across her memory. Light and the sound of thunder.

A storm. Yes—a storm! She'd been on her way to interview Judge Wainright... She remembered rain splattering her face as she hurried from the parking lot into the building.

Into the building?

Her heart slammed against her ribs. Something about the building. She gripped the bedrail, struggling to remember.

Shifting shadows.

The taste of terror on her tongue.

A flash of light.

Her gaze leaped to the door of what she supposed was the bathroom, strangely unsettled by the darkness beyond. And like a rubber band stretched to the breaking point, the string of impressions snapped.

Shuddering, she released the railing and stared at her open hand, unsurprised to see the imprint of the metal bar on her palm. She rubbed at the ache and took a shaky breath. "It's all a blank."

Luke took forever to settle into the room's only chair, an eternity of time during which her anxiety level went up several notches. His guarded expression, when he finally raised his eyes, made her tense in anticipation.

"At approximately seven-thirty last night, a guard at the Justice Center called the police to report a homicide."

She clutched at the sheeting. "Judge Wainright?"

Luke touched her fisted hand and nodded.

"How?"

For several moments she feared he wouldn't answer. Head bent, he loosened her grasp from the sheet and, with elaborate attention, smoothed her fingers between his palms. His clumsy attempt at comfort only increased her apprehension.

"Please," she pleaded.

His hands stilled. "A blow to the head. Something heavy enough to crush his skull."

She'd thought she was prepared to hear the details. She wasn't. Her stomach plummeted as an image of Thomas Wainright's benevolent smile formed in her mind. "He called...left a message..."

Luke lifted his head, slipping into cop mode. "What about?"

"I don't know. I assumed it was something to do with the series I'm working on. He'd been helping me—"

"What's the series about?"

"Drug traffic—the new white-collar crime."

Luke frowned, but didn't comment. "Did you erase the machine?"

"There wasn't time. I jumped in the car and—" She swallowed convulsively and gripped his hand. "He wasn't there. At least, I thought—"

Something stopped her, an elusive scrap of memory that fluttered ghostlike on the edge of her consciousness.

"Tell me what you remember."

"I heard something." The tape holding the gauze in place tugged at her skin as she knit her brows, but the harder she tried to concentrate, the farther away the memory slipped.

"I can't remember."

"Take your time. It works better if you don't try to force it."

She recognized the tone. She'd heard him use it often enough on others. Accident victims and hysterical witnesses—they all responded to his quiet concern and spilled their guts. But Cassie had nothing to spill. No explanation. No insight. Nothing except a vast void.

And a lump on her head.

"We found you just inside the door to Judge Wainright's chambers, unconscious," Luke explained, his gaze fixed on her face as if hoping the telling would prompt her memory. "The attacker probably hit you with the same object he used on Wainright."

The same object? With Wainright's blood still dripping—

Cassie jerked her trapped hand free, then stiffened, tormented by fragmented images. *Shifting shadows. A flash of light. Thunder.*

"I don't remember..." she whispered, fighting against a queasy sensation in the pit of her stomach. "Anything."

If her response frustrated him, Luke was careful to hide it. His expression remained neutral as he leaned back in the chair. "Okay, Cassie. It happens sometimes. Especially with head wounds. Given time it'll come back. Meanwhile we'll see what we can get from the tape."

His composure grated on her nerves. She hated the way nothing bothered him. She'd always hated it. No matter how bad things got, Luke remained calm and unruffled. Even when...Cassie turned her face away to hide the tears that suddenly welled in her eyes.

If only her head would quit pounding. If only she could forget the past as easily as she'd forgotten last night. If only...

She'd fallen asleep. Somewhere between protest and angry silence, she'd drifted away. Luke moved to the side of the bed, noting the dark smudges beneath Cassie's eyes, the dried tear tracks on her cheek.

She whimpered and stirred restlessly. Without thinking, he brushed back the damp curls that clung to her forehead, and she stilled beneath his touch.

Vulnerable. Defenseless. And in desperate need of a champion.

Abruptly he withdrew his hand and shoved it deep into his jeans pocket. Cassie was anything but helpless, no matter how she seemed right now. He would only end up looking like a fool if he let himself believe otherwise.

Before self-pity could gain a fingerhold, he strode out of the room, nodding to the cop on guard duty outside the door. Luke had a statement, for what it was worth. There was nothing more he could do here. Only pausing long enough at the nurses' station to leave his phone number and call Cassie's father, he hurried through the empty corridors and out into the early morning.

His battered Ford sat at the far edge of the parking lot, looking like a poor relation to the half dozen or so late-model cars scattered around it. As he made his way down the aisle, the sun pushed its way above the trees, burning off the remnants of last night's storm. The world sparkled with color, crisp and sharp. Not even a hint of breeze disturbed the air. It was going to be a scorcher.

Before climbing into his vehicle, Luke followed the progress of a slow-moving car on the opposite side of the street. Bundled newspapers shot from the passenger window, thudding against concrete driveways at regular intervals. Last night's events had probably made the morning edition. Thank God, the press had agreed to withhold Cassie's name. He would have hated to see it spread across the front page, especially now, when she seemed to be the only lead.

Weariness washed over him. He was getting too old for

these all-nighters, he decided as he climbed into his car and started the engine. He felt like one of those ads that showed a plate of scrambled eggs: "This is your brain on..." Insert *lack of sleep*.

Shaking his head, Luke tried to clear his mind. Right now all he wanted was a steaming shower and a few hours' rest, but first things first. Chief Bradley expected a report. Pulling from the parking lot, Luke began reviewing the previous night's events.

Cassie was the last person he'd expected to find at the scene of a murder. When he'd returned to Colorado three weeks ago from temporary assignment with the Dallas Police Department, he'd known he stood a good chance of running into her. Boulder's size made it inevitable their paths would cross. He'd prepared for a casual encounter, not the heart-stopping experience of identifying an unconscious victim as his ex-wife. Not since his rookie days had he felt so utterly helpless. And then anger had overwhelmed him—raw, pulsing rage that made him want to smash his fist against skin and bone. Unfortunately there'd been no one to punch.

Well, he needn't worry about inappropriate reactions much longer. Bradley was certain to invoke the unwritten rule against working on an investigation that involved family. And rightly so. Luke's marriage to Cassie was history, but too many memories remained. Memories that would certainly play havoc with his objectivity.

Memories.

Like that first morning when she'd slipped through the doors of the police station. In one swift glance from across the room he'd taken in her white blouse, black skirt, pale blond hair pulled into a tight knot at her nape and had tagged her—a teenager masquerading as a grown-up.

He'd amended his assessment when she confidently approached the front desk and questioned the clerk. A woman. Small and delicate, but definitely a woman. He revised his estimate of her age upward several years. He didn't know he was staring until she scanned the room, searching for some-one. Him, he realized, when she met his curious gaze and started toward him.

A current of electricity shot through him, and hot coffee nearly overflowed his mug. At the last instant he looked down and released the lever on the coffee machine, battling a sudden case of nerves that left him feeling more like a gawky boy than a seasoned cop.

And then she was standing before him, smiling. Open and friendly, her smile was hard to resist. But Luke's fate was sealed when he gazed into her eyes.

Cassandra Bowers had eyes the color of Amazon rain for-ests.

She'd laughed when he told her that the first night they made love. "How do you know?" she asked. "Have you been there?"

"No," he replied, letting the strands of her hair run liquid through his fingers. "I've only dreamed."

"A poet," she whispered and kissed his lips with gentle urgency. "I've fallen in love with a poet."

She hadn't been entirely wrong.

Because of her, poetry had sung in his heart. He just couldn't speak the words out loud. And somehow, when trag-edy had struck, the words became lost in the cadences of sorrow.

A growl of almost physical pain reverberated in his chest. Savagely he ground the car's gears in his haste to put distance between himself and his memories.

A horn blared.

He slammed on the brakes and skidded to a halt a few inches past a stop sign as the other car crossed the intersec-tion, its driver raising his hand in a one-fingered salute.

Luke grimaced and continued down the street, ticking off the names of men who could take over the investigation. Burns, Jessup, Haggerty—all competent replacements.

Competent, but unimaginative.

They'd follow the book, track down leads and patiently wait for Cassie to regain her memory.

And not one of them would worry about what she was going through.

Just as he hadn't two years ago when they'd lost their child.

Luke pulled in at the station and turned off the ignition, trying to convince himself there was no comparison. The two situations were entirely different. He'd been going through hell himself.

Still, the fact remained—he could have done something.

Wrong, he argued, staring out the windshield. Cassie hadn't wanted his help. Hadn't wanted *him* after the baby had died. And he couldn't blame her. After all, the entire tragedy would never have played out if Luke had not authorized a high-speed police chase.

He rubbed the back of his neck to work loose a knot of tension and climbed from the car, feeling every one of his thirty-six years. Hindsight was easy. Easy and useless. He couldn't change the past, no matter how much he might wish to. And, unfortunately, there was nothing he could do about Cassie's current problems.

In an hour he'd be off the case.

Chapter 2

"I feel fine," Cassie protested.

"And you'll feel *finer* tomorrow." Dr. Denning's tone brooked no argument. "A concussion, however mild, is nothing to mess with, young lady. I wouldn't be doing my job if I let you walk out tonight. I'll stop by first thing in the morning, and if things check out, you can go home then."

"So what's to check out?" Cassie grumbled, resentful of her forced inactivity. Headache or no, it felt wrong to be lying in bed like an invalid instead of up getting things accomplished.

The doctor smiled as though he understood her impatience. "Try to get a good night's sleep," he suggested before leaving.

Sleep! Since when did people sleep in hospitals? Between the staff's poking and prodding, visits from overly cheerful volunteers and the shrill demand of the telephone, Cassie hadn't managed to nap once today. Even the painkillers she'd been given didn't make her tired.

Woozy, yes. Sleepy? No way.

Rebelliously she stared at the white tiles marching across the ceiling. If Denning wanted her to get some rest, he should send her home.

When the phone rang, she considered ignoring it. The last thing she needed was more sympathy from her family or another round with Peter Eckhart.

Peter, her boss and editor at the *Denver Tattler*, had expressed the same concerns as her father and brothers, but once satisfied Cassie was all right, he'd focused on her articles. His emotions had roller-coastered from fear she wouldn't finish on time to elation over the possibility for a dramatic conclusion to the series.

Cassie didn't blame him. He was only doing his job. But the thought of another such conversation stayed her hand. Five rings later she decided the caller wasn't giving up. With a sigh she rolled toward the metal nightstand and lifted the receiver.

"Cassandra Bowers?"

Cassie had always hated her given name, and no one used it but her father. No one, she amended, except Luke, and he only did when he wanted to get a rise out of her. The certainty that this wasn't Pop or Luke cooled her response several degrees. "Yes?"

"How's your head?"

"Okay." Her head felt like a helium-filled balloon, although she'd be darned if she'd admit it. Easing it back onto the pillow, she began a tally of tile holes.

"Such a tragic accident. A woman isn't safe anywhere these days."

The slight emphasis on the word *tragic* caught her attention, halting her tile-hole count. "Who is this?"

"Just call me a...concerned citizen."

The caller's chuckle gave Cassie the uncomfortable feeling she'd missed a joke. She shifted the phone to her other ear. Wishing she'd refused the painkiller the nurse had brought half an hour ago, she tried to focus on the raspy whisper.

"A smart girl like you should be more careful."

Why was everyone always telling her to be more careful? First her father and brothers, then Luke, now some crackpot with a frog in his throat. It wasn't as though she went looking for trouble.

"Course, some people claim there's no such thing as an accident. They talk about being stupid, sticking your nose in where it doesn't belong."

Borrowed trouble. That's what her father had once called her job, and she'd denied it, laughing. I'm only reporting trouble, not borrowing it, she'd answered. She wanted to laugh now, but instead, a chill trickled along her spine.

"Play it safe. I'd hate to see more accidents happen."

The caller's voice droned on, scraping her nerves like a nail file against sensitive fingertips.

"...to your car some morning on the turnpike or to that cute little dog..."

A noose seemed to tighten around her neck, cutting off her air. Whoever this was, he knew far too much. About her. About the assault. About her life. An inner voice urged her to slam down the phone, slice off the rambling monologue, yet some contrary part of Cassie's brain wouldn't let her.

It took Luke, who chose that instant to walk in, to end the one-sided conversation. One glimpse of her frozen expression and, without a word, he pulled the phone from her numb fingers. He listened for only a minute, then carefully returned the receiver to its cradle. For long seconds he stared at the instrument, the muscles of his jaw clenched. From the hall came a burst of laughter.

"Recognize the voice?"

Cassie shivered, recalling the hoarse whisper. Mutely she shook her head.

Luke dragged a chair to the side of the bed and straddled it. Hooking an arm over the padded vinyl back, he took her limp hand in a grasp that belied the careful control of his voice. "What did he say?"

Warmth radiated into her cold fingers, giving her courage to relate what she remembered in a matter-of-fact tone. The caller had upset her more than she cared to admit. Now, reading Luke's obvious concern, she experienced something she thought she'd long ago purged from her heart.

You're a case, nothing more, she reminded herself. But as her fear slowly ebbed, she confronted the truth. Much as she hated to admit it, Luke's presence made her feel a little safer.

"How many people did you call today?" Luke asked.

Puzzled, she met his intent gaze. "Dad and my editor. What difference—"

"The creep knows your name, knows you're here. Since the papers and TV kept quiet, someone you talked to—" For an instant his grip tightened painfully.

Cassie's sense of well-being disappeared in a wave of indignation. Pointedly she withdrew her hand from his grasp. "Now I've heard everything. Some kook calls and it's *my* fault? What about reporters, police, ambulance drivers—even the coroner's office? Anybody could have mentioned the murder, mentioned my name."

"True," he conceded with obvious reluctance. "But it's obvious that *someone*—"

"Next, you'll be saying this whole thing—" she motioned to her bandaged head, irritation smoldering "—wouldn't have happened if I hadn't been working on a series on local drug trade."

"It wouldn't have." He ignored her scowl, picked up the phone and punched in a number.

Trust Luke to be literal, she thought resentfully as he filled Chief Bradley in on her call. Following his logic, if she hadn't been working on the articles, Judge Wainright wouldn't have called and she'd never have gone to the Justice Center that night! And if Thomas Wainright hadn't been a good friend of her father's, she might never have gotten his cooperation. And if Pop had never been a judge, himself... Well, she could go on forever.

She tuned back in to Luke's fractured conversation in time to hear him deliver a curt "Yes, sir" before hanging up. His use of the phrase, more than the clipped tone, told her he wasn't pleased with whatever the chief had said, though his carefully schooled expression told her nothing.

"Bradley wants someone with you when you go home tomorrow."

"Don't be ridiculous. I can get myself home."

"Getting you home's not the problem. It's what happens after you're there."

"Are you talking surveillance?"

Luke nodded. "Routine patrol, at the least. Possible round-the-clock if he can find the manpower."

Cassie's heart sank. Even she could see the sense. She was the sole witness to a murder, living alone. But the thought of strangers invading her home, watching her every move… No. She wouldn't stand for it.

"Maybe your father or one of your brothers could stay—"

"You've got to be kidding!" She didn't dare tell him she'd already turned down the same suggestion over the phone four different times today. While she loved her family dearly, their concern was stifling. No, Pop would smother her with attention, and her three brothers—well, they still treated her like a tagalong little sister. "They'd drive me crazy in minutes."

Her face must have reflected horror because Luke suddenly grinned. "You're probably right, but—"

"I'll be okay," she insisted. "I have a phone, locks on the doors and Duffy."

"Duffy?" Luke raised a skeptical eyebrow.

Cassie's lips twitched in an effort to maintain a suitably serious expression. While she'd be the first to admit the little terrier had problems following directions, she didn't consider his behavior a laughing matter. At least not now, when she was trying to portray him as protection. "I've been taking him to obedience classes," she said primly.

"I wondered why he raised one paw when I brought out the dog food."

His comment pulled her up short. "You went into my house?"

"I had to get the tape of Wainright's message off your answering machine, and since I was there, I couldn't let Duffy starve."

He remembers where I keep the spare key.

The thought of Luke walking through the rooms they'd once shared, touching her things, absorbing the nuances of the life she'd created without him was disturbing, but she dared not examine her feelings too closely. Shutting her eyes, she concentrated on important issues. Murder. Judge Wainright. The voice on the phone. She shivered.

"No one's trying to curtail your freedom, Cassie. We only want to protect you."

Her eyes snapped open. "I know," she answered, wondering how he still had the ability to read her mind. "I just hate not having a choice."

"There's always a choice."

Cassie felt a knife edge of guilt as she remembered past choices, ones he had every right to censure her for. She darted a glance at him. His expression remained unreadable. Maybe she'd imagined the blame in his tone.

She sighed. "All right. I guess I can put up with anything for a while. I'll just have to make the best of it."

Luke lips thinned into a tight smile. "You always do."

"Don't be a damned idiot!" From behind his cluttered desk, Chief Bradley glared at Luke.

Knowing the chief of police was only venting frustration on the nearest target, Luke refused to take offense. Besides, in the last hour he'd called himself far worse. He knew how his request would be viewed. Friends would suspect him of living in the past, Cassie would accuse him of meddling, and his colleagues would say he'd taken leave of his senses.

Hell, he didn't know, himself, why he was insisting on being put back on the case, and adding surveillance to his other duties was crazy. But he had to do it. Maybe because of the mess he'd made of things two years ago. Maybe to erase his one big mistake. And maybe because he had a weakness for people in trouble. Whatever the reason, he couldn't just walk away now. He had to help her or carry the guilt for the rest of his life.

"You know the rules. No family. Period." The chief's chair squealed in protest as he leaned back, arms crossed over his massive chest.

"There's nothing on the books. I checked."

"Okay. So it's unwritten. It's still damned good policy." Bradley's scowl deepened. "Bad enough when the creeps get off on technicalities. Imagine what a good defense lawyer would do with an investigation headed by the victim's nearest and dearest."

"She's hardly nearest and dearest. It's been two years."

"Doesn't matter," Bradley grumbled. "They'd have a field day. You wouldn't be able to hear the charges over the screams of prejudice and conflict of interest."

Luke latched onto some of the infinite patience for which he was known and kept his mouth shut, aware of the chief's propensity for arguing both sides of the issue without anyone else's help.

"Crackpot lawyers," Bradley muttered. "Whadda they know?" He stared glumly at Luke, who raised an eyebrow and shrugged.

Swearing, Bradley launched himself from his chair and paced across the room. "I've already had three calls from the D.A.'s office and one from Mayor Brannigan. 'Shocking state of affairs when we're not even safe in the Justice Center,' he tells me. Says to make the investigation 'top priority.'" Bradley jabbed one finger at the duty chart on the wall. "McCormack's tied up with the Swenson case, Haggerty's too green, and Jessup's already whining about not enough manpower. And the *mayor* wants top priority."

Stretching his legs before him, Luke crossed one foot over the other and studied the tips of his dusty loafers, a perfect picture of unconcern.

"Crazy bureaucrats expect miracles. How am I supposed to deliver when they cut budgets and tie my hands?"

"Sure looks as though they have you over a barrel," Luke observed.

"That's what they think." The chief swung around, eyes narrowed. "It's been two years, you say?"

Luke nodded.

"Should be long enough to put things in perspective."

"Plenty long enough."

"No regrets?"

"None."

"And you *were* first on the scene."

Luke confirmed the chief's statement with another nod.

"Then it's settled." Bradley lowered himself into his chair and shuffled the folders on the desk. "You're back on the case. Investigation and surveillance."

"Thanks."

"Just make damned sure she stays out of trouble."

"Guaranteed." Luke unfolded himself from his seat, ignoring the chief's snort of disbelief. "And if I can't, you'll be the first to know."

"She won't appreciate it, you know."

The chief's words halted Luke as he reached for the doorknob.

"She never did like you interfering. I never met anyone so headstrong—" Bradley shot him a sly look from beneath bushy brows "—except for a certain bullheaded detective."

Luke acknowledged the truth of his statement with a wry smile. He *was* bullheaded. No doubt about it. Which was exactly why he could handle Cassie. Resolutely he shut his mind to a voice that reminded him of the many occasions when he'd been less than successful handling her.

It wouldn't be easy. Nothing concerning Cassie ever was. But, by God, this time he'd make sure she was all right, no matter how furiously she resisted his efforts.

As he left the office, he thought he heard Bradley chuckle.

"So when does she get here?"

"Who?" Luke watched Cassie stretch to retrieve two ceramic mugs from her kitchen cupboard, her shorts riding high on her bottom. She had no right looking so good when she'd been released from the hospital only this morning.

"My bodyguard—protector—whatever you call her." Her bare heels plopped to the floor, and she threw him a puzzled look.

He swallowed, his mouth dry. "Oh, *her*."

A scratching sound saved him from an immediate answer. Grateful for the reprieve, Luke opened the unlocked back door and let Duffy in. Knowing from past experience it would do no good to lecture Cassie about her bad habits, he merely closed the door and threw the bolt. The terrier bounced around him, his tail wagging furiously. Luke leaned down to scratch behind the dog's ears.

"I can see he really missed me," Cassie said, arching one delicate brow.

Luke shot her a sheepish look, remembering how the puppy he'd given her for a birthday present, the same puppy whose affection she'd courted with biscuits and hugs, had always preferred Luke's company. "He just remembers I fed him last."

"Right." She poured coffee and brought it to the table. As she settled into her seat, Duffy wiggled past her and waited expectantly next to Luke's old chair. Luke reluctantly took his assigned place, wondering how long it would take for Cassie to return to her original question.

Not long.

She stirred two spoonfuls of sugar into her coffee, then looked up. "Well, when does she arrive?"

Luke met her curious gaze and decided to get it over with. "She's here."

"Where? Outside?"

"No, here."

Her mug poised halfway to her lips, Cassie glanced toward the living room, then back at Luke.

"No." He shook his head. Shifting one ankle to rest on the opposite knee, he dropped his bombshell. "She's a he. *Me.* I'm your surveillance."

Disbelief clouded Cassie's expression. "You've got to be kidding."

Luke shook his head.

"Chief Bradley assigned *you?*"

"Yep. At least, when I'm not needed on the investigation."

Her eyes narrowed. "And if I say no?"

"Doesn't matter."

"But I don't want you," she snapped, slamming down her mug for emphasis. Brown liquid sloshed onto the oak surface of the table.

"Too bad, baby. You've got me."

She glared.

Luke feigned stony indifference. This was one battle she wasn't going to win, no matter how hard she fought, because he was doing this for her own good.

Cassie was the first to look away, down at the puddle on the table. Her mouth tight, she grabbed a rag from the counter and dabbed at the mess, as though the spill was her biggest concern.

Luke knew she was using the time to regroup.

He waited while she tossed the rag into the sink. Waited while she stood with her back to him, staring out the kitchen window. And waited while she returned to her chair and studied her mug in silence.

He recognized the strategy as one of his own. Forcing the suspect to wait, stretching minutes they seemed like hours, raising the anxiety level. She was half-bad at it. Even though he was aware of what she was doing, his nerves felt like strings on a fiddle, anticipating, bow stroke.

"There's no way I can change your mind?"

"Nope."

She gritted her teeth, releasing an exasperated breath of air. "So I'm supposed to sit around all day, staring at the walls."

"No," he replied, unsuccessfully trying to suppress a grin. "Just when I'm not here. When I am, you can stare at me."

The look she threw him was murderous. "This may be funny to you, Luke Slater, but I'm dead serious. I can't stop living my life because of some nebulous threat. I have a job, a social life...."

Something twisted inside him. He'd spent the last two years censoring his thoughts about who she might be seeing, who now shared her bed. Too much of a realist to believe she'd remained alone and celibate, he still wasn't prepared to hear details. "Don't worry," he told her grimly. "I don't plan to play chaperon to you and your current boyfriend."

Indignation crossed Cassie's face. She opened her mouth to respond, but before she could speak, he cut her off. "As for your job, have you considered the possibility that Wainright's death might have something to do with what he wanted to see you about?"

"Don't be ridiculous. There could be dozens of motives for his death. Revenge, for instance. Or robbery—maybe he interrupted someone in the process of burglarizing his office."

"We checked that angle with his secretary. Nothing was taken. No files were missing. No jewelry. He still had two hundred dollars in his wallet."

"Maybe my arrival scared the robber off."

He knew from her haunted expression that she was grasp-

ing at straws. Cas...dn't want to believe Wainright's death
had anything to ...with her, but even *she* wasn't naive
enough to believ...urglar would choose the Justice Center
as a good place...pick up loot. He locked gazes with her
and let his sile...efute her reasoning.

Biting her li...he looked away, but not before he caught
the shimmer...ars in her emerald eyes. As she gazed unseeing out the window, Luke fought back an overwhelming
desire to erase the stricken look from her face. He longed to
trace the curve of her cheek and feel the velvet of her lips
turn into his palm, seeking the comfort he could offer.

He didn't dare. For her own good, she had to face facts,
had to accept reality, no matter how harsh.

Cassie took a deep breath, then slowly released it. Her
expression, when she caught his gaze, was calm.

Too late, a cold shiver of premonition shot through him.
He stiffened, primed to speak, to defuse the quiet determination he read in her eyes.

"I'm going to finish my articles."

Chapter 3

"Damn it, Cassie." The chair legs screeched on the linoleum as he leaped up. Startled, Duffy scrambled to his feet, shooting Luke an injured look. Cassie laid a soothing hand on the dog's head to assure him he wasn't the cause of the outburst, but he continued to eye Luke warily.

Luke paced across the kitchen. "Why can't you listen for once? This isn't a game. It's real life. Make the wrong move and you lose more than your two hundred dollars for not passing Go."

"I don't play games with my life."

"Could've fooled me," he muttered without looking at her.

Choking back another retort, Cassie watched him pick up the coffee carafe and refill his cup. "For your information, Thomas Wainright was a family friend. And in my book you don't just sit quietly by and let someone get away with murdering a friend."

"So you're on a crusade."

"No. Yes." She floundered, stung by his obvious disdain. "This is more than a crusade. It's..." She ducked her head, fighting resentment at his unwillingness to hear what she said.

The stutter of a lawnmower drifted from a nearby yard, accenting her discomfort.

Why did it always seem as if the two of them were speaking different languages? No matter how hard she tried to explain, he would never understand. "You can't stop me," she repeated, keeping her tone reasonable.

"Anything for a story, huh?"

"For this one, yes. Judge Wainright didn't often give interviews, but he talked to me because he thought what I was doing was necessary. Important. I owe him."

"Owe him?" Luke resettled in the seat across from her, conveying cynicism with a quirk of the lips. "Or owe yourself?"

Cassie clamped her teeth together to prevent angry words from spilling out. Why did he always attribute the worst possible motives to her? Did he really think she wanted to end up just another statistic on the police files?

She took a sip from her mug, hoping the jolt of caffeine might kick-start her brain and supply her with the way to win his cooperation. Instead, the acrid taste of cooled coffee coated her tongue and brought a grimace to her face. She shot a glance across the table. Luke's dark eyes glittered beneath lowered brows. Arms folded across his chest, he was obviously primed for a fight. Abruptly she changed tactics. "I suppose you're right. I am thinking of myself."

He showed no surprise at the admission, but a subtle softening of the lines that bracketed his mouth prompted her to plunge ahead. "If my...digging...set things in motion, then I've as good as murdered Judge Wainright myself. The only way I can think of to make up for it is to not let his death be meaningless. I have to figure out what he wanted to tell me and finish the articles.''

Luke shook his head. ''I don't buy it. Wainright made his own choices. You didn't force him. And if his death was due to information he had, you're risking *your* life trying to ferret it out.''

His cavalier disregard of her emotions, to say nothing of the ease with which he shrugged off her reasoning, blew Cassie's composure. ''Risk? With you playing bodyguard?'' she scoffed. ''The only risk I'll be taking is tripping over you.''

Luke's gaze swept over the front of her T-shirt in blatant appraisal, and despite an obvious effort to maintain a serious expression, his lips twitched with amusement. ''Well,'' he drawled, in a passable imitation of a Texas accent, ''just make sure you're facing me when you fall.''

His bantering caught her by surprise, and even knowing he wasn't serious, she couldn't stop the onslaught of tactile memories. The crispness of his chest hair grazing her swollen nipples. A tangle of legs as they sprawled across a bed, laughing. Hot kisses. Building passion.

Heat crept up her neck. If such a display weren't guaranteed to inflate his ego, she'd have covered her breasts in a virginal attempt to shield herself from his gaze. Silently she cursed her unruly senses and wished she dared kick Luke in the shins for not playing fair. Their relationship was history. Dead history. And no amount of playacting on his part could convince her otherwise.

The thought, repeating itself like a mantra, enabled her to pin him with a quelling glance that wiped the amusement from his face. ''I don't plan to take risks,'' she announced firmly. ''I'm perfectly willing to play the game your way—cautious and careful. What I'm not willing to do is run scared.''

''It's not running scared to give us time to do our job.''

"I don't have time. I have a deadline. Eckhart has guaranteed me lead-story status if I wrap everything up within the week. Waiting will only give people the chance to cover up."

"It'll give *us* a chance to solve the case without you messing things up," Luke retorted, his impatience getting the best of him.

"Me?" She turned and widened her eyes in pretended innocence. "You're forgetting who trained me. You should have more faith in the job you did."

She was playing with fire. She knew it from the familiar look of exasperation that narrowed his eyes and wrinkled his brow. Then, amazingly, his expression softened. Leaning forward, he covered her hand with his much larger one. "Let me do my job, Cassie," he said softly.

Let me protect you.

The unspoken message was so seductive, Cassie was tempted to give in and do it his way. But she couldn't. She'd battled too hard, too long, to yield now and let others dictate what was best for her.

She wasn't asking much, and she knew she wasn't being reckless. She'd agreed to delay action until he could be with her. He was just being bullheaded.

"I have to do this," she insisted. "Now, not later."

Luke jerked back his hand as though burned. "You haven't changed a bit, have you?"

Stung by the bitterness in his voice, she thrust out her chin. "Neither have you. You still issue orders and expect everyone to jump."

"Maybe if you'd jumped instead of insisting on having your own way—" He clamped his mouth shut, then catapulted from his chair, as though he couldn't bear looking at her one minute longer.

Cassie felt the blood drain from her face. She didn't need to hear the words to know what he'd almost said.

If you hadn't insisted on having your own way, Danny wouldn't have died.

Her heart twisted in agony, the same agony she'd lived with for two years: because she'd tried to have it all, do it all, their child was dead.

She would carry the guilt to her grave.

Everyone had warned her to slow down—Luke, her father and brothers, even her boss—but she'd thought she knew better than any of them. She was young and strong, a modern woman. And her doctor had backed her up, giving his approval to continue working as long as she felt like it.

Six months pregnant, she'd jumped at the chance to show them all she was capable of juggling career and motherhood as easily as any other female reporter. She begged for the assignment of interviewing a man being held at the county jail for murder. Everyone had a theory about why he'd killed his wife, then calmly turned himself in. Cassie planned to get the story from his own lips.

The meeting itself seemed to pose no risk. Held in a secured room under the watchful eyes of two guards, it had promised to be as tame as an afternoon tea. How could she have known the man would take her hostage in a desperate bid for freedom? And who could have foreseen the results of the police chase that followed, the chase ordered by Luke to rescue her?

She still had nightmares of the car careening off the highway, trees rushing at her and the bone-jarring impact. The ride to the hospital was blurred by pain, and it was only the next day, when she saw the pity on the nurse's face, that she knew for certain she'd lost her baby. She'd wanted to scream denial, but one look at Luke's stricken expression had silenced her. He was having enough difficulty dealing with the death without her falling apart.

Maybe she should have followed her first instincts and loosed her tears. At least then, Luke might have acknowledged her pain. Instead he'd acted like the loss was his alone, a grief she couldn't possibly share because she hadn't wanted to be pregnant—at least not initially.

And when his despair left no room for hers, she'd done the only thing she could—hide her sorrow and crowd the hollow in her life with activity.

In silence Cassie cleared the mugs from the table and carried them to the sink, sneaking a glance in Luke's direction. Hands thrust into jeans pockets, he stood at the kitchen door, seemingly absorbed with something in the backyard, though the rigid set of his shoulders and his widely spread legs betrayed his inner tension.

For an instant Cassie felt an urge to step close, to wrap her arms around his waist and lay her cheek against his back, to whisper she was sorry, the way she'd done in their early days together. Things had been so easy then. One simple gesture and Luke would shake off his irritation and laugh at himself. He'd gather her close and tell her he loved her just the way she was—ornery and contrary and too damned independent.

Not for long. After they'd married, he called her headstrong, foolhardy, and she'd found his attempts to protect her stifling. Maybe people were right when they said the things you loved best about a person were what chafed the most as time went by.

No, she told herself, picking up a wet sponge, their differences couldn't be settled with a simple apology.

She blotted a coffee stain from the countertop, wishing it were as easy to wipe out past mistakes. But hers had seeped into the very fiber of their marriage, like printer's ink across a sheet of newsprint.

The curtains at the open window stirred briefly, and the hot, dry air seemed to suck all moisture from her body, leaving behind an empty, brittle husk. She closed her eyes and wished Luke would leave. She had enough to deal with with-

out resurrecting the past. Things like a throbbing head and
weary muscles.

Shifting her weight from one leg to the other, she felt a
nudge against her bare calf. Even before she turned, she knew
Duffy was regarding her with a hopeful look. Grateful for
the diversion, she joined in the familiar game by cocking her
head skyward and pretending not to notice. Duffy settled
back on his haunches, pricked his ears and whined.

Though Luke turned at the sound, Cassie avoided meeting
his gaze. Focusing, instead, on playing out the ritual with the
dog, she stared at the ceiling and feigned indifference to his
whimpers. He gave a sharp bark—her signal to look aston-
ished and ask, "What's the matter, fellow?" In response, he
balanced on his hindquarters and raised his front paws, unashamedly begging.

Cassie dipped a hand into the cookie jar, all too aware that
Luke now leaned against the counter, arms crossed over his
chest, narrow hips outthrust in a flagrantly male posture.

Watching.

His pose was so achingly familiar, she hesitated, her fingers curled around a dog biscuit. Memories flooded through
her, memories of other times when he'd assumed the same
stance, following her every movement with such passion-
filled intensity, she'd grown faint with longing.

A second bark from Duffy broke the spell. Quickly she
withdrew her hand from the jar and held the biscuit a few
inches over Duffy's head. He caught it midair and settled to
the floor, crunching happily.

"I guess you can teach an old dog new tricks."

"Some old dogs," Cassie muttered, then looked up in surprise when Luke chuckled.

No one, seeing Luke at this moment, would imagine him
other than the most easygoing of men. He'd shrugged off his
anger easier than a dog shook water from wet fur, but Cassie

didn't buy it. She studied the lazy smile playing across his lips and wondered what he was up to.

"We won't solve anything by losing our tempers," Luke said as though responding to her unspoken thoughts.

Cassie stiffened. "*I* was explaining my position. *You* lost your temper."

Although a nerve twitched along his jaw—an obvious sign he wanted to throttle her—he merely shook his head in resignation. "Have it your way." He even managed a half-hearted grin as he held up his hands in exaggerated surrender. "Truce?"

She eyed him with suspicion. Luke never gave in unless he'd already come up with an alternate strategy. She wondered what new surprise he had up his sleeve.

"Hell, Cassie," he growled, his patience snapping. "I'm not the enemy."

"Trying the 'catch more flies with honey' approach?" she asked in saccharine tones.

Even before he bridged the short distance between them, she knew she'd finally pushed him too far.

"Would it do any good?"

His husky whisper raised hairs on her neck. Cursing her runaway tongue, she took a hasty step backward and ran into the counter. Her retreat cut off, she took the only available course of action—she tensed and stood her ground.

Calmly, deliberately, he moved closer. Close enough for her to feel the heat of him. Close enough to read intent in his dark eyes.

Anticipation skittered up her spine. Surely he wouldn't—

His fingers curled around her upper arms.

Sensation jolted through her, making a mockery of her efforts to remain indifferent. As her pulse leaped, she realized she'd been deluding herself. She was as susceptible to his charm as she'd been the first time they met.

Her mouth turned to parchment when he drew her to him,

but she could no more break free of the gentle pressure he exerted than stop her heart from beating. His palms cupped her face, and she shut her eyes, feeling the soft caress of his breath as he dipped his head.

An alarm sounded in her mind.

She couldn't respond to it.

Didn't want to.

The touch of his mouth, coaxing and featherlight, took her breath away, and when he brushed her lips with his moist tongue, she thought she'd melt from pleasure.

It was insanity. Sheer madness. Yet Cassie was powerless to halt the swell of emotions that blossomed within her. As she surrendered to them, inhaling his familiar, masculine scent, the long years of separation vanished as though they'd never been.

His kiss transported her back to the beginning, when their relationship was fresh and new and full of wonder. Power radiated from his lean body; tenderness, from his stroking fingers. Her pulse leaped in an erratic dance of desire.

And then his hands dropped away, releasing her. Cool air slipped between them. She opened her eyes.

Luke's face was expressionless, his gaze assessing.

"Enough honey?"

As his meaning penetrated, her stomach clenched and a bitter taste filled her mouth. It was a game to him, a cold-blooded experiment. She doused the pain in her heart with a surge of anger. Clenching her hands into fists, she opened her mouth to deliver a scathing put-down.

The phone rang.

No fighter, down for the count, could have felt more relieved than Luke did when Cassie whirled to grab the telephone. Her flashing eyes and thin-lipped glare had informed him she was furious.

Not that he blamed her. He was a fool to have pulled such a stunt, especially when he was trying to be reasonable. If she hadn't thrown his good intentions in his face, he might have been able to carry it off, but her challenge had pushed him over the edge. There was only so much a man could take before setting the record straight.

Crouching, he scratched behind Duffy's ears and tried not to eavesdrop. Unfortunately that left him replaying his colossal blunder. The instant she'd melted in his arms, he'd seen his error. Trouble was she'd felt so good, tasted so sweet he didn't care. Tearing himself away was the hardest thing he'd done in a long time.

He glanced across the kitchen, noting Cassie's still-angry posture. So much for teaching her a lesson. All he'd proved was their libidos were as healthy as ever, and he'd better make damn sure he never got that close again.

"What do you want?"

In spite of Cassie's attempt to keep her conversation private, Luke caught a sharp edge in her voice. His senses sprang to red alert.

"What things?" she snapped. Then, as though sensing Luke's interest, she lowered her voice and repeated the question in calmer tones.

Luke wasn't fooled. Her white knuckles and stiff spine betrayed her. Rising swiftly, he crossed the tiles on silent feet and peered over Cassie's shoulder, noting the caller ID display on the phone. *Out of Area.*

"I don't know what you mean," she said with a swell of bravado, "but if you're threatening me—"

Intuition told Luke the person on the other end was no ordinary crank caller; instinct warned him to tread with care. Cautiously he touched her shoulder to attract her attention. She shrugged from beneath his hand, then went rigid in response to whatever the caller was saying.

With sudden clarity Luke realized he would never win Cassie's cooperation if they continued to fight. If he didn't give in to her demands—or at least give the appearance of doing so—she was apt to bolt and ruin any chance he had of protecting her. Gritting his teeth, he resisted an urge to wrestle the phone from her grip and tell the creep what he thought of him in no uncertain terms.

Cassie slammed the receiver down so hard it rang in protest.

"What did he say?"

"He's watching," she replied without turning.

Reacting to the thread of fear weaving through her anger, Luke reached out to touch her but was deterred by her rigid stance. Frustrated, he punched in the numbers that would set in motion a trace of the call, by the phone company, when what he really wanted to do was wrap his fingers around the caller's neck.

She faced him. "It's the murderer, isn't it?"

"Possibly," Luke hedged.

"Probably," she corrected. She rubbed at her upper arms, as though warding off a chill. "He described the house. The rooms. Duffy. He said he hoped I was a good girl who kept her opinions to herself."

Though the quaver in her voice wrenched at his gut, Luke knew better than to offer assurances. "So what are you going to do about it?"

"Do? I already went back over my notes like you asked. No likely suspects. The people Wainright mentioned by name are either dead or in prison."

"You said you intended to continue digging so you could wrap up your story. Have you changed your mind?"

Indecision clouded her eyes for the merest fraction of an instant. Then, just as he expected, defiance replaced it.

"No."

It was time. Time to convince her he was on her side. Time to secure her cooperation and make sure she didn't go off half-cocked. "Okay. Where do we start?"

"We?" Her eyes widened in surprise. "But you said—"

"I've changed my mind." When her expression conveyed disbelief, he motioned toward the phone. "The caller changed my mind." Infusing his voice with what he hoped sounded like resignation, he continued. "Besides, what's the point in working at cross purposes?"

Cassie stared at him, obviously unconvinced of his sincerity, but Luke knew when to hold his tongue. Given time, she would realize that the advantages of his offer far outweighed her reservations.

After long seconds his patience was rewarded when she gave a reluctant nod. "Okay, we work together."

"Equal partners," Luke agreed with a smile.

Chapter 4

Judge Wainright's clerk, Chelsea Sparks, was every male's fantasy. Tall and willowy, with a liquid fall of hair so platinum it could only have come from a bottle, she was padded in all the right places. Indeed, her ample curves strained the limits of her smartly tailored suit in a manner that was nearly indecent.

Feeling like nothing more than a mushroom in comparison, Cassie poked at her own wild mass of permed curls and watched Chelsea's pouty Elizabeth Arden lips form into an expression of profound sorrow.

"He was the greatest boss a girl could have."

Cassie shifted uncomfortably under the syrupy flow of sentiment and wondered how long the woman had practiced the slight quaver in her voice and the sad flutter of mascaraed eyelashes. The display was so blatantly false, it curdled Cassie's stomach. How could the woman just sit there, a room away from where her boss was murdered?

Deliberately Cassie looked at the closed door, ignoring her

clenched stomach and clammy skin. Luke had expressed doubts about returning so soon to the scene of the crime, but Cassie had overridden his concern. Now, forcing herself to breathe deeply, she admitted he might have been right. Thank goodness she'd skipped breakfast.

She darted a glance at Luke, who leaned against a bank of metal file cabinets, pen and notepad in hand. He was eating up Chelsea's performance, if the silly smile on his face was any indication.

Not that Cassie minded. As far as she was concerned, Luke could play the fool over any woman he wanted. Even one so obvious as Chelsea Sparks.

A throbbing ache settled in the spot between Cassie's shoulder blades. She wished she hadn't insisted she and Luke combine their efforts. It had seemed a logical solution at the time. Luke could conduct some of the interminable interviews necessary to a murder investigation while she tried to pinpoint the reason for Judge Wainright's call and work on her articles.

Perfectly logical, mocked an inner voice, except for one small detail.

Watching Luke in action was driving her crazy. His slow smile. The lazy focus of dark eyes half-hidden behind heavy lids. His loose-jointed stance. His demeanor was so potently male it conjured up visions of sultry nights in shadowed bedrooms.

She squirmed in her seat, dismayed at the direction of her thoughts. The last thing she needed was to once again fall under the spell of raging hormones. She was far too familiar with where that could lead. With conscious effort she forced her thoughts back to what had brought her here—drugs, mayhem, murder. Not the most soothing of subjects, but definitely safer, she decided as she caught Chelsea's murmur of distress in response to something Luke had said.

"I realize this is difficult for you, Ms. Sparks," Luke commiserated.

Chelsea managed a tremulous smile that would have done credit to a vestal virgin. "I don't mind. I know you're just doing your job."

Luke nodded approval of her attitude as he thumbed open his notepad. "I'll be as brief as possible, since I see you're busy."

"Busy?" Chelsea followed his gaze to the half-filled cardboard boxes on the floor. "Oh, yes. I'm moving. But I have plenty of time to get things in order. I don't start my new job for a couple of days."

"New job?"

"Judge Kimball's clerk recently retired, and he was kind enough to offer me the position." Spurred by Luke's raised brows, she elaborated. "He and Judge Wainright worked so closely, it's rather like keeping it in the family, you know." She fingered the gold chain at her neck and sighed.

The movement drew attention to her deep cleavage, a fact Cassie concluded was not wasted on Luke, based on the pregnant silence that followed. By sheer force of will, she refrained from shooting him an exasperated glance before she steered the conversation back on course. "What was Judge Wainright like to work for?"

"Wonderful. He was positively wonderful." Chelsea appeared ready to launch into a soliloquy about her former boss, but before she could start, Luke segued to the next question.

"So you were aware the judge was working late?"

She nodded. "Yes, he had a trial starting first thing Monday morning and wanted everything ready. He often stayed late. Lots of people do here. There are fewer interruptions at night. And on Fridays almost everyone's gone by six."

"You didn't know he was expecting anyone?"

"No."

"Is that usual? I thought you kept track of his schedule."

"I do—did. Judge Wainright was a stickler for proper procedure. He insisted I record every appointment."

Luke frowned. "Yet he didn't mention a meeting with Ms. Bowers."

Annoyance painted twin creases between Chelsea's penciled brows. "If Ms. Bowers did, indeed, have an appointment..." She shot Cassie a skeptical look that indicated she wasn't entirely convinced of the veracity of Cassie's claim. "Judge Wainright was undoubtedly being considerate. He knew I was expecting my mother for dinner."

Cassie refused to take offense at the insinuation she might be lying. Chelsea was obviously miffed she hadn't been informed of all her boss's activities. To tell the truth, Judge Wainright's secretiveness puzzled Cassie as much as it did the clerk. Not for a moment did she consider it an oversight. The man was too conscientious to be forgetful.

No, he'd had some reason for not advertising the meeting. But what could it be?

Resisting the morbid lure of the closed door, Cassie glanced around the sunlit anteroom while Luke continued to question Chelsea. The room seemed no different from when she'd first interviewed Wainright. File cabinets still lined one wall, and the clerk's oak desk sat in exactly the same spot, centered on a carpet of bright crimson, guarding the entrance to the judge's chambers. Nothing to indicate a violent crime had occurred a few feet away.

"That's where they found the judge."

Chelsea's voice cut through Cassie's thoughts, making her aware the conversation had stopped. And to make matters worse, she'd been caught staring once more at the very door she'd tried to avoid.

"But then you already know that's where it happened, don't you?" Chelsea said, her tone hushed with morbid curiosity.

A lump lodged in Cassie's throat, making speech impossible. Suddenly fearful the clerk would offer to open the door, she wet her dry lips and resisted an urge to wipe her palms against her cotton skirt. She didn't want to see the room. Even if it proved to be the only way to remember what had happened, she couldn't look.

Her overactive imagination, abetted by a year on the police beat, supplied a much-too-vivid picture of what probably lay beyond the closed door. Gaping holes in the carpet where investigators had cut out bloodstains. Empty chalk outlines identifying the original location of possible evidence. A coating of powder on every stick of furniture that might yield fingerprints.

She shuddered. So little to mark the passage of a man's life.

''Ms. Bowers doesn't remember.''

The sound of Luke's voice wrenched Cassie from her grisly thoughts. Startled, she threw a glance over her shoulder. When had he crossed the room to stand vigil behind her chair?

''Not yet.'' Luke patted Cassie's shoulder.

Chelsea's bright lips formed into a perfect *O*.

Cassie felt her cheeks flame at Luke's theatrical gesture. She realized he hoped to keep the killer guessing, but did he have to act so proprietary? If it weren't for the clerk's sharp eyes taking in every move, Cassie would have shrugged off his hand.

''How dreadful,'' Chelsea commiserated, widening her eyes in elaborate sympathy.

''A temporary condition, I'm sure,'' Cassie replied evenly.

''Since I'm through for now, why don't you go ahead with your questions, Cassandra?'' His thumb grazed the nape of her neck as he withdrew his hand.

Heat zinged along her spine.

Startled, she stiffened, fighting the surge of awareness spreading through her body. His touch had lingered just a fraction too long to be accidental, but whatever message he'd intended was lost in her efforts to ignore her tingling nerves.

She wedged herself into the corner of the chair, as far from his wandering hand as possible, but he didn't take the hint. Instead, he rested his hands on the top of the chair, hovering over her like a tenacious palace guard.

Still much too close. But since she wasn't about to give him the satisfaction of knowing how much his presence flustered her, she turned her attention to Chelsea. "I'm sure you were aware Judge Wainright was assisting me with some articles I'm writing for the *Denver Tattler*."

"Of course." She sniffed. "After your interview he ordered transcripts from a long list of trials. He said he wanted to check his facts. It took me two trips to carry them all."

Since Cassie had hauled her share of records while doing research, she could empathize with the clerk's vexed air, but Chelsea's remark raised an interesting possibility. Maybe Judge Wainright had found something Cassie had missed. "I don't suppose you still have those transcripts?"

"Certainly." Chelsea motioned toward the steel filing cabinets. "I never throw anything away without express orders."

Too easy, Cassie thought. "Could I take a look at them?"

Uncertainty flickered across the clerk's face. "I don't know. I should probably get approval." She picked up a pen. "Do you want me to try Judge Kimball?"

"I'd appreciate it. The transcripts might give me a clue to why Judge Wainright called."

And whether his death had anything to do with me.

While Chelsea wrote herself a note, Cassie fingered the nubby fabric of the armrest and framed her next question with care. "You're quite certain he didn't mention anything? Some vague reference to a case, something that puzzled him?"

Chelsea shook her head.

Disappointed, Cassie changed tack, aware that approaching

the problem from a different perspective sometimes jarred loose a subject's memory. "You seem to have been quite close to the judge."

"I worked with him for two years," Chelsea informed her stiffly. "He often said I was indispensable." She raised one brow and lowered her voice as though imparting a secret. "You should have seen the state this office was in when I got here."

Cassie widened her eyes.

It was all the encouragement Chelsea needed to unbend. "Chaos. Complete chaos. Important papers mixed with department memos, files strewn everywhere. You couldn't find a pen if your life depended on it." She wrinkled her nose in distaste.

"Sounds like a real challenge."

"How did you manage?" Luke asked, evidently forgetting it was Cassie's turn to ask the questions.

Chelsea blinked. "Well," she said, studying the appointment book in front of her, "I'm nothing if not organized." She trailed one finger lightly over the book's embossed surface, a look of genuine regret flickering across her face.

Regret for the job...or for the man? Cassie wondered.

With an impatient movement, Luke straightened and moved toward the file cabinets. His thoughts must have run in a similar vein to hers, for while Cassie fished for a way to tactfully get at the truth, he again butted in. "What can you tell us about his personal affairs?"

"Personal affairs?" Chelsea's gaze was startled.

"Yes. Friends, people he socialized with, anyone he might have had disagreements with—things like that."

"I only handled official engagements. Receptions, public appearances. You'll have to ask his wife about his personal life."

Cassie would have loved to explore the reason for the bitter twist of Chelsea's lips as she pronounced the word *wife,* but the gleam of interest in Luke's eye warned her she had to act fast if she didn't want to lose control of the interview completely. Filing the clerk's reaction away for later consideration, she asked the first thing that came to her mind. "What about enemies? Someone with a grudge?"

"Judge Wainright didn't have enemies."

"No enemies?" Luke asked in exaggerated surprise. "Odd. Most men accumulate one or two on their way up the ladder, and a man in Wainright's profession..."

With startling clarity, Cassie saw where Luke was headed. He was deliberately provoking the clerk, hoping anger would force her to drop some useful piece of information. Unfortunately, in the process, he would ruin any chance for Cassie to gain the cooperation she needed.

In an effort to avert disaster, Cassie protested. "Detective Sl—"

"Not Thomas," Chelsea insisted stubbornly, her attention focused entirely on Luke. "Everyone liked him."

Luke's uplifted eyebrow conveyed his skepticism more eloquently than words. "Even the people he sentenced?"

"Of course not," Chelsea snapped. "But I'm sure they realized he was only doing his job."

As she glanced from Luke's disbelieving smile to Chelsea's tightly compressed lips, Cassie heard the toilet flush on her interview. It was evident she'd get no more information from the clerk today, if ever.

Slapping shut her notepad, she stowed her tape recorder in her shoulder bag while Luke gave Chelsea a card and suggested she call if she remembered anything pertinent to the case. Not until Cassie and Luke were safely in the hallway did she vent her frustration.

Hands on hips, she rounded on him. "I should have known."

"Known what?"

"That you wouldn't keep our bargain. That you'd mess things up."

"What did *I* do?"

His feigned innocence fueled her anger. If it hadn't been a supremely childish gesture, she would have stamped her foot. "Do? What *didn't* you do? We were supposed to take turns."

"I guess I forgot."

Forgot! The Luke she knew never forgot anything, nor made a single move without careful, advance consideration. Refusing to honor his bald-faced lie with a rebuttal, she listed the rest of her grievances. "First you act as though I'm an hysterical female about to shatter at the slightest provocation, then you butt into my interview and spoil everything, just when I was getting somewhere."

His eyebrow shot up. "You were getting nowhere. That inane woman was feeding you a line, and you were taking down every word like it was gospel. All I did was get to the heart of the matter."

"I didn't believe her—I was drawing her out. She was about to open up when you had to jump in like a moose in a china shop."

He grinned. "Bull."

"What?"

"It's a bull, not a moose."

"I don't care if it's a ten-foot gorilla. You did it." She swung away and marched up the hall, propelled by his chuckle at her back.

"Haven't you ever heard of 'good cop, bad cop'?"

Cassie planted leather-soled sandals against the marble floor and skidded to a halt. Evidently caught off guard by the abrupt maneuver, Luke bumped into her. An electric current rippled as the full length of his body pressed against her. Disconcerted, she shook off his steadying grasp. "We're not playing cops and robbers."

"Aren't we?"

His familiar masculine scent, mixed with a hint of spicy aftershave, teased her nose. Startled, she met his stare and lost the thread of conversation. He was standing too close. She took a quick step backward and bent down, making a display of adjusting the strap of one sandal, while trying to ignore the heat coiling in her belly.

"Did you catch her slip?"

Cassie straightened, grateful for the excuse to steer her thoughts in a different vein.

"She called him Thomas," he said.

"Big deal. Lots of secretaries—clerks—use their bosses' first names. I hardly consider that cause for suspicion." *Except when coupled with obvious bitterness at his married state.*

"Anyway," she continued, picking up the thread of her earlier grievance, "in spite of what you believe, antagonizing people isn't always the best way to encourage them to spill their guts."

"It's a good interrogation technique." Luke fumbled his notepad from his pocket and flipped back the front cover.

"I was conducting an interview, *not* an interrogation, and you can't just jump in every time you decide I'm not handling things right."

"You're absolutely right," he agreed, his attention on the first page of notes. "I won't do it again."

Cassie's mouth dropped open. Admitting they were wrong was hard for most men; for the old Luke it was well nigh impossible. What was he up to?

He closed the pad and looked up, his gaze piercing. "Did you remember anything?"

The abrupt question sent a chill up her spine. "No." She took a step back, shaking her head. "Nothing."

"It's all right, slugger," he assured her, his manner subdued by her obvious discomfort. "From what the doctor says, when your head wound heals completely, your memory will probably return. These things take time.''

Time she didn't have, not if she intended uncovering a killer. Not if she ever wanted to feel safe again. Still, she managed a lukewarm response that seemed to satisfy Luke.

"I need to check in and see if Haggerty or Jessup have turned up anything on your elusive caller,'' he said. "Then let's see if Judge Kimball's free this afternoon. He's on my list, and you can check about those transcripts you want.''

"Good idea.'' She started up the hall, her spirits taking an upward swing. "Uncle Harry will be happy to help.''

"*Uncle* Harry?''

As Luke fell into step beside her, she smiled, taking a measure of satisfaction in throwing *him* off balance. "Harry Kimball. I'm sure you've heard Pop mention him. He's another old family friend—the one who *couldn't* make it to our wedding.''

Old friend hardly described the urbane individual who entered the office where Luke and Cassie waited after lunch. Judge Harold Kimball appeared to be in his early forties, closer in age to Cassie's brothers than to her father. And the man certainly didn't treat her like any uncle that Luke had ever known.

"I hope you didn't have to wait too long, honey,'' Kimball said, settling a much-too-affectionate kiss on Cassie's cheek.

"I'm so sorry about your loss, Uncle Harry,'' she said.

"Terrible, terrible. It's always hard to lose a good friend, but this kind of thing...'' Kimball shook his head sadly. "So senseless, so unnecessary. A true tragedy.''

Maybe it was Kimball's overblown manner or just the intimate way he clasped Cassie's hands, but Luke couldn't work up much sympathy for the man. Yet his grief seemed genuine.

"It must have been an awful shock,'' Cassie said to him.

"You can't imagine." He paused, then seemed to pull himself together. "But what about you? I couldn't believe when your father told me you'd been attacked. Are you sure you're not overtaxing yourself?"

Not waiting for an answer, he grasped her chin between thumb and forefinger and tilted her head to inspect her healing wound. To Luke's amazement, she allowed the familiarity, although she pulled away when the judge raised a finger as if he intended to probe the bruises around her bandage.

"I'm fine, Uncle Harry. Pop always claimed I was hard-headed. I guess I proved him right."

"Not hard-headed, my girl. Determined." Kimball patted her cheek and smiled. "There's a difference, you know. And with Benjamin for a father, I'd say you came by the trait naturally."

Luke's lips curled in disgust. If there was one thing he hated, it was hearing someone whitewash the truth to make it more palatable. A spade was a spade whatever you called it, and anyone who knew Cassie knew her stubbornness ran far beyond the bounds of ordinary determination. His estimation of the judge dropped a notch, and he cut in before the man could make an even greater fool of himself. "Excuse me, Judge Kimball, but I'm here on official business."

One arm draped across Cassie's shoulders, Kimball turned to Luke while Cassie performed the introductions. "Slater?" He rolled the name across his tongue as though trying to solve a puzzle, although Luke suspected he already knew everything he needed to know about Luke. "Weren't you and Cassie once..."

"Married? Yes." It was obvious the judge expected more of an explanation, but Luke refused to elaborate. Uncle or not, it was none of Kimball's business why Cassie and Luke were together.

Evidently, good manners won out over curiosity, for after

a moment's hesitation, Kimball extended his hand. "Pleased to meet you, detective."

Like most cops, Luke dealt in impressions, and early on he'd learned to draw conclusions about a man based on the way he shook hands. If asked to guess, Luke would have pegged Kimball a political, two-handed shaker, for despite the manicured nails and custom-tailored suit, he wasn't the least reserved. Unfortunately, Judge Kimball's generic handshake netted Luke little new about his character.

"How about it? Do you have time for a few questions?"

Tilting his right wrist, Kimball exposed a slim Rolex. "I'm due in court in forty minutes."

"Plenty of time. Shall we adjourn?" Without waiting for a response, Luke stepped into the judge's private office.

Seemingly unconcerned by Luke's presumption, Kimball ushered Cassie through the door. Only a slight tightening of muscles around his mouth betrayed his true feelings. Luke pretended not to notice. This was an investigation, not a cocktail party, and the sooner Kimball cut the social amenities, the sooner they could get down to business.

Attempting to curb his impatience, Luke settled into a chair and mentally inventoried the room. Although not an exact duplicate of Judge Wainright's chambers, it was similar in size and shape. Cases filled with leather-bound legal references and a few mementos took up most of the open wall space. He focused on a grouping of framed certificates that proclaimed Harold Kimball to be a graduate of Harvard Law School, as well as a member of the Illinois and Colorado Bar Associations.

Money, Luke guessed. Conservative, old money, he added as he noted the lone photograph of a younger Kimball shaking hands with Ronald Reagan in the Oval Office.

Cassie, accompanied by the scent of wildflowers, slipped into the chair next to him. Just as they already had a dozen times today, his thoughts scattered before the tantalizing odor, and his body responded to her nearness. Grimly he squared one leg over the opposite knee, his foot aimed away from her.

Waiting only long enough for Kimball to settle behind the desk, Cassie edged forward on her chair, sending her snug, cotton skirt a few inches up her thigh. "Uncle Harry, I need a favor."

A person would have to be blind not to notice how Kimball ogled the exposed expanse of tanned leg she was displaying, and Luke wasn't blind. The fact that he himself hadn't missed the mouth-watering sight was beside the point.

Oblivious to Luke's chilling glance, Kimball smiled. "A favor? Name it, sweetheart."

Kimball's proprietary air and the syrupy names he called Cassie rubbed Luke the wrong way. Nerves twitching, he wondered how far the judge would like to stretch the tenuous bonds of kinship.

"Judge Wainright ordered some transcripts I'd like to look through. Nothing confidential, but I thought they might provide me with additional information for my series."

"Say no more." Kimball lifted a rock paperweight and offered Cassie the single manila folder trapped beneath. "Chelsea called, and when I found you had an appointment scheduled with me after lunch, I decided to save you the trouble of going back. That was the only one Chelsea found." Taking care not to mar the spotless surface of the desk, he set the rock down, turned it a few degrees, then settled back to admire the effect of the glittering amethyst crystals at its hollowed center. "Now I want to know how you really are. Your father assured me you were doing fine, but I couldn't believe you'd be out so soon."

"You don't need to worry, Uncle Harry. Luke's looking after me."

"Not *too* arduous an undertaking, I trust."

Figuring the comment was rhetorical, Luke met the judge's unctuous smile with impassive silence.

Cassie tightened her lips in obvious irritation, but evidently decided her best course of action was to ignore the silent innuendo. "Luke's a little overcautious. Judge Wainright's death had nothing to do with me, and as far as I can tell I wasn't even a witness. But—" she shot Luke a sly glance, "—you know how cops are."

"As far as you can tell?" Kimball's brows knit in confusion.

"I don't remember anything that happened. Blank. Zippo."

"No?" Kimball gazed thoughtfully at Cassie and rubbed the side of his neck. "Even so, it's usually better to err on the side of caution."

Cassie stiffened. "Not you too, Uncle Harry."

"I just wonder if it might not be best for you to— What's the term?" He glanced toward Luke for help, then supplied the answer himself. "'Lay low.' Until the police have cleared up this matter."

The murderous look Cassie threw Luke told him she suspected him of collusion, but he was too surprised at the judge's unexpected support to do more than shrug.

"I have work to do," Cassie insisted.

"I'm not suggesting you abdicate your responsibilities, merely that you table them until the police have done their job. Until it's safe for you to be out and about."

"And how long will that be? A week, months? What if they never solve the case?" Cassie was indignant. "No. I have a deadline, and I'm going to meet it whether you help me or not."

Luke's heart warmed to see someone besides himself provoking Cassie to rebellion. For a split second he nearly felt sorry for Harry Kimball.

"Now don't get yourself worked up. I didn't say I

wouldn't help." It was apparent from his placating tone that Kimball had dealt with Cassie's stubbornness in the past. "I just haven't had a lot of dealings with drug cases. It's why I referred you to Thomas in the first place." He paused, then added hopefully, "Surely by now you've collected enough material…"

"I thought so until Friday, when Judge Wainright called," she admitted. "But now my instincts tell me he had something more—something important. I have to find out what."

"Knowing Thomas, he was probably making sure he wouldn't be misquoted." When his attempt at levity fell flat, the smile faded from Kimball's face. Frowning, he stared at Cassie for several moments before picking up a pen from the desk blotter. "Tell you what. I'll make you a deal."

Cassie waited, her expression wary, as Kimball rolled the pen between his palms.

"Go through the papers." He nodded toward the file in her lap. "I'll see what I can find out. We'll give it—say, three days. Then, if nothing new shows up, you write the articles with what you already have. Deal?" His hands halted their restless movement while he waited for Cassie to respond.

Luke didn't have time to wait. Each second that ticked away was one less question he could ask, one less answer to analyze. In a few minutes Kimball was due back in court, and Luke still hadn't gotten in word one. It was time to take matters into his own hands. "Sounds like a good idea to me, Cassie," he said with only a hint of impatience. "Why don't you think about it while Judge Kimball and I talk?"

Then, before she could voice an objection, he began his questions.

Leaving the chilled building half an hour later felt like stepping into a sauna. Hot, dry and sweat-popping. By the time they'd crossed to the parking lot, Luke was longing for nothing more than a cold shower and a frosty mug of beer.

Cassie hadn't spoken a word since they'd left Kimball's office, not even after Luke called the station again. He'd expected her to be as frustrated as he over the delay in tracing yesterday's call, but she'd brushed aside his explanations with an irritated wave of her hand.

He glanced sideways. Bright spots of color stained her cheekbones. She was angry all right, but not over having to wait for a subpoena of the cellular company's records.

"I'll drive," he offered when they reached her car.

Grabbing a folded paper from beneath her windshield, she unlocked the passenger door, then silently handed over the key.

"What is it?" Luke indicated the paper in her hand.

"Advertising," she answered curtly and ducked into the car.

Whistling tunelessly, he circled to unlock the driver's side. If he'd had as much sense as God gave mud, he realized, he'd have kept his mouth closed when they left Kimball's office. Only, the judge's condescending responses to Luke's questions had left him feeling like a cat whose fur had been rubbed against the grain.

Hell, instead of being upset, Cassie ought to be damned grateful he'd held his tongue as long as he had. The way he saw it, he'd shown remarkable restraint in waiting until they were out of earshot before muttering, "Pompous ass."

He yanked open the car door and leaned in. Hot air sucked the moisture from his eyes. Visible waves of heat rose from the vinyl upholstery, making him feel like nothing more than a strip of bacon about to be tossed into a cast-iron skillet. Steeling himself, he settled gingerly behind the steering wheel, giving silent thanks that, unlike his own, the cooling system in Cassie's car worked.

"Uncle Harry happens to be an extremely intelligent man."

Since Cassie seemed to be addressing the front windshield rather than Luke, he didn't bother to respond. Impatiently he turned the key in the ignition and flipped on the air conditioner, adjusting the vents so a blast of arctic air slapped him in the face.

"I'll have you know he's a highly respected member of the legal community."

"And damned full of himself," Luke added, shifting the car into reverse. He stretched one arm along the seat top and looked out the rear window. The hairs of his forearm stirred as Cassie exhaled in exasperation. Without thinking, he turned his head.

And found himself drowning in the stormy depths of her eyes.

The scent of wildflowers clung to her as she leaned forward, glaring at him through thick chestnut lashes. A strand of her hair grazed the back of his hand, and he had a sudden urge to slide his fingers beneath the silky curls and brush her nape.

"Full of himself?" she sputtered, wagging the paper in her fist at him. "Because he took offense at some of your questions? You treated him like a suspect."

She had a comeback for everything. Always had. But the bitterness bleeding through her words was new. His gaze slid to her mouth. He remembered when it took only a look to bring a smile to her lips, make her body melt. A surge of heat roughened his voice to a growl. "Until I have proof otherwise, everyone's a suspect, even Harold Kimball."

Cassie's face registered shock. "Don't be ridiculous. Uncle Harry wouldn't hurt a fly. I'd trust him with my life."

Luke released the clutch and backed from the parking space, avoiding her gaze. "If I were you, I'd think twice about trusting anyone right now."

"Even you?"

Especially me. He clenched his teeth in frustration and concentrated on exiting from the parking lot, wishing he dared angle the air vent at his lap.

Her heavy sigh broke the silence. "I'm sorry. I didn't mean that."

She sounded sincere. Luke shot her a sideways glance. She sat with her head bent, fingers pleating the paper in her lap. Maybe she'd finally realized he was only trying to protect her.

As if sensing his scrutiny, she looked up. "I'm being a real witch, aren't I?" Her halfhearted attempt at a smile was doomed to failure by her bottom lip. It trembled.

Startled, Luke raised his gaze a few inches, then wished he hadn't. Uncertainty muddied the clear green color of her eyes, reminding him of the ordeal she was going through.

Luke hardened his heart. On top of all other emotions raging through him, he didn't need to start feeling sorry for her. Deliberately he kept his tone light as he braked at the intersection. "How're you spelling that?"

"Probably with a *b*," she admitted and fell silent, staring down at the paper fan she'd fashioned.

A ripple of air fluttered a curl against her cheek.

His grip tightened around the steering wheel. Damn, but this had to be the longest red light in creation.

He flexed his fingers and shot another glance across the seat.

"Do you know what really scares me?" Head bowed, she unfolded the paper fan and spread it across her lap. "Not some faceless thug out to keep me from talking."

He followed her hands as she smoothed the creases from the paper.

The air conditioner hummed.

Her hands stilled. "Do you know what really scares me?" she repeated.

He strained to catch her softly spoken words.

"What if I never remember?"

He didn't want to understand what she was saying, but, God help him, he did. It was one thing to fear something tangible, something or someone you could fight. But what happened when your fear was faceless and had no substance? What happened when no matter what you did, no matter how hard you tried, there was no defeating it?

A chill chased down his spine.

His gaze skipped from her face to the unfolded sheet in her lap. Smeared, block letters marched across the wrinkled paper like a first-grader's labored attempt at penmanship.

Frowning, he sharpened his focus. The letters shifted and blurred, then formed into words.

"What the—"

Somewhere, from a long way off, the sound of a horn threaded between the purr of the engine and the hum of the air conditioner.

Luke looked up. The damned light had finally changed. Stamping on the gas pedal, he sped through the intersection.

Chapter 5

With one arm outstretched, Cassie braced herself against the dashboard as Luke whipped into a parking space and stomped on the brakes. They stopped mere inches from the rear bumper of a shiny, red sports car. Gasping, Cassie rubbed at the sore spot where the shoulder harness had bitten into her chest. "What kind of a crazy stunt—".

"Give it to me," he demanded, turning off the engine with a flick of his wrist.

Puzzled, she followed his gaze to the paper clutched in her fist. Rather than the printed advertising flier she expected to see, hand-printed letters marched across the page. "So someone left me a message. What's the big deal?"

Instead of answering, Luke snatched it from her. Holding it by the corners, he stretched it out on the seat. "Not that there's much chance of lifting any prints off this now."

"I didn't realize it was important." Guilt shaded her indignation. She should have checked it out before telling him it was just an advertisement, but she'd been too mad.

Uneasily, she glanced at the sheet between them. "Curiosity killed the cat,'' she read upside down. Apprehension prickled along her neck, and she fought an urge to glance over her shoulder. Who would leave such a message? She looked at Luke. "Do you think the caller left it?"

"Possibly." He held the paper to the light, turning it this way and that as if looking for clues.

"Why would he risk being seen?"

"People leave notes on cars all the time. Who's going to wonder?"

"But we could have returned at any moment."

"All he has to do is keep an eye on the building. As soon as he spots us, he can wander off."

Watching their every move. Goose bumps pebbled her skin. She opened the side window a couple of inches, then dropped her head back against the seat, hugging her arms close to her body. Heat seared her cheeks while the rest of her body remained chilled.

Curiosity killed the cat.

Her stomach flip-flopped. In the distance an ambulance siren rose and fell and blended with the disharmonic sound of passing traffic.

Curiosity…

The odor of gasoline fumes and car exhaust set a pulse throbbing behind her eyes.

…killed the cat.

Perspiration beaded her forehead. Suddenly she didn't want to go home, didn't want to stay in the empty house alone. She wanted Luke to stay with her, hold her through the night, and keep her fear at bay. The way he used to.

"Are you all right?" Luke folded the paper and slipped it into his pocket. "You look pale."

"I do?" Cassie took a gulp of air and opened her eyes. Lowering the sun visor, she grimaced at her reflection in the small mirror. She looked ghastly. "It must be the heat," she suggested, concentrating on keeping her lunch down.

"The heat?" He slid her a doubtful glance as he turned

the key in the ignition and released the hand brake. "The heat's never bothered you before."

Like a kindergartener fibbing to the teacher, Cassie avoided his eyes. She prayed he wouldn't look at her too closely. The rosy pink she felt creeping up her neck was a dead giveaway. If he noticed, he'd pry the truth from her in seconds, and she didn't dare let him know she was scared spitless. It would be all the incentive he needed to move in. And no matter how tempting that sounded at the moment, it was out of the question. Luke was too controlling, too protective.

Luckily he seemed preoccupied with pulling into traffic. Each passing second of silence eased the knot in Cassie's stomach. The apprehension generated by the note shrank to manageable proportion. Grateful for the reprieve, she risked a sideways glance from beneath lowered lashes.

Luke drove with the same economy of motion as he did most things. Everything about him spelled *mellow,* from his careless slouch to his loose-fingered grasp on the steering wheel. But Cassie knew it was all façade. Beneath the calm exterior, Luke was about as relaxed as a bobcat in deer country.

The car slowed in preparation for a turn, and she watched tendons flex beneath the dusting of hair on his forearm as he gripped then shifted the gears. His movements were oddly seductive in their familiarity. Her gaze traced his profile, lingering on the dark hollows beneath his cheekbone and the sexy curve of his full lips. Longing lodged in her chest.

"I'll drop the note at the station after I take you home."

Startled from her musings, she glanced up and found herself staring into his eyes. For one breathless instant she thought she read an answering gleam of desire in their dark depths, but then his expression altered, and he shifted his attention beyond the front windshield.

All imagination, Cassie told herself, but unaccountably the street outside the window blurred. It was obvious the spark was still there—ready, willing and able to trip her up if she let down her guard.

She blinked several times and tried to swallow past the lump in her throat as she realized the equilibrium she'd worked so hard to establish these past two years was a pathetic illusion. All it took was proximity to him, and her defenses crumbled more easily than the walls of Jericho.

Mentally she shook herself. *You made your choice. Live with it.* Luke hadn't changed—he still wanted to wrap her in cotton and cut her off from the world—but she'd grown too used to making her own decisions to listen to his. It would be dishonest to invite him back into her life now. She'd be making promises she couldn't keep in exchange for a few hours of counterfeit security.

By the time they pulled into her driveway, Cassie's head was throbbing in earnest. An instant after the car came to a halt, she spoke. "Don't bother coming in."

Luke ignored her words and cut the engine. "Cassie, we agreed—"

"We agreed you'd come with me whenever I left the house. Nothing else. Well, I'm not leaving." She opened the car door.

"I have to check for intruders."

She threw an annoyed look over her shoulder as she swung her legs from the car. "Duffy's inside, and you installed new locks yourself three years ago. Who's to intrude?"

"Duffy wouldn't scare a cat away."

"Well, if a cat attacks when I open the door, I'll scream, okay?"

He obviously didn't find any amusement in her attempt at humor. Features set in uncompromising lines, he exited the car and headed for the front door.

Knowing it would do no good to argue further, she turned over the key. "Okay, check the darn house. Check the whole neighborhood if it makes you feel better," she grumbled, trailing him through the door.

Just inside, Luke came to an unexpected halt. Unable to avoid a collision, Cassie bounced off his back. To steady herself, she clutched his upper arms. The muscles beneath his shirt were tense. Cautiously she raised herself on tiptoe and peeked over his shoulder.

Caught in the updraft from the opening door, bits of foam swirled toward the ceiling, then fluttered downward to settle on the carpet like a sprinkling of confectioner's sugar.

The vibration of a muffled oath transmitted itself to Cassie, warning her she was pressed intimately against Luke's back. Chagrined, she tried to spring away, but Luke caught her by one wrist.

"Stay here!" His narrowed gaze swept the room.

Cassie rolled her eyes in exasperation, yanked her hand free and took a step toward the kitchen doorway.

"Duffy!" she snapped.

Warned by her exasperated tone, the culprit poked his head around the corner and slunk into the room, his tail wagging feebly.

"What is this?" Cassie demanded, pointing a finger at the throw pillow in the middle of the floor.

Duffy sniffed at the mangled mess, then looked from her to Luke with exaggerated surprise, plainly hopeful blame would be fixed on someone else.

When Cassie continued to regard the dog with obvious disapproval, he switched tactics. Stiff-legged, he approached the offending pillow, caught it in his teeth and shook it vigorously, growling all the while. Once he was certain it was dead, he dropped it at her feet.

A strangled sound escaped from Luke, although his expression remained sober. "You were right, after all."

Puzzled, Cassie knit her brow as he motioned to the terrier.

"You said there was nothing to worry about." His mouth twitched. "You have Duffy to protect you."

Cassie tried not to smile. She turned a stern face on Duffy.

Head cocked to one side, the dog waited, obviously expecting praise for his bravery.

Her lips quivered as she met Luke's amused gaze, and before she could stop herself, she burst out laughing.

A board creaked somewhere downstairs.

Cassie peered into the muffling darkness of her bedroom. Positive she was imagining things, she nevertheless held her breath and waited for the sound to repeat itself.

Had she locked the back door?

Of course she had, she reassured herself. Even so, an eternity of silence passed before she finally released stale air from her lungs. Shivering, she tugged the cotton sheet and blanket to her chin and forced her muscles to go limp.

You're paranoid, she scolded herself. Luke checked every door and window this afternoon and pronounced the house secure. No one could get in, not even Houdini.

Warm milk with a shot of bourbon. Cassie heard the suggestion as clearly as if Luke had whispered it in the darkness. Defiantly she folded her arms across her chest. The only insomnia remedy she needed was for Luke to disappear from her life. She hadn't had any trouble sleeping before he'd charged back on the scene.

Frustrated, she threw back the covers and padded to the window. Though it took some effort, she managed to shove the lower pane upward as far as it could go. Caught on the hint of a breeze, one gossamer curtain lifted and brushed her cheek. She swept aside the delicate fabric and gazed out across the silent neighborhood. As a child visiting her grandma, she'd stood here and imagined herself a princess imprisoned in a high tower.

Cassie's gaze skimmed the shadowed treetops of what had once been her enchanted forest, seeking the fire-eating dragon that guarded the gates to her castle. Yes, she could just make out Flagstaff Mountain's faint outline against the night sky at the western edge of town.

Curling her toes against the worn floorboards, she remembered waiting night after night for her prince to appear. She'd pictured him, tall and blond, riding to the castle gates, engaging the dragon in battle and rescuing her from her imprisonment.

Her lips twisted in a wry smile. She'd been a sucker for fairy tales. Not until she grew up did she discover the truth. There were no princes. At least, not for her. Only frogs.

It was funny—she'd still believed in princes when she met Luke. If not the fairy-tale kind who rode astride white chargers, at least the sort who saw beyond outer blemishes to the inner beauty of the soul. She'd thought Luke just such a prince, though he wasn't classically handsome and his manners were far from courtly. Yet somehow, when he gazed at her from beneath his dark brows, her heart had done a triple loop. And his voice…well, suffice it to say, the gravelly sound had grazed intimately along nerve endings and sent sparks flying across synapses.

It still did.

The unwelcome thought wedged through her musings like the insistent chirp of a cricket. Cassie fretfully brushed back a lock of hair, wishing it were as easy to brush aside her feelings. They couldn't recreate the past. Truth be told, she didn't want to. The ecstasy she'd found in Luke's arms wasn't worth the pain of his rejection.

Sadness swept over her. Sighing, she flattened her palms on the low sill and stared across the patchwork of yards toward the twinkling streetlights of downtown Boulder. A cloying scent of lilacs drifted from Mrs. Ogalvie's yard. A chill skittered across her neck as she thought of a single spray of lilac adorning a small grave.

Danny's grave.

Eyes squeezed shut, Cassie clenched the sill, heedless of the texture of chipped paint beneath her fingers. Despite her efforts to divert them, memories washed over her until she was trapped in an undertow of sorrow and guilt.

Pop and her brothers had been there that day, giving support and comfort in the only ways they knew—with awkward pats on the back and senseless promises of future children. She'd wanted to scream she didn't want other children, she wanted Danny, but the words lodged in her throat when she'd met Luke's bitter, unforgiving eyes.

Carefully Cassie loosened her grip. Eyes stinging, she brushed her palms across the soft weave of her nightshirt, watching intently as tiny paint chips floated to the floor like ghostly flakes of snow.

She hadn't meant to kill his unborn son—*their* unborn son. It wasn't her fault a madman had forced her to accompany him on an insane dash for freedom. The crash wasn't her fault, either. Yet, when the pains began ripping her apart during the long ride to the hospital, she'd glimpsed the truth in Luke's hard jaw and bleak eyes. She herself had sown the seeds of tragedy with her recklessness, but a defenseless infant would pay the price.

That realization had sealed her lips and kept her dry-eyed through the weeks that followed. In silence, she'd waited, but Luke continued to avoid her, until she finally faced the fact that whatever they'd had together had died with their child.

Cassie hugged her arms close to her body and let the pain wash through her, knowing that trying to ignore it would only make it worse. Aching for what was lost, for what could never be, she turned, then halted as a flicker of movement caught her attention.

Someone was out there!

A giant fist squeezed her chest. Spinning from the window, she plastered herself against the wall. Air passed in and out of her lungs in gasps so loud she feared she could be heard on the ground. *Was it the caller?* Heart hammering against her ribs, she clamped shut her lips and edged back to the window, praying for a clear view. Cautiously she scanned the sidewalks, the street, then the adjacent yards below.

Nothing stirred.

No sound disturbed the night.

Her muscles began to cramp, and her eyes ached with the effort of plumbing shadows, but she willed herself to remain still. She was *not* imagining things.

Just when she was about to give up and listen to her body's complaints, she saw it again.

There! Nearly hidden by the hedge of Russian olives that marked the boundary between her yard and Mrs. Ogalvie's. As Cassie narrowed her eyes, the shape detached itself from the shadows and crossed the open lawn. Stale air burst from her lungs. *Luke!*

She didn't need to ask herself why he was there in the middle of the night. It was obvious. She'd refused to let him stay in the house, so he was doing what he considered the next best thing—running surveillance outside. She stepped to one side of the window to avoid being seen while she located his car half a block away. How long had he been there? She hadn't seen the car when she closed the downstairs drapes earlier.

Frowning, she plopped onto the mattress and ran her fingers through Duffy's thick coat. If she had the slightest bit of compassion, she'd relent and invite Luke inside.

But she couldn't. He would know she'd been awake, staring out the window in the middle of the night. Without her confessing anything, he'd know how badly the note had unnerved her, and she couldn't give him that power. No, better to leave him believing her to be stubborn and foolhardy than weak and vulnerable.

Cassie scooted Duffy over and slipped beneath the covers. Guilt niggled at her conscience. Firmly she pushed it away. It was warm out, and Luke had always claimed to be a night owl. It was no concern of hers if he chose guard duty beneath her window over a good night's sleep.

Fatigue tugged at her eyelids.

A smile curled her lips as she fell asleep to the sound of distant hoofbeats.

* * *

Luke was not smiling four days later when he pulled into Cassie's driveway. Four nights surveilling the neighborhood—four *sleepless* nights—had taken their toll, to say nothing of intervals at the station, meeting with the rest of the team and sifting through mounds of useless data.

The occasional catnaps he'd managed only emphasized his exhaustion. This morning the face peering back at him from the bathroom mirror had had raccoon eyes with lids at half-mast. Even after showering and shaving, he had looked more like an alcoholic recovering from a weeklong binge than a respectable member of the community. His wrinkled summer-weight blazer didn't help matters. It made him look like Humphrey Bogart after three days aboard the *African Queen.* The only thing needed to complete the picture, he thought as he felt a muscle jerk next to his left eye, was a nervous tic.

Angling the rearview mirror to catch his reflection, he waited for the twitch to repeat itself. When it didn't, he shut off the engine and ejected from the car. His joints creaked ominously. He was definitely getting too old for this kind of thing.

The slight flutter of an upstairs curtain next door informed him Mrs. Ogalvie was standing lookout over the neighborhood. Her view of Cassie's backyard was obscured by hedges and mature trees or Luke might have been tempted to enlist the old lady's help, despite her advanced years. He definitely needed some nighttime backup.

Luke hit the doorbell, scowling at the memory of what he'd learned at the station. Much as he'd like to, there was no keeping it from Cassie. She had a right to know what they'd found out.

As the door swung open, he smoothed the frown from his face, noting when Cassie greeted him that she looked far more chipper than anyone had a right to be a week after nearly being killed. The fading bruise on her forehead was hidden by unruly curls, her smile was sunny, and *she* looked rested.

As well she should, he thought begrudgingly. She'd been in bed by ten every night, instead of standing a lonely vigil on the street.

"You're early," she announced. "I was just getting my things together." When she took in his appearance, her smile faded. "Something's happened."

There was no question in Cassie's voice, only certainty. Luke pushed from the door frame with a curt nod. He should have known he couldn't fool her. She'd always managed to sense his moods no matter how hard he tried to conceal them. "I'll tell you on the way over."

Mutely she shut down her laptop computer. He didn't ask how the articles were going. Her grimace as she shoved papers into a haphazard pile on the desk told it all. Once in the car, he could tell from her furtive glances that she was dying to question him. But instead of deluging him with chatter, as she might have in the past, she remained silent. When they turned north on Broadway, he put her out of her misery.

"We heard from the cellular company."

"About time," she grumbled.

"Yeah…well, a subpoena takes time, and they don't give away information without one. Part of what their customers pay for is privacy."

Cassie cut off his explanation with an impatient wave. "So who's making the calls?"

"We don't know."

"You don't know! I thought you heard from the cellular company."

Luke's gaze slid over Cassie's pursed lips. Kissable lips. "They told us who the phone belonged to, but the information isn't much help."

"Why? Who's the owner?"

She leaned close, near enough to tease him with her scent. Tightening his hands on the steering wheel, he stared at the

street ahead and tried to blame sleep deprivation for his reactions.

"Judge Thomas Wainright."

"The phone belongs to Judge Wainright? Then who..."

Shrugging, Luke rolled down his window to let some air
into the car. "Almost anyone, including his wife."

"So, arranging this interview for me had an ulterior motive."

Luke clenched his teeth. It wasn't so much the words as
her tone that triggered his resentment. Why did she look for
hidden meaning in everything he did? Just once couldn't she
accept his actions at face value?

"Combining our efforts was your idea, not mine," he responded, not quite managing to control his irritation. "And
just to set the record straight, it wasn't your excellent cre-
dentials that got you an interview. It was your father's name
and my personal assurances as to your integrity. Lydia Wainright has a special aversion to the press, now more than
ever." In the silence that followed he hit the turn signal and
pulled a sharp left off the main street.

Mapleton Hill took its name from the deciduous trees that
lined the center median and shaded the manicured lawns on
both sides of the street. Just driving its length was a soothing
antidote to anger. Luke breathed deeply, feeling the tension
slip from his shoulders, and slid a glance at Cassie. "I'm
sorry I lost my temper. The case is getting to me."

She smiled. "No problem."

The ease with which she replied surprised him. Two years
ago she'd have carried a grudge for hours. He decided he
liked the change. "How is it you haven't met Lydia Wainright before now?" he asked.

"I don't recall Pop ever socializing with the Wainrights,
although they may have before Mom died and I was just too
little to remember. Pop and the judge were golfing buddies.
They'd stop at the house for drinks after playing eighteen
holes."

The smell of honeysuckle and roses drifted through the window, adding to the sense of having stepped back in time to an era of afternoon teas, calling cards and coming-out balls.

As though picking up on his thoughts, Cassie said, "It's hard to imagine modern families living in these houses. I keep expecting to see a horse-drawn carriage turn the corner."

Luke grinned in agreement as he rolled to a stop in front of the Wainrights' home. Cassie didn't wait for him to unpeel himself from the vinyl seat. Before he rounded the car, she was halfway up the front walk, head tilted to take in all three stories of the granite-and-brick house. Even a hundred years ago it would have cost a fortune to build. In today's inflated market, he wouldn't even hazard a guess as to its value. Out of *his* range, that was for sure. Joining Cassie on the wide front porch, he acknowledged her "Wow" with a grin of agreement.

The mellow sound of the doorbell echoed softly from within, and he waited, half expecting a poker-faced butler to answer. Instead, the door swung open to reveal a large-boned woman dressed in a faded oxford shirt, gabardine slacks and leather gardening gloves. Her white hair was cropped close around a weathered face.

"Lieutenant Slater, Mrs. Wainright. I called earlier."

She nodded and shifted her gaze to Cassie.

"And Cassie Bowers."

Lydia Wainright inclined her head. "I made your father's acquaintance a number of years ago, just before your mother died. I trust he's handling retirement well?"

"He stays busy," Cassie answered briefly. "He asked me to convey his sympathies, Mrs. Wainright."

The older woman arched an eyebrow and smiled as if Cassie had passed some test. Taking a step back, she motioned them inside. "Call me Lydia. We'll talk out back."

Without waiting for an answer, she led the way to the

library where a set of French doors opened onto a flagstone patio. "I'm in the middle of trimming the potted plants," she explained, "and if I don't keep going, I'll lose momentum. I just don't seem to have the energy I used to."

From the manner in which she attacked a geranium with a pair of wicked-looking gardening shears, she was either a master of understatement or in the throes of a near-religious frenzy. Not caring to find out which, Luke sat down on a wrought-iron bench well out of range. After a moment's hesitation Cassie joined him.

"As I told you earlier," Mrs. Wainright began without preamble, "my secretary handles the bills, and since she hasn't mentioned anything, I hadn't given Thomas's cellular phone a thought. I have no idea where it is. He used it for business, and since he didn't like being disturbed at home, I assume he kept it in his car. Naturally, your call piqued my curiosity, so I've already checked there." Without looking up from the geranium, she waved the shears wildly in the direction of a stone building at the back of the yard.

The garage, Luke assumed, fighting an impulse to duck.

"It isn't there. Perhaps he left it in his office at the Justice Center."

"The possibility occurred to us," Luke admitted. "We've checked with his former secretary, but she informed us it wasn't among his things."

"Chelsea Sparks?" Lydia's disdainful sniff spoke volumes. "That floozy couldn't find her brassiere if it leaped up and bit her on the—" Moving to a pot a few feet closer to the bench where Luke and Cassie sat, she continued, "I don't know why Thomas kept her on." She eyed the bedraggled collection of blossoms before her. "Then again, I suppose she had her uses." With a competent snap of the wrist, the widow amputated one mangy limb from the plant.

Next to him Cassie winced, and Luke avoided meeting her gaze, afraid he'd laugh aloud.

Lydia set down the shears and smiled serenely as she peeled off her gloves. "Lemonade?"

Chapter 6

Cassie managed to keep a straight face until they reached the car, but when Luke looked at her as he turned on the ignition, she caught a sparkle in his eyes. Biting down on her bottom lip, she glanced away, searching for something to focus on, something to halt the laughter welling in her chest. Unfortunately the profusion of blooms along the Wainrights' front porch only served as a reminder of Lydia flourishing a pair of gardening shears like a broadsword.

Cassie tried to look serious, but Luke's expression undid her. His lips twitched, and she knew without a doubt he was having the same problem she was. As the car pulled from the curb, she let her laughter burst forth. Seconds later Luke joined in.

By the time they reached the stop sign on Broadway, tears rolled down his cheeks and Cassie was doubled over, her arms pressed across her aching stomach.

"I kept imagining the Red Queen from *Alice in Wonderland* shouting, 'Off with their heads!'" she gasped.

"Or appendages farther south," Luke suggested.

His horrified exclamation set her off again as she recalled how he'd flinched when Lydia waved her shears in front of his torso.

"You're warped." He flung her a reproachful look, then refocused out the front windshield. "Definitely warped," he muttered.

Cassie grinned. Her earlier misgivings about being around Luke had faded. Not only was he looking out for her, he'd smoothed the way for her to talk with Lydia Wainright. Thinking about his late-night vigils the past four nights filled her with gratitude. His presence had enabled her to drift into peaceful slumber, something she hadn't done for quite a while. And he hadn't expected anything in return. Indeed, he couldn't know that each night, before she went to bed, she stood hidden in the dark of her room and drew comfort from the sight of him on the sidewalk below. And now, their shared laughter forged another link between them.

The car climbed the curving sweep of street that led into her cul de sac, slowing to turn into the driveway, then glided to an effortless stop, inches from the garage door. Luke set the brake and lay his arm along the seat back, shifting a little to face her.

Silence filled the car. Friendly, accepting silence that made Cassie's lips curve upward. Contentment was an unfamiliar emotion for her lately, but right now she felt strangely content.

Luke lightly touched the indentation on her cheek. "It's nice hearing you laugh, seeing you smile."

Her pulse fluttered erratically at the husky timber of his voice.

"But..." He trailed his fingertip along her jawline, his gaze fixing on her mouth.

She ran her tongue over her lips. Why was it suddenly so difficult to breathe?

"...we can't forget Mrs. Wainright is a murder suspect."

Cassie stiffened and drew back, her eyes widening in protest. He *couldn't* suspect that spunky old woman. His unrelenting gaze told Cassie he could. Would. In his book, everyone was guilty until proven innocent.

She couldn't blame him, not if she were honest with herself. Lydia Wainright had fairly bristled with resentment when she spoke of her husband's secretary. It didn't take a genius to figure out why.

Luke's chuckle pulled her from her thoughts. "Duffy must be tired of his own company."

Following Luke's gaze, she caught sight of Duffy in the front window. His ears were pricked forward while his front paws performed a little dance. Since only his upper body poked from between the drapes halfway up the window, he appeared to be suspended midair.

Cassie knew better. He was using the couch back as a stage.

She muttered an expletive under her breath and scrambled from the car, afraid to imagine the newest destruction inflicted on her hapless couch. Intent on catching the terrier in the act, she covered the distance to the front door at a run, too incensed to pay attention to Luke's shout.

As she fumbled the house key from her purse, he caught up to her and laid a restraining hand on her arm. "Something's wrong."

Cassie froze. What on earth did he mean? The door and the window beside it looked perfectly normal. No signs of forced entry, as far as she could tell. She threw Luke a puzzled look. He was crouched, studying the wooden planks of the porch.

"Someone knocked into one of your pots," he said quietly. Straightening, he motioned to the smear of dirt beside the railing.

"You saw that from the driveway?" Cassie couldn't keep the skepticism from her voice.

"No, I noticed the pots weren't lined up."

He was right. The second pot from the end sat closer to

the edge of the railing than the rest. It had been turned a few degrees, and the petunias inside looked traumatized.

"Maybe I moved it when I watered yesterday."

His silence told her what he thought of that possibility.

Cassie had to agree. As Luke had pointed out a few days ago, she was a creature of habit. If she'd moved the pot herself, she'd have automatically returned it to the right spot. "Maybe a salesman was here?"

"Maybe."

Luke's lack of conviction made her uneasy, but when he drew his gun from beneath his jacket and motioned her to one side, her apprehension soared. Flattening against the house siding, he positioned himself between her and the front door. Then, with nerve-racking care, he turned the knob.

An airplane hummed overhead, and from several streets away Cassie heard the shriek of a child. She focused on a bead of sweat forming at Luke's hairline and followed its painstaking descent to his damp collar. As it slid from sight, he threw a glance at her over his shoulder. More clearly than words, his expression warned her to stay where she was.

The thought of convincing her leaden limbs to obey any command made Cassie want to laugh.

Luke eased the door open a crack, and the accompanying high-pitched squeak made Cassie wince. He nudged the door with the toe of one loafer. Cassie held her breath as the narrow gap widened. And then, between one moment and the next he sent the door flying inward with a swift kick.

"Police!"

She knew the drill, but jumped anyway, then plastered herself so tightly against the siding that wood grain dug into her spine. The blood drained from her head, leaving her weak and sick to her stomach, while at the same time she had the incongruous picture of how she and Luke must look to any neighbors glancing out their windows. Fighting back hysteria, she scanned the few houses visible from her front porch. No one seemed to be watching, not even Mrs. Ogalvie.

Strange, since Luke's shout had split the quiet afternoon like a sonic boom.

Cassie returned her attention to the house she was propping up with her stiff body. Shouldn't she be hearing something? Footsteps? Sounds of struggle? A gunshot?

The silence coiled around her, pressing tighter and tighter until she felt like a moth imprisoned in a cocoon. Surely Luke would have called out if everything was all right. Holding her breath, she forced her unwilling feet to inch closer to the open door.

Her heart nearly stopped when she heard a tapping, like typist fingers across a keyboard. Several moments spun past before she identified the sound as canine toenails against a wooden floor. The resulting rush of adrenaline left her so drained, she nearly dropped Duffy when he leaped into her arms. An eternity later the pounding in her head lessened enough for her to continue a slow advance through the doorway. The closed drapes cast the house into deep shadow, but as far as she could tell, everything was in place.

"Luke?" she called, her voice pitched low.

From somewhere upstairs came a muffled response. Though the words were indistinct, the tone reassured her. Evidently, whoever had entered her house was gone. She moved from the entryway into the living room, then peered at the oak floor. Smudges? Squinting, she followed them across the Navaho rug onto the couch.

She pressed her lips together in irritation at the thought of cleaning up another mess in the living room. "Bad dog!" she admonished as she crossed to the window. Duffy squirmed in response, but Cassie kept a firm grasp on him and snagged the drapery cord with her free hand.

Sunlight streamed between the parting cotton panels, laying a bright path across the room. Blinking against the sudden glare, Cassie looked down at the couch to determine the extent of Duffy's mischief. Damp splotches formed a haphazard pattern across the Southwestern print.

Footprints. Doggie footprints. What had he gotten into?

Propping the dog on one hip, Cassie crouched down to touch a spot. Her finger came away sticky. Duffy wiggled against her, and to keep from toppling, she rose. Shifting his weight, she rubbed her finger and thumb together, wrinkling her nose at the pungent odor. It smelled like—

Duffy jammed four feet into her midsection, knowing from past experience that she'd release him if he made her uncomfortable enough. A rebuke died on her lips as she caught sight of the red streaks patterning her blouse. Paint. Where had Duffy found red paint when she didn't have any in the house?

Puzzled, she stared at the paw prints on the floor and tracked them backward. Nothing but the door to the garage was visible from her current position, but for some reason, she was reluctant to step closer to the doorway. Tightening her grip on Duffy, she forced herself to move one foot, then the other.

"Don't go into the kitchen."

Luke's sharp command from the head of the stairs halted her midstride. In reaction to the sudden sound, her heart thudded heavily against Duffy's small body.

"Someone's been here," Luke explained as he descended the last steps and crossed the hallway. His voice was pitched to soothe, to keep her calm, and that fact alone raised her apprehension several notches. By the time he took Duffy from her and shut him in the bathroom, her nerves felt like someone had rubbed them with sandpaper.

"What's going on?" she asked. "What's in the kitchen?" When Luke didn't immediately answer, she took a shaky breath. "It's my house."

"Right now, it's a crime scene."

Crime scene? Cassie swung away. "I won't go in." Before he could stop her, she hurried to the doorway. What greeted her went far beyond her wildest imaginings.

Red paint.

Everywhere.

Smeared across cabinets. Streaked along counters and floors. Splattered on the ceiling.

And across one wall, glistening in the afternoon light, was scrawled the macabre message: "Judge not, that ye be not judged."

Red. Bloodred. Cassie swayed, spots of light dancing before her eyes as the room seemed to swell, then recede. Bile rose in her throat. But she couldn't tear her gaze away.

She nearly jumped out of her skin when hands touched her shoulders. She'd been fighting so hard for control, she hadn't heard Luke approach. Now he stood close enough for her to feel the strength emanating from his lean body. She resisted an urge to turn and bury her face in his chest, to let him shelter her in his arms. She felt too brittle. One soft word, one gentle caress, and she'd shatter into a million pieces.

"Why?" she asked without turning her head.

"A warning," he answered quietly.

Cassie shuddered. First the calls, then the note left on her car, now this. Luke didn't need to say anything else. She could read the signs herself. Someone didn't want her digging. The more information she unearthed, the more nervous they grew. And if she didn't stop—what then?

In the silence she heard Duffy scratching at the bathroom door. But neither the thought of the destruction he was causing nor his piteous whines swayed her. Any decent dog would have sunk his teeth into a stranger's ankle, but not Duffy. The intruder must have had a good laugh over the hyperactive terrier.

At least he hadn't harmed him.

She shivered as the words whispered through her head and she pictured what she could have found when she entered her front door.

"I've called the evidence crew. They're on their way." Gently, Luke turned her from the kitchen. "Take care of Duffy, and I'll bring you a clean shirt."

Feeling stiff, and decades older than when she'd entered

the house, Cassie got some mineral spirits and rags from the garage and began scrubbing at the paint on Duffy's coat. The task should have distracted her from the desecrated kitchen, but whenever she relaxed her concentration, the room flashed vividly through her mind. Just the thought of cleaning it was enough to send her spiraling into despair.

By the time the first patrol car arrived, her nerves were strung tighter than her grandmother's clothesline. With Duffy stashed safely in the backyard and a clean blouse on, she let Luke persuade her to go with him to question the neighbors. He didn't have to work very hard. The last thing she wanted to do was watch an investigation team tromp through her house.

They hit pay dirt at their first stop.

"Why, yes," responded Mrs. Ogalvie. "A delivery truck arrived about three o'clock, right after you two left."

The birdlike woman had answered their knock with such speed, Cassie was sure she'd been waiting for their arrival. When she invited them in for tea, Cassie's suspicions were confirmed.

"I'm quite sure of the time, Cassandra, because *Days of our Lives* had just started."

"Which was it, Mrs. Ogalvie, a truck or a van?" Luke asked, balancing a delicate teacup and saucer on one knee.

"I'm quite sure it was a van. A white one like the florist uses, but it wasn't theirs." She cocked her head to one side, squinting into space. "I don't recall where it was from right now, but it'll come. It usually does if I pretend I don't care."

Luke shook his head when Mrs. Ogalvie offered a plate of cookies. "Why don't you tell us what happened. As I recall, you have a pretty good memory for detail."

Normally Cassie would have been amused by Luke's diplomacy. She knew he remembered how close a tab Mrs. Ogalvie kept on things—a One-Woman Neighborhood Watch Program, he used to call her. But with everything that had happened this afternoon, she was having trouble finding anything humorous.

"Let's see," Mrs. Ogalvie said. "The lad carried a large cardboard box to the front door. I don't think it was very heavy because he balanced it on one hip when he rang the bell. Of course, he had to set it down when he knocked into one of your flowerpots." She wagged her head in disapproval. "I considered offering to keep the box for you, but before I could get out my door, he went around the house and left it in the back. Terribly careless of him, I must say, but then, he was in a hurry."

Luke leaned forward. "Why do you say that?"

Mrs. Ogalvie sipped her tea, then set the cup on the side table. "He seemed impatient. On your front porch he looked at his watch several times, and when he left he drove so fast he nearly took the corner off my flower bed." She shook her head in dismay. "Luckily he didn't damage anything. I checked after he was gone."

"How long would you estimate he was in Cassie's back-yard, Mrs. Ogalvie?"

She gazed thoughtfully at the mantel clock. "Five or ten minutes."

Cassie flashed on what she'd seen in her kitchen and felt like crying. Five or ten minutes—such a short time to wreak such terrible havoc.

"I'm quite sure it wasn't longer than that," Mrs. Ogalvie added. "Bo hadn't made it to the crash site yet."

"Bo's a character on *Days of our Lives*," Cassie explained when Luke looked confused.

"He and Hope were going to get married when she returned from the Himalayan expedition, but her plane went down," chimed in Mrs. Ogalvie. "Now he'll probably drown his sorrows in booze and wild women. Unless Rosalyn convinces him—"

"A description would be extremely helpful. Can you recall

what he looked like?'' Luke interrupted, bringing the conversation back on track.

"I don't see as well as I used to," Mrs. Ogalvie said uncertainly.

"Just do your best."

"All right." She tapped one finger thoughtfully against her lips, then folded her hands in her lap. "His hair was frightfully long. He wore it in a ponytail."

She glanced from Luke to Cassie. "In my day you could tell the difference between men and women. Now..." Lips pursed, she shook her head in disapproval before her expression lightened. "Personally, I much prefer your hair, Luke."

The look she turned on him would have done a teenage vamp justice, but Luke just smiled. "What hair color?"

"Dark. And he was about your height. You both hit about the same spot on Cassandra's front door."

"Did you see his face?"

"Not very well." She tapped her glasses. "I think I need a new prescription."

"You've done fine, Mrs. Ogalvie," Luke said. "Most people wouldn't have spared a delivery man a second glance. If there were more people like you, my job would be easier."

"What did he do? I hope he didn't harm your little dog."

The quaver in Mrs. Ogalvie's voice brought a lump to Cassie's throat. The old lady loved Duffy almost as much as Cassie did, often saving little treats for him from her own meals.

"Duffy's fine," Luke reassured her. "This is a matter of malicious mischief."

"Oh, dear. What is the world coming to?"

Cassie patted Mrs. Ogalvie's hand. "I'm sure the police will catch the culprit quickly."

"I certainly hope so. A thing like this can make a person think twice about going out on the streets."

Since nothing ever cowed Mrs. Ogalvie enough to keep

her indoors, Cassie struggled to keep a straight face while Luke wrapped up the interview.

At the front door the elderly woman gave Cassie a fierce hug. ''If you need help, you just give me a call and I'll be right over.'' Then she turned to Luke. ''And I'm certainly glad you're back in the neighborhood.''

Before Cassie could set her straight, Mrs. Ogalvie patted Luke's arm and confided in a stage whisper, ''I suffer from insomnia, too, you know, so if you ever want company late at night, don't be afraid to ring my bell. I'll make you some tea.''

Waving goodbye as the door closed, Cassie stepped from the porch and pretended she hadn't just heard Mrs. Ogalvie blow Luke's cover sky high.

Behind them, Mrs. Ogalvie's front door popped back open. ''Mitchell's Delivery Service,'' the old lady piped triumphantly. ''It was written in green-and-black letters on the side of the truck.''

Luke shot her a V-for-victory sign. ''If you ever decide to come out of retirement,'' he said solemnly, ''we could use you on the force.''

Her wrinkled face lit with an indulgent smile. ''You couldn't afford me, young man.'' Her chuckle hung on the air for long moments after she closed the door.

Grinning, Luke trailed Cassie across the lawn to her driveway. As he'd hoped, taking her to question the neighbor had diverted her from the horror they'd found in her kitchen. But the brief respite was over. Even before they left Mrs. Ogalvie's yard, Cassie's face took on a melancholy cast. The haunted expression in her eyes made him want to capture her in his arms and murmur soothing sounds against her hair.

He couldn't risk it. In the doorway of her kitchen, he'd seen her spine stiffen. Now, the set of her head, the lift of her shoulders, her entire demeanor telegraphed her unwillingness to be comforted.

Luke grimaced. Much as he liked Cassie's father and

brothers, there were times when he wanted to chew them out for how they'd raised her. Not that they'd deliberately done anything wrong. They'd just been…male.

With no mother around to set an example, Cassie had denied her gentler, feminine side. Her father's initial tendency to protect his little girl had forced her to prove she was as strong and capable as her brothers. And because she equated tears with weakness, she learned to do her crying alone.

Luke hadn't helped any, he admitted, studying the brave tilt of Cassie's chin. Ever since his teens, he'd tried to look out for others. First his sister, then his parents and finally, when he went into law enforcement, an entire city. It was his Achilles' heel—the compulsion to step in and take care of everyone around him.

Cassie, not surprisingly, had fought him every step of the way. Just as she had her father and brothers. And at first her grit had intrigued Luke. Later, after they'd married, it became a bone of contention.

Luke needed to be needed, and Cassie needed no one. Ironically, the one time she'd sought his comfort, he'd had none to give.

"I want to see how he got in." Cassie paused near the gate to the backyard just long enough to state her intentions, then sailed through without waiting to see if Luke would follow. He did. At times like this, arguing would get him nowhere.

Ahead, Cassie was talking to Archer, one of the evidence guys. The two had been friends back in the days Cassie worked the police beat, and they appeared to be renewing their acquaintance. Feeling like an outsider, Luke joined them.

"Yep. He came prepared. Used some kind of metal crowbar," Archer said.

Luke pretended not to see the triumphant look Cassie shot him. He knew what she was thinking—for once she'd remembered to lock the door and someone had still managed to break in. Luke curbed his impatience and waited while Archer explained, in excruciating detail, how the intruder had gained entry. As if the gouged door frame and splintered wood weren't apparent enough for any fool to figure out.

Through the screen, Luke caught a glimpse of a video camera panning the kitchen, and although he couldn't see the person, he knew someone would already be dusting for fingerprints and collecting paint samples.

Luke made a mental note to have Jessup check out local paint stores. It was possible the vandal was stupid enough to buy his supplies locally.

Frankly, Luke doubted it. Someone had carefully planned this whole thing to leave Cassie a message. But, for the life of him, he couldn't figure out why. Why would someone who was worried she could identify them as a murderer, merely try to scare her? It would have made more sense for whoever it was to try to eliminate her from the picture. Ditto if there was a connection to the drug series she was writing. The big boys didn't play head games. If they wanted a silent witness, they offed him.

Nothing added up.

Unless he'd missed something.

He rubbed his eyelids and pinched the bridge of his nose in an attempt to relieve the dull ache that had taken up permanent residence in his skull. Nights of standing watch followed by days of overseeing the investigation and serving as a bodyguard were taking their toll. At times he could barely remember his own name, let alone make sense of what anyone had said days earlier. Small wonder nothing added up.

Aware that Archer's monologue was winding down, Luke stepped closer, determined to get Cassie away before the evidence crew finished up. Away from the ravaged kitchen, away from the house and away from danger. She needed to be safe, and *he* needed sleep. Badly. He'd be worse than useless to her if he didn't get some rest soon.

Draping an arm across her shoulders, he bid Archer goodbye. "We've got to check upstairs to see if anything's missing," he explained, urging Cassie toward the gate.

A tremor quivered across her shoulder blades, but she nodded assent. Even so, Luke kept his arm around her as they circled the house and entered through the front door. On the second floor, they went from room to room, the noises from below muffled and indistinct. By the time they approached the rear of the house, their movements had taken on the familiarity of ritual.

Without a backward glance, Cassie entered her bedroom. Luke stopped in the doorway. When checking on things earlier, he'd made a cursory examination here. Now he couldn't avoid a closer look at the room he'd vacated two years ago.

It looked the same—lacy curtains at the window, the carved pine dresser with its matching framed mirror. The little Shaker table they'd found at an antique store in Nederland still sat next to the bed. The room looked the same, but not quite. Somehow it seemed more delicate, more feminine now.

He gave himself a mental shake. It was probably the lack of masculine clutter. Cassie had always complained he was sloppy. With a wry twist to his mouth, he stepped inside and watched his ex-wife scan the room, then shake her head. Nothing out of order.

"Check the closet and dresser." His tone more brusque than he intended, he added, "We need to be sure."

When she opened the drawers, he caught the scent of spring flowers, a scent so much her signature, the faintest whiff evoked memories of satin skin and spiraling passion.

Luke's body responded. Automatically. Painfully.

Cassie eased the closet door shut. "Everything's here." Her gaze collided with his, then skittered away as though she shared his discomfort at being alone together in this room. Their room.

Abruptly, with more awkwardness than she usually displayed, she presented her back and crossed to the window.

Hands braced on the sill, she tilted her head to look down into the yard. "How much longer do you think they'll be?"

Luke shifted his weight from one foot to the other and avoided glancing at the bed. "Another half hour at the most."

Silence greeted his response. A total, all-consuming silence that hampered further conversation. Frowning, he realized that now was the time to convince her she couldn't remain here alone. Tonight especially.

After a moment's hesitation he drew closer, stopping near enough to touch her—if he wanted. The afternoon heat had glazed her skin with a thin layer of perspiration. Damp curls clung to her slender neck. His glance settled on her lower lip as she worried it between her teeth.

He shoved his hands into his pants pockets and fought against offering comfort he knew she'd reject. Staring past her shoulder, he watched Archer get into an unmarked patrol car and back out of the driveway.

"The messages...they've gotten..."

Luke swayed closer. "Menacing?"

"No." She shook her head. "More...more flagrant."

"They're meant to scare you."

"They do," she whispered, her gaze focused beyond the trees.

He touched her nape, took heart when she didn't pull away. "Then call your family. You can stay with one of your brothers or your d—"

Before he could finish, she shook her head.

"Why not? They love you. They'll take care of you."

"Exactly." She swung to face him, shaking off his hand.

Luke frowned, catching echoes of other, more heated arguments from the past. "I know you think they're overprotective—"

"Stifling is more like it." Her expression tightened. "No, it's taken too long to convince them I can manage my own life. If I run to them, I'll never hear the end of it."

A sharp pain stabbed behind his eyes. His head throbbed. He gritted his teeth, knowing he was on the verge of losing his temper—and the battle. With as much calm as he could muster, he shrugged, communicating lack of concern at her refusal. "There's only one other alternative."

She raised a skeptical eyebrow.

Deliberately, he let the silence drag, catching and holding her gaze until uncertainty flitted across her face. "You'll come home with me."

Chapter 7

Duffy obviously hated his leash. He alternately yanked and dragged Cassie across the parking lot to the apartment building, apparently hopeful she would let him run up the outside staircase and explore. Finally tiring of the hassle, Luke scooped him up beneath one arm. On the second-floor landing, he turned the dog back over to Cassie while he unlocked his apartment door.

The refrigerated air inside was a welcome relief from the late-afternoon heat. Luke made a quick survey of the room. A week's worth of *Daily Cameras* were piled beside the L-shaped, sectional couch. On the other side of a low wall, the sink was full of unwashed dishes.

Not too bad. No dirty socks or empty beer cans.

Moving a book from the couch to the glass-and-chrome shelving that housed his sound system and barroom-sized TV, Luke sketched a bow. "Welcome."

Cassie shooed Duffy off the couch and smiled. "Where shall I put my things?"

"I'll take care of it." He shrugged out of his jacket and

hung his shoulder holster over a kitchen chair before heading down the hall to the bedroom with her suitcase. By the time he returned, Duffy was curled up on the overstuffed couch.

"It's okay," Luke said when Cassie apologized.

"But if you let him stay on it, he'll stake a claim." She lowered her voice ominously. "Are you prepared for the consequences?"

Luke recalled the snowfall of foam in Cassie's living room. "The salesman told me the upholstery's like iron. It'll withstand anything."

Cassie wasn't convinced. "I'll bet they didn't run terrier tests on it."

"It doesn't matter. I can get another." He picked a CD from the stack on the shelf and turned on the player. Cool, easy jazz curled softly through the air. "Sit," he insisted. "I'll make us some coffee."

While the coffee dripped, Luke piled dirty dishes into the dishwasher and kept one eye on Cassie. Following orders, she now reclined against the gray velour cushions, eyes closed. Completely at home.

Although it had been his idea, having her here suddenly set his nerves on edge. It was one thing to assure his boss he could remain objective enough to handle this case, another to find himself cooped up in a 1000-square-foot apartment with his ex-wife. An apartment that grew smaller with each passing minute.

The last of the silverware rattled into the basket, and Luke closed the dishwasher door. He filled two mugs with coffee, spooning a little sugar into Cassie's, and carried them into the living room.

She was asleep.

He shifted both cups to one hand and swiped dust off the glass-topped coffee table with his shirtsleeve, then carefully set them down. Duffy followed his movements without raising his head from Cassie's lap.

Luke eased onto the far end of the sectional and lifted a

steaming mug, inhaling the rich scent before taking a gulp. Normally, after a day of Colorado dry heat, he unwound with a tall beer. Not today. He had to get Cassie settled and check with the lab. In a few more hours he could let down and relax, but the beer would have to go on hold.

He glanced over at her. She hadn't stirred, but Duffy was regarding him with something akin to suspicion. Maybe the little mutt had watchdog potential after all. Luke certainly hoped so. It would help to share guard duty, even if his relief was only a skittish terrier.

From the speakers on either side of the room a saxophone spun an intricate web of notes around the main melody. Elbows propped on his knees, Luke cupped his hands around his mug and studied Cassie over the rim. Sunlight danced along the curve of her cheekbone, slid across her slightly parted lips. The week's strain showed in the sharp contrast of dark lashes against pale cheeks. Somehow, in repose, she seemed younger, more vulnerable.

Right. His lips twisted in self-derision as he realized how easily he'd fallen into the old trap. Cassie might look vulnerable, but inside, his ex-wife was as tough as granite. Exwife. What an innocuous word for someone with whom he'd once shared so much. Passion and laughter, joy and pain.

And a child.

With the suddenness of a summer storm battering the earth, regret slashed through him. Then, just as swiftly, it vanished like the last drops of moisture beneath the sun's fierce glare.

Strange how sadness never really went away. Just when you thought you had it controlled, something triggered a memory and all the old feelings sprang back, full-blown.

He stared into his cup, searching for enlightenment in the murky liquid it held. Maybe, if they'd stayed together, had other children…

Coffee sloshed perilously close to the rim of his mug as Luke jerked upright. Life wasn't predictable, and survival depended on putting mistakes behind you, not looking back. Besides, between the two of them, he and Cassie had made might-have-beens impossible.

From where they'd lodged in a dark corner of his mind, he heard Cassie's angry words echo across time. "I want this baby as much as you do, but I'm sick of you telling me what I should and shouldn't do. I'm pregnant, not an invalid."

He'd ignored his intuition, let her interview Durell at the county jail. And their baby had died.

He searched Cassie's face for the woman with whom he'd fallen in love, the woman to whom he'd once given his heart. Did she ever feel regret? Did she, too, lie in the dark, consumed by an aching core of emptiness? Did she sometimes wonder what would have happened if they'd both made other choices?

Grimacing, Luke took another gulp of coffee. The hot liquid scorched his throat but did nothing to dissolve the tightness lodged there or ease the tension in his soul.

The woman he yearned for was gone. Hell, she'd probably never existed. For all he knew, he'd fashioned her from whole cloth, imbued her with all the qualities he longed to find and then trapped himself in his own fantasy.

He'd expected too much of her.

Or too little of himself.

Before he could assimilate that startling thought, Cassie's lids fluttered open. Her forehead wrinkled, and her gaze leaped from point to point around the room until it lit on Luke.

In the instant before she came fully alert, an easy smile curved her lips, reminding Luke of summer mornings. His body stirred at the memory of waking face-to-face and pulling her close. His skin prickled to the remembered sensation of soft flesh pressing against him.

As though aware of his thoughts, Cassie frowned and looked away. Pushing Duffy from her lap, she stretched her legs and studied the room with an elaborate interest that didn't quite hide her nervousness.

"Nice pad," she said, addressing the far wall.

Luke grimaced as the throbbing in his groin settled to a dull ache. Irritated, he thrust his memories into the past where they belonged. "It's close to work."

"Great sound system," she offered, her voice overly bright.

He grunted, stalling the conversation.

When Cassie next spoke, her voice was tentative. "I'm sorry I'm such a bother. If you want, I'll call Pop and stay with him."

Luke knew what such a concession cost her, but it hurt anyway. She'd even put up with her family to avoid him.

"No need," he replied with more ease than he felt. "You know how I thrive on trouble." He picked up the mug he'd poured for her. "Have some coffee, and we'll figure out what to do about dinner."

As she took it, their fingers brushed. Lighter than a butterfly's wing, the unintentional caress sizzled across his synapses to lodge suggestively in his brain. For a frozen instant before he relinquished the mug, their gazes locked, and Luke knew, by her sudden intake of breath, that she'd felt the same leap of awareness. Then her glance skittered away.

"I'm not very hungry."

"Just as well," Luke replied, speaking gruffly to cover the fact his insides felt like mush. "There's not much to choose from."

The CD picked that moment to end. A final, melancholy note hung in the air, underscoring the awkward silence and the distance between them.

Cassie looked everywhere but at Luke while he shifted his weight and wondered how to ease the situation. Duffy, as though sensing the mood, lay beneath the table, head on his front paws, his gaze flickering between the two humans.

Finally unable to stand the tension, Luke unpleated himself

from the couch. After putting some ragtime on the player, he inventoried the contents of the refrigerator. If he'd been alone, he'd have settled for popcorn and a beer, but it somehow didn't seem quite like company fare.

He considered ordering pizza, but before he could suggest it, Cassie asked to use the phone to check her answering machine. By the time she returned from the bedroom, he'd changed his mind and was breaking eggs into a cast-iron skillet.

Like a sudden Chinook wind, nostalgia swept over Cassie, taking her by surprise. Her breath caught in her throat at the sight of Luke whistling while he stirred the mixture in a pan at the stove.

"Huevos rancheros?" she asked as nonchalantly as possible, though she didn't need an answer to confirm her suspicions. *Huevos rancheros* was Luke's only claim to culinary fame, the one dish he'd always fixed when they were too sated from an afternoon of lovemaking to go out.

It's only eggs. He probably doesn't even remember. But the look in his eyes when he nodded told her differently.

"I'll shred the cheese," she said, half wishing he'd taken her up on her offer to stay with Pop, even though she didn't really want to go. With Luke she felt safe. It was only when he wasn't there that fear began creeping in, wrapping itself like bindweed, tighter and tighter around her heart, cutting off her oxygen and chilling her blood.

She grated cheese into a bowl and tried to avoid contact with him in the cramped kitchen. Unfortunately, every time he swung from the stove to the refrigerator or reached to the cabinets overhead, she felt his heat like a physical presence. Her traitorous body felt soft and feminine in contrast to his solidness. She could even smell him—the same scent that used to fill her lungs when he'd take her in his arms.

Desperate for distraction, she set the bowl of shredded cheese next to the stove and leaned back against the counter. "Peter told me to take my time getting the articles in."

"Didn't I say he'd understand?"

Cassie watched the tendons in Luke's tanned forearm shift as he spooned scrambled eggs, cheese and *picante* sauce onto flour tortillas, then rolled them up. "Yeah, he told me my safety came first—right before he informed me Smitty had turned in a riveting piece about city graft that could be stretched into a three-part exposé."

"And that's bad?" Luke slid their plates onto the chrome and glass dinette table and waited for her to sit down before settling across from her and picking up his fork.

"It means he's taken me out of the loop. Next he'll probably suggest I take a few months off."

"It might be a good idea." Luke chewed thoughtfully.

"Good idea!" She almost choked on a mouthful of food.

"To anyone with a lick of sense."

Fighting words if ever she'd heard any, yet the soothing tone in which they were uttered rendered her speechless.

"You don't know who's out to get you. You can't even guess which direction the next threat's going to come from," Luke told her, as if he didn't notice her dumbfounded expression. "Maybe you should take Peter's advice."

"And maybe you should mind your own damned business," she retorted without thinking.

His gaze narrowed a fraction. "I'd love to, slugger," he drawled in imitation of a Texas accent. "But you forget. You are my business. At least for now. Guess you'll just have to make the best of it." His smile didn't quite reach his eyes, and though she glared at him, he never wavered.

Cassie looked away first, using Duffy's approach as an opportunity to rein in her temper. She didn't really expect Luke to be fooled by the attention she lavished on the dog, but at least he dropped the subject of her taking a leave of absence.

In silence they finished eating, then began cleaning up, falling without conscious thought into their old way of splitting the job. Luke cleared and wiped the table while Cassie

rinsed dishes and stacked them in the dishwasher. Leftovers
went into a bowl on the floor for Duffy.

It felt so much like their last months together—so civil, so
distant—Cassie wanted to scream. Instead, she wrung out the
wet rag with which she'd been wiping the counters and
draped it over the faucet. Muttering something about checking with the lab, Luke disappeared down the hallway as she
dried her hands and returned to the living room.

Duffy was once again curled on the couch, but it didn't
seem worth the effort to get him off. Even working on her
articles on the laptop computer she'd brought along held no
appeal. Listlessly she scanned the CDs on a shelf. She wasn't
used to wasting time anymore, not since the baby.

Wheeling from the music selection, she crossed to the window. Nearly eight o'clock, the sun had just dipped behind
the cluster of red rocks on the western hillside. In spite of
the late hour, she heard muted laughter echo through the glass
from the postage-stamp lawn below. She looked down and
spotted several small children vying for space in an inflatable
wading pool. At its edge, a towheaded toddler in droopy
swim trunks clung like a limpet to his mother's leg, obviously
leery of the splashing children in the water.

Cassie felt a familiar tightening in her throat. Her son
would have been just about that age.

Abruptly she averted her gaze, seeking out the slice of
Canyon Boulevard visible in the distance through the trees.
By concentrating on the street, she managed to hold back the
tears prickling behind her lids and resisted taking another,
covetous glance at the tiny figure below.

Anger washed over her, white-hot and sudden, driving the
pain back to its hiding place in a dark corner of her mind. It
wasn't fair. One stupid mistake, and she'd lost her child. And
when she'd tried to forget by burying herself in her work,
she'd lost Luke, too. Driven him away. Even after two years
she read the questions in his eyes, sensed his unspoken accusations.

Dusk fell, shadows crept across the lawn, and the wading pool was abandoned as Cassie continued to gaze, unseeing, into the distance.

Why did Luke have to show up now, when she'd finally mended the torn fabric of her life and learned to stand alone?

Why did he have to come and reawaken hope?

Less than an hour later Cassie turned out the bedroom lights, opened the window and slipped beneath the covers of Luke's bed. Her family might call her stubborn, but she'd given in easily this time. Luke had insisted he often fell asleep on the mammoth-size couch, and she hadn't had the strength to argue that as the guest she shouldn't usurp his bed.

She closed her eyes.

It felt peculiar after all this time to be living with Luke again. Well, she amended, not exactly *living* together. More like being roommates. But strange, nevertheless. She grimaced, remembering the bathroom she'd just left. There she'd discovered towels tossed in front of the clothes hamper and the cover off the toothpaste tube—old habits he apparently still hadn't broken. Not that it mattered, since he lived alone. No one to complain about the mess.

Or was there?

She inhaled sharply, and her lungs filled with a tantalizing smell—a teasing combination of spice and musk. Too late, she identified Luke's scent clinging to the pillow beneath her head.

Her eyes snapped open. She stared into the dark, realizing she hated the idea of him sharing his apartment—and his bed—with anyone. Not that she ever pictured him celibate. He was too masculine, too virile. And women liked him.

Her heart twisted. She didn't want to think of Luke smiling into some woman's eyes, tracing a fingerpad along her cheekbone, trailing kisses…

Tossing the pillow to the floor, she squeezed her eyes tight and willed her muscles to go limp. It didn't work, for though her body felt leaden, her mind wouldn't shut down.

The room was full of movement and sound. Miniblinds swayed and slapped insistently against the glass in response to a faint breeze, and every time they swung outward, a parking lot light sent spots of brilliance splattering across her eyelids. A fly buzzed near her ear, and outside on the street, cars sped past with a sound like flowing river water.

She'd never get to sleep with all this racket.

Throwing back the covers, she went to the window and slid it shut, trading fresh air for silence. With a sigh, she sprawled facedown on the bed, shifting around until she'd made a soft nest for herself.

With the outside noises muted, her ears now picked out the drone of the television from the living room. She wondered if Luke was really watching or if he'd fallen asleep with it on.

If things were different, she would have tiptoed out to see. If he were asleep, she'd have turned the TV off, then slipped onto the couch and spooned around his sleeping form, flattening her breasts against his back.

If he were awake... She shivered as memories bled across the canvas of her mind. Luke following her progress across the room, his lazy gaze hardening her nipples against the worn cotton of her T-shirt. His hands working magic, sending heat spiraling within her womb.

A soft gasp whispered past her lips.

She was wet. Wet and ready.

And all alone in the dark.

Misery fissured through her. She knew him so well. Well enough to know he'd never come to her. Not when she'd destroyed what he wanted most—a home, a wife and a son. It didn't matter that she'd wanted their baby as much as he had. All he saw was how she grabbed for it all—baby, husband, career. He only remembered how her actions, her overconfidence, had ruined everything.

She'd had her chance for happiness, and she'd blown it. Life didn't hand out lots of second chances, not to people like Cassie.

Turtlelike, she buried her head beneath the covers, praying for the strength to keep from crumbling into a million pieces.

Arms folded beneath his head, Luke stared at the ceiling. The last few nights of guard duty had left him feeling like one of the walking dead. Earlier this evening he'd have wagered everything he owned that he would fall asleep within two minutes of closing his eyes. Instead, here he lay, wide awake at—he turned his wrist to check the time—nearly 2:00 a.m. One leg bent, he stretched the other out and wiggled his bare toes.

Having Cassie a mere wall away had turned him into an insomniac.

After she'd gone to bed, he'd tried to concentrate on the television. But when the sitcom ended an hour later, he'd had no idea what it had been about.

On the other hand he knew the exact second Cassie had left the bathroom and turned out the lights, and he could testify in court as to the moment she got up to close the window and crawled back into bed.

His bed.

Therein lay the problem. His imagination had gone into overdrive at the thought of her draped in his sheets. Soft, compliant, yielding. It didn't matter that she was as stubborn, headstrong and argumentative as she'd ever been. Neither did it matter that with one toss of her head she could send his blood pressure skyrocketing. None of it made sense, but it didn't matter. He wanted her.

As badly as the first time he'd seen her.

He wanted to caress her silken skin, rediscover each dip and curve of her delightful body. He wanted to taste the moistness of her mouth and bury himself within her. He wanted to make her beg for release.

His jeans tightened. He shifted his hips to relieve the discomfort.

He couldn't act on his thoughts, no matter how many erotic images danced across his brain. Cassie was in his care, under his protection. His job was keeping her safe from harm. From him.

What they once shared was gone, eradicated by his decision to force a chase with the escaped prisoner who'd held her hostage. He hadn't planned the crash, but it was his fault, as surely as if he had. His orders had triggered a chain of events ending in the death of their child. What woman could forgive that? Was it any wonder she'd first avoided him, then severed all connection by serving divorce papers?

Regrets added nothing to Luke's peace of mind. Annoyed, he flexed his shoulders, seeking a spot that would allow him to relax.

How does anyone sleep in all this heat?

Frustrated, he swung his feet to the floor and padded to the kitchen. Turning on the dim light over the stove, he checked the thermostat on the wall. Something was wrong with it, he decided. He tapped the box with two fingers, but since the readout continued to register seventy-three, he turned the setting down several degrees.

Back in the living room, he paced, waiting for the air to chill. Still too damned hot. His T-shirt clung, damp and sticky, to his body, and his jeans had become restrictive— thanks to an overactive libido. His original decision to keep his clothing on, in concession to his houseguest, seemed quixotic in his present state.

He peeled off his T-shirt and tossed it to the floor. Duffy, who'd been sleeping half-under the coffee table, raised his head and sniffed at the wadded material, then settled his chin back on his front paws.

Hooking his thumb in his waistband, Luke undid the metal fastener on his jeans, then reached for the zipper.

A piercing scream jettisoned Duffy from his hiding place and sent Luke scrambling for the gun he'd left lying under the couch.

Chapter 8

Centering all his energy into his leg, Luke kicked out. The bedroom door slammed into the wall, rattling windows. Adrenaline spiked through his veins, sharpening his vision to near nightscope level. The gun with which he swept the room became an extension of his hand.

No one was there except Cassie.

She huddled at the head of the bed, eyes rounded. Her fear was tangible. He could smell it, feel it roll off her in waves. Instinctively he moved closer, his heart squeezing at the way she shrank away.

"It's all right," he whispered. "It's Luke."

She remained frozen in place, not seeming to hear him, and it was all he could do to make himself cross to the window and raise the blinds before going to her.

No sign of attempted entry.

Puzzled, he snapped the safety in place on his 9mm and shoved the gun into the waistband of his jeans at the small of his back. What had frightened her? With a brief word of reassurance to Duffy, who crouched in the doorway growling, Luke crossed to the bed. In the dim light Cassie's eyes were twin mirrors of terror.

"Bad dream?" he asked quietly, and when she didn't respond, he flicked on the bedside lamp. Light pooled on the oak surface and spilled onto the carpet, pushing back the dark a fraction.

It was enough. Her shoulders slumped, and the wary expression faded from her face, though she still clenched the bedding to her chest. Luke edged closer, reached out and loosened her grip. Her fingers felt icy. The mattress sank beneath his weight as he settled beside her and clasped her hands between his.

"Do you want to talk about it?"

She shook her head, yet didn't resist when he drew her close. He moved his hands in slow circles across her back, alternately massaging and soothing. Beneath the worn cotton of her T-shirt, her rigid muscles slowly relaxed.

"Better?"

He took her head movement for assent and continued his gentle ministrations, trying not to think of the length of leg she displayed nor the soft flesh separated from him by a thin layer of cotton fiber. She stirred, the small motion indicating she was about to speak. The tip of her tongue flicked across her lips. Luke stopped the movement of his hands as she began whispering.

"I was in a dark room. So dark I couldn't see anything. But I knew someone was in the room with me—I could hear him breathing."

She released air from her lungs in a quavering rush that signaled her reluctance to continue. Luke smoothed her hair back from her forehead. He knew better than to force her to talk. Only by giving her space would she find the strength to share whatever horrors were in her mind.

"I tried to touch the man, but I couldn't lift my arm. Something was pinning me down."

Abruptly Cassie released her grip on his waist and pushed

herself upright, retreating with the same determination she had two years ago. Now, as then, Luke experienced a flash of pain at her rejection, but he let her go, refusing to hang on if she no longer wanted him.

A frown furrowed her forehead. She gave her attention to the striped, navy comforter, letting long moments pass before continuing.

"There was a flash of light. It was bright—so bright, I closed my eyes. When I opened them I was all alone." Again she stopped. The loose thread she was tugging slipped unheeded through her fingers as her gaze darted around the room. "Something felt wrong. I touched my head, my body, and when I lifted my hands I saw blood."

Luke reached for her hand. He'd have to be a monster not to feel compassion. But beneath the layer of sympathy his detective persona kicked in.

A voice warned him not to get his hopes up. The nightmare might just be Cassie's way of dealing with the events of the day. It didn't necessarily mean she was beginning to remember what had happened at the Justice Center. But despite the admonition to proceed with caution, he couldn't stop a rush of anticipation.

"I heard someone crying." Her whisper was harsh with distress. "It was you. Luke…"

He leaned forward, straining to catch her muffled words, knowing what he was about to hear could break the case wide open. When she wouldn't look up, he stroked her arm, urging her to turn. She did, gazing intently into his eyes.

"Luke…why did Danny have to die?"

It felt to Luke as though all his blood had frozen in his veins. The walls of the room advanced and receded, and his gut ached as though he'd been sucker punched. It didn't help to hear a small voice in his head sneer, *You* have *been*. While he'd waited to hear details about the recent murder, she'd brought him face-to-face with a time in his life he'd rather avoid.

A stifled moan forced its way through Luke's paralysis. From far away, he observed his hands wrapped around Cassie's upper arms, and though he didn't remember tightening his hold, he could measure the pressure he exerted by the pain in her eyes.

Belatedly, as things snapped into focus, he loosened his grip and flexed his stiff fingers. "I don't know, honey," he answered, his voice raw with emotion. "Life's not always fair."

Cassie studied him for several heartbeats, sadness distorting her features. "No, it's not," she agreed. Her expression crumbled, and her cries came in deep, wracking sobs. Luke pulled her to him, propping his back against the wall at the head of the bed. He hugged her shaking form, appalled by the anguish she'd kept bottled inside for so long.

Cassie, following in the footsteps of three older brothers, had always prided herself on never crying. Now, releasing the controls of a lifetime, it seemed she would never stop.

Luke recalled all the times he'd thought her untouched by the tragedy that had laid him low. He remembered how he'd turned his face away, unwilling to share with her his understanding or his grief. He'd denied her comfort, left her to suffer alone in the only way she knew how. Silently. And then...

A giant hand squeezed his chest.

Then he'd branded her insensitive, cold. Unloving.

And unlovable.

Long after her sobs had subsided and her breathing had settled to a steady rhythm, punctuated by an occasional hiccup, he continued to hold her. It was only when his arms grew numb that he turned off the lamp and eased her onto the mattress. The bedsprings creaked as he rolled away and stood.

Cassie whimpered. He halted midstride.

"Don't leave."

The smoky voice curled around his heart. The plea drew

him back to the side of the bed. And when she reached up and captured his fingers, he succumbed to her whispered need. ''Stay.''

Slipping his gun from his waistband to the bedside table, he slid full length on the bed beside her and took her in his arms. She snuggled against him with a sleepy hum of contentment.

''You make me feel safe.''

Safe?

Her trusting pronouncement set guilt twisting in his gut. Luke was familiar with the emotion. As a child, he'd felt guilt over being the favored offspring and had tried to make it up to his older sister by becoming her confidant and sounding board. When she'd run away to become a flower child in Haight-Ashbury, he'd blamed himself for not stopping her. Even his parents' deaths in a car accident several years later had left him feeling culpable, as though in some unfathomable way, he should have been able to prevent it.

No, Luke was no stranger to guilt. It had molded him into a man obsessed with responsibility and propelled him into a profession where he could be responsible for an entire community. And to be perfectly honest with himself, he rarely failed in his responsibility.

Cassie, he'd counted as a double failure because he'd been unable to prevent her from first placing herself in danger and then from losing their baby after the car chase. It was only tonight that he'd learned of his ultimate failure—a failure to see *her* pain and grief because he'd been so blinded by his own.

Lying in the semidark, feeling Cassie's trust in her gentle breathing, her peaceful slumber, he knew redemption lay within his grasp. All along she'd needed him, and he'd ignored the signs. This time, he vowed, would be different.

Sunlight warmed Cassie's back, trapped against her skin by her worn T-shirt. She yawned and tried to twist from her stomach to her side, but something stopped her—something heavy and unyielding across her waist. Curious, but still too sleepy to check it out, she inhaled a lungful of air. A familiar smell filled her nostrils, a scent that teased her memory and awakened longing. As she snuggled against her pillow, a part of her brain wondered why it felt so firm, so scratchy.

Scratchy?

She opened her eyes and frowned at the chest mere inches from her nose. She blinked to clear her vision. It was a chest, all right. In the seconds it took for her to register *whose* chest, events of the previous night splashed across her brain. She remembered the nightmare and her awful despair. She replayed Luke's arrival, being held in his arms, begging him to stay.

Heat rose in her cheeks.

Surely she hadn't begged?

But as she weighed her present circumstances, her heart sank. There was no way Luke and she would be together—in bed—if she hadn't. She lifted her head a fraction and studied his face.

She'd forgotten how much younger he looked in repose, less troubled by the cares of the world. So unlike the worried, weary expression he'd worn for the past week.

Tender, sweet feelings flooded through her as she recalled the sensitivity and compassion he'd displayed last night. She itched to smooth the thick brown hair back from his brow, to feel the morning stubble on his cheek, to trace his firm, wide lips—the way she used to.

Temptation was so powerful, she nearly succumbed. Indeed, her fingers were within inches of his jaw before she caught herself.

She squirmed, tearing her gaze away, then abruptly stopped when she realized exactly *what* she was squirming against. Her inner thigh lay sprawled across faded denim, and Luke's zipper—his *straining* zipper—pressed intimately against her. Cassie froze. Her gaze leaped back to his face.

Luke was inspecting her from beneath lazy, half-lowered lids. A chuckle rumbled deep in his chest.

"Don't stop."

The heat in her cheeks spread until she felt like a lobster tossed in a pot of boiling water. Why had she let him talk her into staying at his apartment? She should have realized the danger involved. Instinctively she stiffened her elbows and tried to pull away.

The muscles in Luke's forearm tightened against her waist. Cassie's dismay must have registered on her face because, instantly, he relaxed the pressure. She was free to escape.

She didn't.

She ran her tongue over suddenly dry lips, aware of a tension building inside as Luke followed the movement, then recaptured her gaze. His pupils were dilated, turning his eyes to the liquid chocolate she always felt she would drown in. Against her chest, his heart thudded an increased tempo. Hers followed the lead.

You court danger. Luke's words echoed in her head. His old accusation had been directed at her penchant for offbeat assignments, but now, as every inch of her body tingled with awareness, it took on new significance.

His fingers speared through her hair, sliding seductively against her scalp. He cupped the back of her head, and an eternity passed while she forgot to breathe.

With the barest bit of pressure, he urged her lips closer.

She didn't resist.

Then his mouth claimed hers. Softly, gently, completely.

Deep inside her something shifted, and control slipped from her grasp. She'd worked hard convincing herself that the last time, in her kitchen, was a fluke. She'd persuaded herself the only reason she'd reacted to Luke was that he'd caught her by surprise. Now, she knew she'd lied to herself.

This was what she'd wanted all along—to once again taste him on her lips, to feel him against every inch of her skin, to soak up his remembered scent through every pore.

Luke licked a trail of moisture across the crease of her mouth, seeking entrance. She obliged by parting her lips. As his tongue thrust within, a moan rose from the back of her throat. Heat coursed through her, making her frantic with longing. It had been too long. Too long without his hands on her body or his breath on her cheek. She shifted restlessly, centering herself above him, reaching downward.

"Please..." She gave voice to a terrible yearning. "Please..."

He caught her hand, pressed it between them against the bulge of his zipper. A look of near pain shadowed his expression. "Are you sure?"

Not trusting herself to speak, she nodded and fumbled with the zipper pull, arching away enough to allow her fingers to maneuver it down. In the seconds it took him to finish stripping, a voice of reason tried to assert itself in Cassie's head. But when Luke rolled her over and edged up her T-shirt, pausing to suckle each breast in turn, she quit listening. And when his fingers plunged inside her panties to stroke her hot, wet core, she gave up thinking, too.

He trailed moist kisses across her stomach while he slipped off the lacy scrap, then slid himself upward, covering her completely. She caught her breath, not because of his weight pressing her into the mattress, but because she loved the feel of muscle and bone against her body—*Luke's* muscle and bone.

She closed her eyes and spread her hands wide across his back, using palms and fingertips to relearn every inch. Amazingly, she discovered, there was little relearning involved. As if by magic—or some internal gridwork of memory—her palms anticipated each ridge of muscle an instant before finding it, and her fingers knew just where to dip and rise along his spine.

He felt wonderful. Warm and wide, and so familiar her throat ached with emotion. She turned her face away, afraid to show her vulnerability, fearful he'd turn it against her as he had in the past.

"What's the matter?" Luke asked, running his fingers the length of her arm, so lightly it seemed he'd used a feather.

She shivered and gave a little shake of her head, her lips curving into a soft smile. Luke continued the teasing touch across her collarbone and up the side of her neck. With his tongue he traced the shell of her ear.

Desire shot through her and settled, hot and heavy in her womb. Hungrily she clasped him closer, wishing it could always be this way between them. He chuckled, kissed her tenderly, then pulled away. The movement was so unexpected, Cassie whimpered in protest, and her eyelids popped open.

"Shh." Luke soothed, running a thumb gently across her swollen lips. "I'm not leaving." Rolling to his side, he reached into the nightstand drawer and withdrew a small, foil-wrapped package.

It didn't really surprise Cassie he used protection. They'd been apart for two years, and although she hadn't been with another man, it was unlikely Luke had remained celibate. No, in view of the circumstances, it made perfect sense to be careful. What *was* illogical was her pain at realizing he was protecting her from getting pregnant. Irrational as it was, the act felt like a denial of all they'd been through.

In the moments it took for those thoughts to race through her head, Luke tossed the empty package to the floor and pulled her back in his arms.

"Sorry, sweetheart," he murmured in apology for his absence.

Cassie wrapped her arms around his neck and kissed him fiercely, in an attempt to blot out her insecurities. Luke responded with equal fervor, nipping at her neck, driving her wild with desire. His teeth grazed her earlobe as he whispered words of seduction that sent her spinning helplessly out of control.

And then, when she thought she could wait no longer, he was there, filling her, making her forget everything but the slick, sweet feel of him inside her.

She'd believed she'd purged him from her heart, and yet every touch of his lips, every caress of his body was hauntingly familiar. Like grass before the summer wind, she dipped and swayed in heated response to his lead, willingly following wherever he led. Without a qualm she abandoned herself to sensation.

In ever-increasing tempo, he moved within her, drawing her with him higher and higher. Then, without warning, he slowed his pace until she wanted to scream in frustration. Again and again, he brought her to the brink of fulfillment, then eased away, forcing her body to fever pitch. Her whole world narrowed to the tension coiling tighter and tighter within her and his passion-dark eyes above.

And finally, when every atom of her body shouted for release, he gave a final thrust and carried her over the edge.

Cassie clung tightly to him as together they rose, hung for one glorious instant, then spiraled downward through a shower of sparks.

Luke lay on his back amid a tangle of sheets, Cassie sprawled across him. He smoothed his palm along the length of her back. She responded with a hum of pleasure. He kissed the top of her head, content to drift in a state of euphoria.

He should be feeling guilty. After all, he'd just broken the first rule of police work—don't get involved. But as he rubbed his cheek against her curls, savoring the silky sensation, he admitted he'd been involved long before this morning. In all honesty, he should never have taken the assignment. Remembering Bradley's attempts to discourage him, Luke realized the chief had guessed the truth from the beginning—Luke still had feelings for Cassie. He'd just been too pigheaded to listen.

And look where his stubbornness had gotten him—smack dab in bed with his ex-wife.

A hell of a predicament, he thought. But the silly grin he felt spreading across his face belied his concern.

He inhaled, capturing Cassie's fragrance deep in his lungs. He finally remembered the name of the scent. Wild honeysuckle. It fit her. Wild and passionate. Honeyed mouth. And suckle—

His mind pictured what he'd like to suckle, and his manhood quivered with interest. He tried to exercise a little mind over matter, but Cassie chose that moment to shift her hips.

Groaning, Luke fought to control his wayward thoughts. He should get up, check with the lab on the results of the blood analysis, see how the investigation was progressing...

Cassie rocked gently.

Luke bit down on his lower lip, painfully aware his attempts at control were proving useless. Not until she cupped her hand around him did he realize her movements were no accident.

"You stinker," he said.

Cassie smothered a giggle and lifted her head. A picture of innocence, she asked, "What's the matter?" while her fingers glided the length of his erection.

All coherent thought disappeared. Gripped by agonizing need, he buried his fingers in her hair and urged her closer. With very little persuasion, she parted her lush lips and met each thrust of his tongue with a counterthrust of her own. Her arms slipped around his neck in a caress that sent shivers down his back, and she pressed against him. His body, the one he'd thought too tired to move, sprang to life and—

The telephone rang.

Luke uttered an expletive that would have done a sailor proud. Looping one arm around Cassie's shoulders, he stretched to reach the phone with his free hand. Frustration turned his greeting into a bark. "What?"

Someone chuckled.

Male, registered a sane, analytical portion of Luke's brain while the rest continued to fume. Not Cassie's father, not a brother. Luke gritted his teeth. He'd have the head of whichever of the homicide team was indulging in—

"Busy?"

His stomach muscles tightened. He recognized the voice, and it wasn't from homicide. The hoarse, sibilant whisper was the same he'd heard on the telephone in Cassie's hospital room. Luke's gaze leaped to Cassie's face, poised atop her crossed forearms on his chest. In response to a questioning look, he shook his head. "No one important," he mouthed, unwilling to alarm her. He ran a lazy finger over the satin skin of her shoulder and neck, and she relaxed, rubbing her cheek against the fur of his chest.

"What can I do for you?" Luke asked the caller, his tone deliberately bored. After all Cassie had been through in the last twenty-four hours, he didn't want to worry her needlessly.

"I thought you might pass on a little friendly advice...to your lady friend."

His *lady friend* apparently intent on distracting him, was tracing his ribs with light strokes of her nails. Luke gripped the phone hard enough to leave dents in his palm and struggled to concentrate on the conversation.

"Till now it's been fun and games, but I'm tired of playing. Get my drift? Tell her from now on it's for real—the majors all the way."

A chill went through Luke and raised hair on his neck. There was no mistaking the menace in the voice, nor the threat in the words. Realizing this was no time to play it cool, he manacled Cassie's wrist with his free hand so he could focus his attention. Cassie frowned and started to complain, but the protest died on her lips when she met his warning look.

Luke's response to the caller was laced with all the scorn he could muster. "This is *friendly* advice?"

"No. *This* is. Tell the lady to keep her nose clean. If she wants to live a long and healthy life, she'd better butt out of things that don't concern her."

"What about—"

A click in Luke's ear signaled the end of the conversation. Slowly he returned the receiver to its cradle and loosened his grip on Cassie. She sat up, cross-legged, and rubbed at her wrist.

"Sorry," he muttered, shoving one leg into the jeans he grabbed from the floor. He was less troubled by the caller's words than the fact the guy had found them so quickly. Luke checked the clock on the nightstand. Fifteen hours. Approximately half a day. A long time if they'd been followed, but he'd made certain they weren't. So, the man either had contacts or knew Cassie well enough to figure where she'd go.

"It was *him,* wasn't it?"

He nodded, rising to pull his jeans up the rest of the way. He filed a mental reminder to check with Cassie's father and brothers for odd calls. Somehow, he doubted there'd been any. The guy was too pleased with himself to have used such ordinary methods to find them.

"What did he say?"

"Nothing. Nothing to worry about." He smiled reassuringly as he sat on the bed, angling his body to face her. Gloriously naked, she glowed honey warm in the morning light, and despite his good intentions, Luke felt his body stir. Suddenly all he wanted was to forget this whole mess, to pull her into his arms and once again taste every golden inch of her. One look at her troubled expression, however, dissuaded him.

"It didn't sound like nothing." Suspicion glinted in her eyes.

"It didn't?"

"No."

"He was trying to impress me with how quickly he'd found us," Luke admitted, hoping to stall her with a half-truth. "The creep should do ads for the phone company. You know—'reach out and touch someone.'" He groped for his T-shirt, then remembered he'd left it in the living room last night. Straightening, he changed the subject. "Why don't I make us some coffee?"

"Not yet." She rose to her knees on the bed and halted him with a hand on his forearm. "I want to know the rest."

Same old Cassie, he thought, struggling to keep his irritation from showing. Couldn't leave well-enough alone. What did she want? To hear she'd been right all along? To know for sure that Wainright's death and her articles were connected? To learn some SOB was going to waste her if she didn't stop snooping?

"Drop it," he advised in a tone most of the men on the Force knew better than to argue with. "It's not your concern."

Her spine stiffened and she released his arm, clenching her fists at her sides. For one moment, before it went up several notches, he thought he saw her chin quiver, but an instant later he knew he was mistaken. There was nothing soft about the woman before him. Indeed, her naked body could have been carved from stone—a rosy marble he knew would feel cool to the touch.

"When are you going to learn you can't protect people—can't protect me—all the time?"

"I'm trying to safeguard your life."

"I know," she said, frustration evident on her face. "But just living is risky. A meteorite could hit me, or I could choke on a piece of steak. You can't protect me from everything."

I can try. I have to. He clenched his teeth, declaring the discussion at an end.

"I guess I just deluded myself into hoping—" Cassie bit her lip as though stopping herself from going on.

He waited for her to finish, for in spite of his irritation, he wanted to hear what she hoped, wanted to know if a few of their dreams still coincided. But when she shook her head and looked away, he knew he'd get no answer to his questions today.

Just as well. There were enough complications to this case without rehashing old dreams. Grimly he watched her rise from the bed and enter the bathroom without a backward glance. The door closed with a soft click, leaving him with a curious sense of disappointment. He heard the shower being turned on. For a fraction of an instant uncertainty raised its ugly head. Could Cassie be right about the way he chose to handle things?

No. Brushing aside his doubts, he reached for his gun on the nightstand. The scent of honeysuckle wafted to his nose.

Honeysuckle and musk.

He froze, assailed by a strong desire to slam open the bathroom door and demand she finish what she'd started. But common sense reasserted itself. With careful deliberation he turned his back on the rumpled bedsheets and the memories they'd rekindled.

He slid the weapon into his waistband. The cold metal raised goose bumps on his skin, but its presence was familiar and oddly comforting. Combing his fingers through his hair, he strode to the kitchen.

Chapter 9

Closing her eyes, Cassie stepped beneath the stream of water to rinse the soap from her hair. The spray beat against her scalp. Normally her muscles would have relaxed in response to the steady tattoo, but not this morning, thanks to a certain lunk-headed detective.

He was doing it again. Telling her what to do and how to do it. Giving orders. Hiding things from her. All in the name of protecting her. She swiped the excess moisture from her face, then lathered the washcloth with a bar of citrus-scented soap.

The sudsy slide of the washcloth over her breasts and belly reawakened memories of Luke's hands.

Fool!

She began scrubbing with renewed vigor in an attempt to eradicate the imprint of his body, the memory of his lips against her skin.

Only a fool willingly jumps into bed with her ex-husband.

What had she expected? He hadn't grown wings in the two years they'd been apart. He was still the same bullheaded, overbearing male he'd always been. Cassie faced into the falling spray, letting water sluice over her body.

How dare he treat her like a child, as though she were too fragile to hear the truth! This whole thing was about *her,* and she had every right to know what was going on. She shut off the water, shoved the shower curtain to one side. Grabbing a white towel emblazoned with Dallas Athletic Club from the rack, she blotted at her dripping hair, then stepped from the tub.

For someone so perceptive, Luke certainly had a blind spot when it came to her. He acted as though he still expected her to go off half-cocked at the slightest provocation.

Not that she'd done a whole lot to change his views, she admitted. She wiped steam from the mirror with a corner of the towel before wrapping it around her. The past two years had taught her patience and prudence, but you'd never know it when Luke was around. Somehow he managed to push her buttons and bring out the worst in her.

Well, not *always* the worst, she amended, her face reddening at the memory of earlier this morning.

Hastily she ran a comb through her hair, then prodded the damp curls into place with her fingers before returning to the bedroom for something to wear.

It was discouraging how easily she and Luke had slipped into old roles with one another. Luke, though sympathetic, seemed inclined to believe her still flighty and needing a firm rein, while Cassie found herself butting heads with him at every turn, even when it wasn't necessary.

Slinging her suitcase onto the floor, she crouched in front of it. Admittedly, not all the old roles were negative. A part of her liked having Luke around again. She'd missed their camaraderie and private jokes, missed sharpening her wit against his.

Realization slammed into her, rocking her back on her heels. In spite of the traumas and terrors of the past week, she felt more alive than she had in ages. Colors were brighter, scents more intense. Even the nerves in her body tingled with renewed energy.

Dear God, if she didn't know better, she'd almost say...

No! She refused to go there.

Grabbing the first thing that came to hand, she dressed and hurried from the room. When she entered the kitchen, Luke was just replacing the receiver on the telephone. Turning on a smile with enough wattage to light a 100-watt bulb, she pointed to a mug beside the sink. "Mine?"

"Unless you've given up caffeine."

Stepping over Duffy, who sat munching from a bowl of kibble, she reached for the pot. "Do you know any self-respecting reporter who has?"

Luke leaned one hip against the counter, pelvis thrust forward, and watched from beneath half-lowered eyelids as she poured her coffee. He looked positively sinful.

Suddenly dry-mouthed, Cassie concentrated on adding sugar to her cup. "Who was on the phone?"

"Jessup."

"And...?" When he didn't elaborate, Cassie shot a glance from the corner of her eyes. His expression told her he was considering what to tell her. The look, alone, triggered a button, but she checked her first impulse and found that restraint brought the results she wanted.

"They've located a Mitchell's Delivery Service out of Fort Collins, but their area doesn't extend to Boulder."

"So what was it doing here?"

"Their regular vehicles are accounted for, but an older van kept for emergencies is missing from their warehouse. We've got an APB out on it, but so far, no luck. It's probably tucked away in a garage somewhere."

Duffy whined and edged hopefully toward the door. When neither human leaped to attention, he gave a single bark.

"I'd better take him out for a walk," Cassie said, setting down her coffee.

PLAY "LUCKY 7" AND GET
THREE FREE GIFTS!

HOW TO PLAY:

1. With a coin, carefully scratch off the silver box at the right. Then check the claim chart see what we have for you — **FREE BOOKS** and a gift — **ALL YOURS! ALL FREE!**

2. Send back this card and you'll receive brand-new Silhouette Intimate Moments® novel These books have a cover price of $4.50 each in the U.S. and $5.25 each in Canada, b they are yours to keep absolutely free.

3. There's no catch. You're und no obligation to buy anything. V charge nothing — ZERO — f your first shipment. And you do have to make any minimum numb of purchases — not even one!

4. The fact is thousands of readers enjoy receiving books by mail from the Silhouette Read Service.™ They enjoy the convenience of home delivery... they like getting the best ne novels at discount prices, BEFORE they're available in stores...and they love their *Heart Heart* newsletter featuring author news, horoscopes, recipes, book reviews and much more!

5. We hope that after receiving your free books you'll want to remain a subscriber. B the choice is yours — to continue or cancel, any time at all! So why not take us up on c invitation, with no risk of any kind. You'll be glad you did!

YOURS FREE!

PLAY LUCKY 7 FOR THIS EXCITING FREE GIFT!

THIS SURPRISE MYSTERY GIFT COULD BE YOURS FREE WHEN YOU PLAY
LUCKY 7!

Visit us on-line at
www.romance.net

NO COST! NO OBLIGATION TO BUY!
NO PURCHASE NECESSARY!

PLAY THE

LUCKY 7

SLOT MACHINE GAME!

Just scratch off the silver box with a coin. Then check below to see the gifts you get!

YES!

I have scratched off the silver box. Please send me the 2 FREE books and gift for which I qualify. I understand I am under no obligation to purchase any books, as explained on the back and opposite page.

345 SDL CY2U

245 SDL CY2P
(S-IM-02/00)

NAME   (PLEASE PRINT CLEARLY)

ADDRESS   APT.#

CITY   STATE/PROV.   ZIP/POSTAL CODE

7	7	7

WORTH TWO FREE BOOKS PLUS A BONUS MYSTERY GIFT!

WORTH TWO FREE BOOKS!

WORTH ONE FREE BOOK!

TRY AGAIN!

DETACH AND MAIL CARD TODAY!

The Silhouette Reader Service™ — Here's how it works:

Accepting your 2 free books and gift places you under no obligation to buy anything. You may keep the books and gift and return the shipping statement marked "cancel." If you do not cancel, about a month later we'll send you 6 additional novels and bill you just $3.80 each in the U.S., or $4.21 each in Canada, plus 25¢ delivery per book and applicable taxes if any.* That's the complete price and — compared to cover prices of $4.50 each in the U.S. and $5.25 each in Canada — it's quite a bargain! You may cancel at any time, but if you choose to continue, every month we'll send you 6 more books, which you may either purchase at the discount price or return to us and cancel your subscription.

*Terms and prices subject to change without notice. Sales tax applicable in N.Y. Canadian residents will be charged applicable provincial taxes and GST.

If offer card is missing write to: Silhouette Reader Service, 3010 Walden Ave., P.O. Box 1867, Buffalo, NY 14240-1867

BUSINESS REPLY MAIL
FIRST-CLASS MAIL   PERMIT NO. 717   BUFFALO, NY

POSTAGE WILL BE PAID BY ADDRESSEE

SILHOUETTE READER SERVICE
3010 WALDEN AVE
PO BOX 1867
BUFFALO NY 14240-9952

NO POSTAGE
NECESSARY
IF MAILED
IN THE
UNITED STATES

Luke pushed away from the counter. "We'll both go. I need some fresh air."

He wasn't going for the fresh air, but Cassie was glad of the pretense that everything was all right. At the moment she didn't want to dwell on murder and stalkers and what she couldn't remember, any more than she wanted to think about the articles hanging over her head like a dark cloud. Having Luke along would be like the old days, when they'd used early-morning walks as an excuse to spend time together.

She scooped up Duffy and waited out on the tiny, concrete landing for Luke to secure the door. "Any special destination?"

"I've seen some of my neighbors take their dogs over there," he said, indicating the weed-clogged field at the far end of the parking lot.

Cassie's vision of a companionable stroll to Red Rocks Park evaporated like moisture on hot pavement. It was just as well, she decided, setting Duffy down. Neither she nor Luke wanted to fall into old habits, and that's all their love-making had been—an old habit. Luke had made it clear he was only here for the duration of the case, and she—well, she wasn't going to settle for another relationship cloned from the first. Resolute, she forced her thoughts into different channels.

"I'm thinking about calling a doctor," she announced.

Luke turned to study her. "If you're feeling bad, I can walk Duffy by myself."

"No, I'm fine…except for an occasional headache. I don't mean a physician." Rubbing at the metal railing with her forefinger, she gazed toward the low ridge at the back of the building. "I mean a psychiatrist. Someone who can help me remember. Maybe they can hypnotize me or something."

"Hypnosis can help people remember details, but it's debatable whether it brings back memory."

Cassie shot him a surprised look.

"The chief already explored that possibility," he explained, sidestepping to let Duffy push close to the railing for a look at the ground. "Besides, we've been warned to go easy on the jogging-your-memory angle. We don't want to jeopardize our case in court."

"How would my remembering hurt your case?"

"A good defense lawyer would jump all over your testimony if someone helped things along. Implanted memories and undue influence, for starters."

Duffy drew their attention with a low growl. Ears pricked forward, he stared over the edge of the concrete landing at something below.

"He's probably spotted—" Cassie made an ineffectual grab for the little dog as he raced down the steps, barking furiously "—a squirrel." She started after him.

Luke stopped her headlong pursuit by grabbing her arm. "No, I'll—"

A sudden flash of sunlight glinting off something made Cassie squeeze her eyes shut. In one time-lapse moment, Luke shoved her, pinning her against the building with his body. Air whooshed from her lungs.

Something thunked against the door a split second before she heard three sharp cracks resonate in the air.

Before her brain could process what was happening, Luke pulled away. Drawing his gun with one hand, he dug in his pocket with the other. He shoved a key into her hand. "Here! Get inside and lock the door behind you."

Struggling to get a breath, Cassie managed one word. "Duffy—"

"I'll take care of him," he growled. "Just do as I say." His tone brooked no argument. With shaky fingers, she inserted the key into the lock and twisted frantically at the handle.

Halfway down the first flight of steps, Luke snapped out one last command. "And stay away from the windows!"

Cassie staggered inside the apartment, turned and threw her weight against the door. It crashed shut. She secured two locks and the dead bolt before slumping against the solid wood.

What in the name of heaven is going on?

Willing her legs to carry her, she stumbled to the kitchen and dialled 911. By the time she gave the pertinent information tremors seized her.

Cold. So cold.

She grabbed the afghan from the back of the couch and pulled it around her as she sat. Feeling as though she'd just survived a winter storm on Mount Evans, she rocked her body and tried to make sense of the last few minutes.

Someone had taken a shot at them! At her. The glint that had momentarily blinded her must have been from the metal of a gun. And Duffy had sensed danger.

Duffy.

Dear Lord, she prayed. Don't let him get hurt.

She stopped rocking.

What was going on outside?

Slowly she uncoiled her body and licked her dry lips. Her ears strained for sounds of gunfire, a struggle. She heard nothing but the hum of the refrigerator in the kitchen.

It was like being inside an isolation chamber.

Her gaze darted across the spill of light on the carpet to the window. From the couch all she could see was a portion of the indigo sky with a wisp of cloud in one corner.

Stay away from the window.

Cassie hadn't answered Luke, hadn't had time to. But if she had, she would have assured him the last thing she wanted was to be mistaken for one of those wooden ducks in a shooting gallery.

But the drapery cord was on the side nearest to her. And if she hugged the wall...

She pulled the afghan closer around her and rose. Taking care to stay out of the range of anyone on the ground below, she sidled toward the window. An arm's length away, she yanked the cord. The drapes swayed shut.

The maneuver left her breathless and wondering how cops managed in similar circumstances.

Counting slowly she tried to convince herself there was nothing to be afraid of as long as she was careful. The tightness in her chest informed her that her body didn't agree. At 100, she reached out and pushed the drapes away from the wall. Only an inch—hardly noticeable unless someone was staring directly at the window. Again she waited. Finally, when her efforts elicited no reaction, she cautiously leaned closer to the opening.

A loud banging on the door jerked her away from the peephole and sent her heart into her throat.

"It's me, Luke. Open up, Cassie."

Weak from reaction, Cassie hurried to the door, undid the locks and let him in. The closed expression on his face announced his lack of success in catching the shooter, but for the moment Cassie didn't care. Luke had Duffy tucked under one arm.

She took the indignant terrier to the couch and checked him over. He didn't have a scratch on him. Ignoring his squirms of protest, she hugged him close.

"Had to chase him all the way to Canyon Boulevard," Luke grumbled.

It wasn't until Luke said "From now on he stays on a leash when we're out-of-doors" that Cassie realized he was speaking of Duffy and not the invisible assailant.

"What about the—"

Luke dropped to the couch. "He got away from us. Had too much of a head start. My backup called in an APB, but they won't find him. Hell, I couldn't even give a description." He leaned forward, elbows on his knees, frustration evident in every tense muscle. "Too many different threats and attacks," he muttered, running restless fingers through his hair. "I'd swear there was more than..."

Cassie stopped stroking Duffy's fur. "Luke..." she said in a tentative voice.

He wasn't listening. "But only one caller. One person directing things—or hiring out the work." He straightened. "That's the only thing that makes any sense."

"Luke..." She tried again.

He gave her his attention.

"Maybe we should reconsider my idea of seeing a shrink."

He seemed to consider the suggestion. "Maybe," he said, leaning back and closing his eyes with a sigh. "You are the common denominator." He remained silent for several seconds. "But not yet."

Why not? It made perfect sense to *her*.

As if she'd asked her question aloud, Luke opened his eyes. "No matter what, our top priorities are finding a killer *and* making sure he doesn't get off on a legal technicality."

"But—"

"No buts." He took Duffy from her and set him on the floor. The dog threw him what could only be interpreted as a grateful look and lay down out of reach under the glass table. Taking Cassie's hand, Luke continued. "I know you think you have to remember or we won't find the killer. You could be right, but give us a chance. We solve lots of cases that have no witnesses."

"But my remembering might make it easier."

"It might," Luke agreed. "But it's not guaranteed."

Turning her hand palm up, he traced lightly over her life line. "Tell you what. If, after a reasonable time, your memory hasn't returned—and if we don't have a suspect in custody—I'll personally take you to the best shrink in Colorado."

"Reasonable time?"

"Two more weeks."

This sounded too simple. Luke didn't normally capitulate so easily. She narrowed her eyes in thought.

"Okay, you got me." Luke grinned. "I already ran it by

the chief. He's given permission. Reluctantly. And only if we wait till after the end of the month.''

The grin convinced her. Open and honest, it told her he would try her way if his didn't work. She nodded agreement. As much as she wanted to remember, as much as it scared her to have a big, blank hole in her orderly life, she could understand the police's reluctance to do anything that might be used against them.

Luke gave her a hug. "Now, we have to get you out of town. It's the only way to guarantee your safety while the team follows up leads.''

"Out of town?" Cassie couldn't keep dismay from coloring her words. "For how long? My article's due in a few days, and—''

"Take your laptop. Wherever we go, there'll be electricity.'' Then, guessing her next concern, he added as he crossed to the kitchen, "And a phone line to transmit it if necessary.''

Cassie's mouth snapped shut. He'd overcome her objections without blinking an eye, leaving her with no good argument against going away with him. She half listened while he discussed diversionary tactics over the phone with someone at the station, grateful to leave the details of their escape to others. His voice rumbled on, deep and somehow comforting. Feeling strangely detached, Cassie quit listening to the words, concentrating instead on the way the cadences dipped and swayed around her.

She jumped when Luke touched her arm. She'd been so deep in thought, she hadn't heard him approach.

"Bradley's arranging for us to use a cabin in the mountains outside of Nederland—Connor McCormack's. Remember him? Used to work undercover. You went to his wedding.''

Cassie nodded, recalling a broad-shouldered Irishman and the pretty probation officer who'd finally snagged him. All she really remembered of the boisterous wedding, though, was an endless sea of celebrating relatives, a staggering number of whom had been cops.

"McCormack's place is isolated, and we'll make sure no one follows us."

"I guess I'd better get my suitcase," Cassie said, making no move to get up.

Luke studied her face, then urged her to her feet. "Hang in there, slugger. Get your things together. In an hour you won't have anything left to worry about." He gave her a little shove toward the bedroom.

Nothing but you, she responded silently as she made her way down the hall.

Chapter 10

"Home, sweet home," announced Luke. The car rolled to a stop in front of a tiny cabin on the edge of the clearing. Juggling her laptop and Duffy, Cassie trailed Luke to the door. While he fished a key from his pocket, she eyed the log structure with suspicion. It looked as though the next strong wind might knock it flat. Evidently sensing her apprehension, he reassured her. "Mac says this place is about as secure as you can get. Besides the road we came in on, the only other access involves an hour hike through the forest. The path starts just beyond the outhouse."

"Outhouse?"

"Mac said a septic tank's next on his list of improvements, but till then…" Her face must have reflected dismay because Luke smiled as he turned the key in the lock. "I'll stand guard if you need me."

"Wonderful," Cassie replied faintly and followed him across the threshold.

The single window on the cabin's rear wall transmitted only token light as the late-afternoon sky darkened outside.

Cassie paused to adjust to the shadowed interior. It reminded her of the three bears' house—or at least the way she'd imagined it as a child. Halfway across the room, two straight-backed chairs and an antique highchair were pulled up to a wooden table. All that was missing were bowls of cooling porridge. Cassie set her computer on the table and released Duffy, who made a beeline for an overstuffed couch in front of a stone fireplace.

"Turn on the light. It's behind the door," Luke called over his shoulder as he carried the grocery bags to a low counter beneath the window.

Cassie groped unsuccessfully in the shadows, a vague sense of unease grabbing her. A distant clap of thunder combined with the darkness to send her fingers scrabbling over the rough logs, frantically searching. Anxiety ballooned in her chest, pushing outward with ever-increasing pressure. She sensed Luke moving around the kitchen, heard Duffy's doggy snores, but they were no more than phantoms hovering on the edge of the mist.

Reality was a sinister, looming shape at her back. It was a growing sense of fright and the certainty that something awful would happen if she couldn't push back the gloom.

Her lungs ached in their effort to suck in air and release it through her constricted throat, until finally, after what seemed like hours, she touched the corner of a smooth plastic plate, then flipped up the lever at its center. Light flared across the open room.

On legs of rubber Cassie crossed the short distance to the couch and lowered herself onto one lumpy cushion. Her body felt oddly limp, like a shirt with no starch. She clasped her hands in her lap to keep them from shaking. Was she going mad? She was no longer a child, afraid of the dark. She'd long ago outgrown the fear of monsters waiting in dark corners. So what had possessed her?

Was she suffering some kind of delayed stress syndrome?

A result of the last few days? Or was she on the verge of a nervous breakdown?

The crinkly sound of paper bags being folded told her Luke was nearly finished in the kitchen. She drew an unsteady breath, telling herself she should check on the stove, decide what to cook for dinner, but her body refused to cooperate. She'd go in a minute, when her heart stopped fluttering against her rib cage and her face felt less like a flour-and-water mask.

She shivered.

"Cold?"

Fingers curved around her shoulder.

Startled, Cassie twisted her head. While she'd puzzled over tricks of the mind, Luke had finished his chores. Now he stood directly behind the couch, so close she could feel the heat of his body. So close that with only a small movement...

She tilted her head so her cheek brushed against the fine hairs on his forearm. The wobbly feeling in her stomach lessened. It took so little to make her feel safe and cared for. She remembered the way he'd cradled her last night so she'd been able to hear the thudding of his heart in his chest.

A soothing lullaby.

She smiled and felt her self-doubts lose ground as warmth radiated from Luke's palm. Warmth and comfort.

After all this time, after all that had happened between them, he still had the power to move her. To anger. To laughter. To tears.

Her smile faded. She was unexpectedly terrified at the direction of her thoughts. For two years she'd managed with no one, yet all it had taken was for Luke to walk back through the door and into her life...

Cassie rose to her feet, steeling herself against the regret that seeped through her as Luke let go of her shoulder. On the periphery of her vision, the window brightened and a second later thunder rolled. She flinched.

"Cassie?" Worry edged his voice.

"I'm fine," she said, wrapping her arms around her upper body. "But a fire would definitely take off the chill."

"Good idea," Luke agreed, but he continued to stare at her for long seconds, and Cassie had the weird sensation he read her fear as easily as if she'd spoken it aloud. He placed kindling beneath the small pile of logs in the fireplace, then hunkered to light it. A flame leaped within the logs, hungrily consuming bits of bark and paper. Without turning, he spoke again. "You're remembering, aren't you?"

"Maybe," she replied in as casual a tone as she could muster. Dread trickled through her. Was that what was happening? Suddenly, contrary to all her earlier declarations, she wasn't sure if remembering was such a good idea. Not if it involved the terror she'd experienced a few minutes ago.

"I don't think so," she amended hastily, relieved that he kept his attention on the fire. "I think I'm just tired."

"That's probably it," he agreed without looking up. He picked up the poker and prodded the logs.

Her tension eased at his easy acceptance. She watched his profile against the flickering light, mesmerized by the way shadows dipped and danced in the hollow beneath his cheekbone and skated across his lips.

The kitchen window rattled in its frame. Rain splattered against the glass. Luke leveled a glance at her over his shoulder. The poker stilled in his hand. "Tell me, Cassie. Since when have you been afraid of lightning storms?"

Her chest tightened. She shook her head vehemently. "I'm *not* afraid. I was just startled."

"And since when," he asked, his tone mocking her denial, "were you afraid to face the truth?"

Cassie bit her lip as the barb struck home, and Luke pressed his advantage. "You're remembering, and for some reason you don't want to."

"Who *would?*" she shot back, letting anger bury the fear. "You seem to forget that I probably saw someone killed—

someone I knew and respected. Isn't that reason enough to not want to remember?''

"Enough," he agreed. "But I think there's something more. Something else you're afraid to face." His expression grew pensive. "Could it be you're afraid something you did caused Wainright's death, something more than your series?"

Throat tight, she tried to smile. "Don't be silly. It's the articles. We agreed."

Luke stood, forcing her gaze upward. "No." His tone raised the hairs on the back of her neck. "*You* decided. The police have continued exploring *all* the angles." His glittering gaze pinned her like a moth, forcing her to listen to truths she didn't want to hear. "Whether or not your articles have any bearing is immaterial. You're the key. You personally. Maybe you didn't cause Wainright's death. Maybe the problem is you can't accept who did."

Unable to look away, Cassie edged backward until she came up against the table. Luke was wrong. She didn't know the person who'd killed Judge Wainright. Why couldn't he leave her alone? Suddenly the cabin felt like a trap instead of a haven. Catching her lower lip in her teeth, she swung toward the kitchen window.

Lightning seared across her retinas, sending her heart into her throat. A drumroll of thunder shook the cabin. When Duffy added his howl to the barrage, Cassie clapped her hands to her ears and squeezed shut her eyes, just as the lights flickered and went out.

It's a storm. It's a storm. Over and over the litany repeated itself in her head, with little effect.

Too wrapped in her private struggle to hear or see anything, Cassie sensed Luke's approach an instant before he touched her. His scent flooded her nostrils, his strength enveloped her. Blindly, like a falling climber grabbing for a handhold, she reached out and hugged herself against him.

He slipped his arms around her, his voice low and comforting. The words didn't matter—she couldn't distinguish them, anyway. It only mattered that he was here, soothing her silent tears, absorbing the shudders that racked her body. Keeping her from slipping off the edge of the world.

Twice in as many days. Luke registered the oddity of Cassie's tears, while inside his chest, something softened, like a lump of clay in a potter's warm hands.

Without halting the flow of soothing words, he turned the puzzle over in his mind. What had brought that pinched look to her face earlier? Why was she suddenly fearful of lightning storms? And most of all, what was she hiding—from him and from herself?

So many questions. Too few answers.

She shifted against him, her muscles no longer rigid and unyielding. Her breath heated his skin through the tear-dampened shirt. Unbidden, the image of the morning's love-making returned to haunt him. His body reacted instinctively, stiffening with want.

Guiltily, before she could feel his arousal, Luke put space between them when what he really wanted was to pull her into his lap, slant his mouth across her full lips and release his insistent desire. He imagined her kisses, hot and achingly sweet, envisioned the moment of complete surrender…

Feeling anything but noble, he trailed his palms down her arms. "Go sit by the fire," he suggested, realizing how impossible it had become to remain objective now that they'd been intimate again.

She stiffened when he nudged her toward the couch, and when he didn't follow, he knew she felt abandoned. There was nothing else he could do. At least, not if he was going to stick to the promise he'd made himself to keep his distance.

For an instant he allowed himself to relive the horror he'd felt when shots rang out on the landing next to his apartment. He remembered the mind-numbing terror that had nearly wiped out all his training.

He'd gotten too close. When he wasn't looking, she'd slipped inside his defenses and made him care again, but he couldn't risk it. Not now, when her life hung in the balance.

His resolve strengthened. No matter how he felt, he had to maintain tight control over his libido. He'd do Cassie no good if he didn't.

While she eased onto the sofa, Luke crossed to the wall by the door and flipped the light switch several times. As he expected, nothing happened. Moving to the kitchen, he lit the kerosene lamp on the counter, then lifted the phone from its wall receiver. Dead air greeted him.

He hung up the phone. Too bad his cellular was out of city range. For long seconds he stared at the log wall. With a wry twist to his lips, he watched fire-cast shadows leap and sway in a primordial dance. He'd gotten what he had aimed for—with a vengeance. Not only were they far from town, now they were completely cut off from civilization.

Rubbing the back of his neck, Luke turned from the shadow show and joined Cassie in front of the fire.

"How about some coffee?" he offered. "I brought a thermos."

She shook her head.

"Some cola? A glass of water?"

"I don't need anything."

From you, he finished mutely, heaving a silent sigh of exasperation. It was as if the last few minutes had never happened. Lightning and thunder hadn't startled her; she'd never trembled in his arms. She was back to being strong and independent. Invulnerable.

When he settled next to her on the couch, he wasn't surprised to have her edge away. He leaned forward, elbows resting on his thighs, hands dangling between widespread legs, and pretended to be fascinated by the fire. Somehow he had to break through her protective armor and convince her she needed help. His help.

Duffy sidled over, nudging his hand with his nose. Luke

scratched absentmindedly behind the dog's ears. "You're not unusual, you know," he told Cassie.

He didn't need to see her face. Her stillness proclaimed her attention. "It's quite typical for people suffering trauma to block out the events leading up to it. Selective amnesia, they call it."

"Psych 101?"

"Victim Awareness 2000," he quipped. He shifted his weight and reached out, gathering her icy fingers between his palms.

She stared pointedly at their intertwined hands, then raised an eyebrow at him. "More VA 2000?"

The smile he'd been trying to hide flitted across his lips. "Second semester."

Cassie didn't return the smile. "You wasted your tuition," she said, tugging loose her hands and wedging herself into the corner of the couch. She crossed her arms over her chest and met his quizzical look with narrowed eyes. "I don't need your armchair psychology."

Luke clenched his teeth. "I'm only telling you for your own good," he replied with as much patience as he could muster.

"That's the excuse you always use when you want me to do things your way."

Although it took some effort, he relaxed against the cushions and kept his voice reasonable. "I'm trying to find a killer." A killer who gave every indication he'd decided to eliminate any witnesses.

"So you can solve your case."

"So I can keep you alive."

"Why?"

He tensed. The question, little more than a breath of air, floated across the space separating them and banged against his heart. Why was he fighting so hard to protect her? He could say he'd do the same for anyone in his care and it would be the truth.

But not the whole truth.

Luke watched firelight play across her face, etching it in stark relief against the inky background of the room. She worried her lower lip with her teeth, the way she did when something troubled her. This time he knew the cause—his expected response. What was he going to tell her? Restless, he crossed one ankle over the opposite knee and scanned the room, as if his answer lay somewhere in the dark shadows.

All she asked for was honesty. All it required was baring his soul. He wasn't sure he could.

The God's truth was, he owed her. For the one terrible time he hadn't protected her, for what she'd suffered. Although a permanent bond no longer joined them, Luke knew he'd never really be free until things were out in the open. Like a spirit held earthbound by unfinished business, he would remain tied to her for eternity...unless he atoned for his mistake.

"It was my fault you lost the baby."

Confession was supposed to be good for the soul, but Luke felt raw and exposed, as though his heart had been wrenched from his body and left to dry in the sun. Disbelief flitted across Cassie's face, followed by an expression of dismay. He tried once again to take her hand, but when she shook her head and raised her palms to halt him, he stood.

He'd always known how she'd react if he admitted the truth. He'd anticipated her rejection, yet it still left him hollow inside, like the way he felt when he arrived at a crime scene—his mind trying to prepare for the carnage he was about to view, his gut wrenching over not having prevented it.

Just like those times, he wanted to turn and walk away, leave the devastation for someone else to clean up.

And just like those times, he made himself proceed before he could lose his nerve. He paced the length of the cramped cabin while he recounted, in controlled tones, how he'd weighed the alternatives.

''The jail personnel handled things by the book. They didn't try to stop Durell when he took you hostage during the interview. They refrained from making him more nervous than he already was. If it'd been my operation at that point, I'd have tried negotiation instead of handing over the keys to a car, but I can't fault them for doing what they did.''

In the kitchen the kerosene lamp cast a spill of muddy light onto the floor. Luke circled it and returned to the couch. ''At least,'' he said, stealing a sideways glance at Cassie, ''they did what they could to ensure your safety.''

Her face, as she followed his progress, looked like one of those you saw in pictures of relocation camps—the ones of women who'd grown so inured to sorrow and adversity, they asked for nothing from life.

Luke looked away, tempted to gloss over the next part to spare her feelings. To spare his own. But it was too late. Once set in motion, he couldn't stop his forward momentum. He didn't want to. If it killed him, he had to set things straight. Now.

Last night he'd realized how much blame she'd taken on her shoulders. For his own peace of mind he had to make it clear she was wrong.

''They took a safe course of action,'' he repeated, stopping beside the fireplace. Duffy looked up expectantly, but Luke ignored him. Before he could sugarcoat what he had to say, he swung to confront her. ''I didn't.''

Shock registered on her face, but no words came from her mouth. Grimly Luke pushed on. ''There may have been safer ways to handle the situation. We could have called for outside help—a negotiator. Hell, we could have even let him run until he felt safe enough to release you. He was desperate, and what I set into motion didn't help.''

Unable to bear her haunted eyes, Luke dug his fists into his pockets and hunched his shoulders. He stared at the rug. ''I forced the issue. I ordered the chase. I insisted they press him, push him over the edge. It was a calculated risk, but one I knew would eventually shove him into our hands.''

Heated sap popped in the fireplace. Luke turned to brace his hands against the mantel, determined to look anywhere except at Cassie while he admitted his failure. ''I never meant for you to be hurt. I never meant to hurt the baby.''

He heard a strangled gasp and knew she'd tried to hide her reaction. He was a coward for not facing her, but it was hard enough to feel her pain without watching it twist her features. He had to see this confession through. Every stinking part of it. That would be impossible if he saw tears well in her eyes, watched them trace paths down her cheeks.

He had just steeled himself to go on when she touched his back. It was indicative of his frame of mind that he hadn't heard her approach. And when she spoke, her words were so soft, for a moment he thought he'd imagined them.

''You did what you had to.''

Self-disgust rose in his throat. *She* was comforting *him*.

''I never blamed you, Luke.''

Her lack of censure, her unconditional acceptance, was the final straw. Knowing what he still must tell her, he couldn't let her go on feeling sorry for him. Scowling, he swung around.

''But *I* blamed *you*.''

As he intended, shock obliterated the expression of pity he didn't deserve, but he still felt like a heel. ''I couldn't face what I'd done, so I told myself it wouldn't have happened if you'd listened to me. I told myself your stubbornness and rash behavior had killed our child.''

Cassie flinched as though struck.

Luke forestalled an urge to apologize by dropping a fresh log in the grate. Then, without looking at her, he took a deep breath and plunged on, hurrying to get the whole mess over with.

''I remembered how at first you'd fought the idea of being pregnant, how you'd said it was too soon. I convinced myself you were glad our child had died, that you'd hidden your resentment so I wouldn't know how you really felt.'' Two years of festering bitterness churned his insides, turning his voice harsh and unrecognizable to his ear.

''God forgive me, I hated you for destroying what we could have had.'' His voice broke, and for long moments all he could hear was the harsh sound of his own breathing. Within the cabin there was no sound, save the crackling fire.

Turn around. Tell her the rest.

But when he tried to speak, dryness prickled his throat. Opting for the coward's way, he crossed to the kitchen cabinet where, earlier, he'd spotted the liquor supply. He grabbed the first bottle that came to hand and took a long swig. Whisky burned its way to his stomach.

Bracing his hands on the counter, he watched the wind whip the trees outside the window and waited for the alcohol to work its magic. Rain splattered against the glass like the tapping of nervous fingers. Though it was hard to tell for sure in the gathering dusk, the storm seemed to be moving on.

''I was wrong,'' he informed his reflection, then repeated the words louder for Cassie's benefit. ''But it wasn't until last night that I realized how wrong.''

He cast her a look over his shoulder, but all he could make out was her bowed head. Guiltily he backtracked to the far side of the cabin, drawn by the vulnerable curve of her slender neck. The closer he moved, the more apprehensive he became. At any moment he expected her to lash out in anger and condemnation, but she remained silent until he was a few feet away.

''There were times…'' She faltered, then staggered on. ''Times when I thought I'd buried my heart alongside Danny's casket.''

Her admission threw him into confusion. The pain edging her voice pulled him closer. He lifted a hand to touch her.

''Don't!''

The single, vehement word, uttered without turning her head, stopped him cold. He dropped his hand to his side.

When she finally continued, her voice was flat and devoid of emotion. "I had nothing to hold on to. No pictures, no souvenirs. I didn't even have memories to help me. I'd never sheltered Danny in my arms, never felt his baby breath against my skin."

Her words sliced his careful control with razor-sharp precision, exposing the full extent of his blindness. By wrapping himself in his grief, he'd refused her the right to admit her own.

"I knew you blamed me," Cassie whispered. "I blamed myself. And the only way I could deal with the pain was to bury it deep inside and get on with my life, my work."

Her shaking shoulders sent Luke around the sofa to crouch before her, balanced on the balls of his feet. For an instant he hesitated, studying the crown of curls that hid her face. Then, with fingers curved beneath her chin, he gently raised her head.

Tears streaking her cheeks, she bit her lower lip and tried to avert her gaze. He wouldn't let her.

"Cassie, I was wrong to punish you by pulling away. My only excuse is fear. I was so afraid of the censure I'd see in your eyes, I refused to look and see the pain." He knuckled a stray tear trickling down one cheek, then raised her hand to his lips. "I'm sorry. Can you forgive me?"

Forgive him? Cassie looked up in surprise. Her eyelids felt hot and swollen, her lips parched. While she searched his face in confusion, she cleared her throat, stalling for time. Not a sign of insincerity, not a hint of disapproval marred his expression. Only a reflection of her own pain.

She swallowed around a sudden lump. Once she'd have given anything to hear those words. Now she wasn't sure they made any real difference.

It had taken so long to confront her failures, to accept herself, flaws and all. But doing so had brought her a measure of peace. And time had worked its magic. If it hadn't quite healed all her wounds, it had, at least, tempered her first, wild grief into something she could live with—an aching hollow at the center of her being.

Did she really dare to upset the precious balance she'd established and shed the guilt that had become a part of her very existence? Because she knew, even if Luke didn't, the magnitude of his request. She could only forgive him if she were willing to forgive herself, too.

Against her palm his breath was moist and seductive. The persuasive pressure of his firm lips sent a shiver trembling through her veins. The mantle of guilt she'd worn for so long slipped a fraction, but instead of frigid air against her skin, she felt hope warm her. If Luke no longer blamed her, if *he* believed…

Cassie took a deep breath and with a slight nod, took the first, hesitant step toward peace.

Tension drained from Luke's face, relieving any lingering doubts she may have harbored about her decision. She'd done the right thing. Maybe now they could both get on with their lives, unfettered by ghosts.

He straightened, urging Cassie from the couch with a gentle tug. He readjusted his grip to encircle her wrists, manacling them so loosely she could have broken free if she wanted.

She didn't want.

"Thank you," he said, his voice rough edged with emotion. He regarded her with a sober intensity that set her insides quivering in anticipation, while his thumbs traced figure eights against the insides of her wrists.

Cassie knew she should break off contact. Now that they'd cleared the air, there was no logical reason to remain standing so close. However, as Luke himself had pointed out on numerous occasions, she'd never concerned herself overmuch with logic. And right now, with all her senses focused on his hypnotic touch, her brain wasn't working too well.

"Have I answered your question?"

"Question?" she asked, distracted from his words as he tracked twin paths on her inner forearms.

"About why I want to keep you alive."

Cassie would have answered in the affirmative, but just then Luke's thumbs moved to the sensitive spot inside her elbows, and her brain shut down. Awareness shimmered through her, firing her cheeks, and try as she might, she couldn't stop a shiver of delight.

When he drew her close, she went willingly, though she knew it was folly. He had made no promise but forgiveness, no pledge but acceptance. Yet, for now, it was enough. She rested against his chest, content to stand within the circle of his arms and inhale his masculine scent.

"This time I'll take better care of you."

The words were disturbingly familiar, but Cassie refused to waste time examining them with Luke's fingers spearing her hair and flexing against her scalp. He cupped the back of her head. Then, with maddening slowness, he lowered his mouth to capture her lips.

So sweet was his kiss, Cassie forgot to breathe. Heat coursed through her, leaving her weak with desire, so weak that if she hadn't clasped her hands behind his neck, she would have fallen.

When he drew back, she moaned, then sighed as he trailed his fingers from her cheek down the column of her throat.

"I don't think this is a good idea," he said hoarsely. "At least, not until the case is over."

Cassie's eyes widened. "Maybe you should have thought of that earlier," she retorted as disbelief warred with frustration.

"I did." He shook his head as though to clear it. "I'm just having trouble following through lately."

If she hadn't felt so thwarted, Cassie might have been flattered. Luke had as much as admitted that being around her played havoc with his precious control. Unfortunately, right now she wasn't thinking too straight, either.

"Besides," he added, avoiding her eyes as he ruffled his hair with agitated fingers, "I didn't pack any condoms."

The realization that his frustration was as acute as hers offset the pain of his words a little, pain she tried to hide with an offhanded shrug. "No problem. It's the wrong time of month to get me pregnant."

Luke jerked as though struck. "Is that what you think?"

When she responded with another shrug, he seized her shoulders. "Damn it, Cassie, look at me," he demanded.

His fingers dug insistently into her upper arms, forcing her to lift her gaze. Holding her breath until her chest ached, she willed her lower lip not to tremble. Her efforts at hiding her feelings proved useless. The muscles clenching along Luke's jaw informed her he'd deciphered her thoughts as easily as he read clues at a crime scene.

With a heavy sigh, he relaxed his grip. "Don't blow this out of proportion, slugger. It's just that it's been two years." He released her and rubbed the back of his neck, his gaze sliding away. "Neither of us have any right to expect…I mean, we both…" He looked toward the window as though seeking an avenue of escape before he drew a deep breath and faced her squarely. "Oh, hell, Cassie. Be realistic."

Cassie frowned and tried to follow the series of incomplete thoughts. Then, as the truth struck her, she felt color flood her face. "I haven't been with anyone since you," she blurted.

Her admission seemed to increase his discomfort, and Cassie felt her throat thicken. *But* you *have.* Wordlessly, she turned away, fighting to hold back the tears stinging her eyelids.

She heard Luke step closer, felt his familiar warmth along the length of her back as he slipped his arms around her. "It's better to play it safe," he whispered alongside her ear.

Safe? How in heaven could he talk about safety after the

last few days? In comparison to being clobbered over the head and shot at...

Safety be damned, she decided. Deliberately she fed her anger, trying to blot out the gray memories. In her heart she knew Luke was right, but right wasn't always best. At the moment best was his arms around her, her body yielding and soft against his strength. She needed him. Needed his physical presence inside her, needed him to complete the healing process he'd started.

And he wanted the same thing, if the rock-hard evidence pressing against her buttocks was any indication. Perversely, she wiggled her fanny, not caring if he called her rash and headstrong for ignoring his warning.

The movement elicited an ego-bolstering groan from deep in his throat. Satisfaction flooded through her. She was right. He wanted her as badly as she did him. Again she swiveled her hips, this time making sure he couldn't mistake the message.

His reaction was a growl of warning. "Stop it, Cassie. I'm not made of stone."

"You couldn't prove it by me." She smiled, arching her neck to throw him a flirtatious glance from the corner of her eye. Her smile ended in a startled gasp when he flattened his palms over her stomach and pressed her close against his hardness.

"So you want to play games, do you?"

Chapter 11

The words rolled off Luke's tongue, as seductive as fine French wine, conjuring up images that fired her blood. She tried to twist to face him, wanting to kiss his mouth and melt against him. He would have none of it. With unyielding obstinacy, he held her firmly against him. She was unable to move.

Unable to do anything but feel.

But Cassie entertained no thought of resistance. Her world had narrowed to a single focus—sensation.

Playing games.

With one gentle palm he caressed her breast to aching fullness. His other palm slid lower, inch by agonizing inch, down the curve of her abdomen, following the faded denim seam of her shorts. Through the worn fabric, she tingled to his touch. Impatiently she tilted her pelvis forward, and his fingers swept the exposed flesh of her inner thigh.

Bewitching, beguiling games.

"Remember this one?" he murmured, his lips skimming

her arched neck while with the back of one finger he traced the hem of her shorts, lightly stroking sensitive skin.

Her breath snagged in her throat. Remember? Oh, yes, she remembered. Anticipation tightened her chest.

When his finger breached the barrier of sand-washed denim, moisture pooled at the juncture of her thighs. He stroked, and pure pleasure sizzled through her. Her head fell back against his shoulder. "You're not playing fair," she gasped.

"Fair depends on whose rules you follow."

His response whispered against her ear and filled her mind, obliterating all logical thought, while his fingers continued to tease and tantalize. She shifted restlessly against the confinement of his arm, needing to touch him, kiss him, make him want with the same intensity she did.

He refused her unspoken request, his words an erotic caress. "You started this, Cassie. But I'm going to finish it."

Cassie quivered, her other senses intensified beyond belief by the absence of sight. "Please," she whispered, wanting to watch the raw emotion evident in his voice play across his face. Tension coiled in her belly as she envisioned desire, a twin to her own, dancing in his eyes.

And then it was too late.

Her muscles clenched. Spasms shook her. And she gained release in a Fourth of July shower of fireworks.

Then, and only then, when she sagged against him, did he turn her toward him, supporting her trembling body in his arms. He lowered his mouth and his breath caressed her, summer warm and smoky with the faintest taste of wild honey. Desperately she clung to him, prolonging the wild emotions he'd set free.

Eventually, exhilaration settled into something tamer and more personal, and Cassie arched back against Luke's encircling arm, feeling for all the world like a contented feline. A purr vibrated in her throat as she felt his washboard muscles and solid thighs pressing intimately against her. Metal against velvet.

A shaft of steel.

Her eyes flew open. Against her belly rested physical evidence of Luke's true state. He was hard—hard and wanting.

Heat stained her cheeks as she understood his sacrifice. "You didn't—"

"Shh." He silenced her with a finger against her lips. "It's all right. We have plenty of time."

"But…" She trailed her palm along his cheek, and he turned his head slightly, trapping one finger between his lips. Gently, he sucked, then nibbled. Her brain fogged with renewed longing. A vision of the second-floor bedroom Luke had mentioned on the trip up the canyon tantalized her.

As if sensing the direction of her thoughts, he gave her one last kiss and set her away with a rueful grin. "Later," he promised. "Right now we need to do something about eating." He interlaced their fingers and led her toward the kitchen. "I don't know about you, but I'm starving."

Cassie cast a longing glance upward as they passed the ladderlike steps to the loft and bit her lip to curb her disappointment. She was less successful, a few seconds later, at controlling an imp of deviltry that urged her to brush her breasts against Luke's arm as he searched the interior of a shadowed cupboard.

Luke shifted away a fraction. "Shall we settle for something that doesn't require cooking?"

"Ummm," Cassie replied, leaning closer.

"Peanut butter sandwiches?" A faint tremor telegraphed from his arm to her breast, but otherwise there was no indication she'd bothered him at all.

Cassie pressed closer and ran her tongue across her lower lip. "Any honey?"

With a muffled sound, he shoved the peanut butter jar and a loaf of bread at her. "Knives in the second drawer," he said, a hint of desperation in his tone.

Smiling, she prepared several sandwiches while Luke took an inordinate amount of time to rummage through the small refrigerator. When he finally emerged with a carton of milk and jar of pickles, he appeared to have regained his equilibrium. Several minutes later they settled in front of the fire to eat their makeshift meal.

Luke seemed disinclined to speak, and after a couple of curious glances, Cassie went along with his wishes. Unfortunately the silence left her with too much time to think—mostly about Luke. Her gaze strayed to the stairway. She imagined the two of them naked on rumpled sheets.

A puff of cold air skittered across the cabin floor, shaking her from her fantasy. Upstairs would be colder than here, she realized. Edging closer to the fire, she adjusted her daydream to include a cocoon of blankets.

Cassie shifted her bottom against the rag rug and threw Luke a surreptitious glance. He was still lost in thought, and from the frown lines that creased his forehead, she doubted his thoughts were following the same road as hers. Glumly she fed bits of crust to Duffy, who curled against her leg. They were safe here. Luke promised. So what could be wrong with trying to escape from reality for a while?

With a toss of her head, she popped the last of her sandwich into her mouth. Just as she swallowed, two things happened simultaneously—the light overhead flared on and the phone rang.

Their gazes tangled. For a long moment, neither moved.

The phone rang again, and Cassie hazarded a guess. "McCormack?"

"Bradley's more likely." Luke unfolded from the floor, brushing crumbs from his jeans. "He's probably just checking in."

Luke caught the phone on the third ring, while Cassie busied herself tossing their napkins into the fire. She watched the wadded paper flare, then transform into curling negatives. Across the room, Luke assured whoever had called that they were fine and the storm had only temporarily disrupted things.

A sudden silence made Cassie turn in time to catch Luke throwing her a swift glance. Just as quickly he hunched his shoulders and swung away.

What was going on?

She felt a spark of familiar resentment at his furtiveness. He had no right. Whatever the caller was saying, she was certain it concerned her, and she deserved to be let in on the conversation.

She remembered the old Luke, secretive and controlled, and knew she should demand to be told everything. Then she thought of the man she'd seen this evening, and tried to convince herself to wait, to trust he wouldn't hide things from her.

But had he really changed?

While she shifted uneasily from foot to foot, debating her course of action, Luke hung up.

"They have Wainright's killer."

Cassie froze in shock. It was over. They'd caught the murderer. No more looking over her shoulder, no more jumping at every sound. Once again she could drive the streets without worry and pick up the phone without dreading who might be on the other end.

She waited for elation to take hold. Instead her hands were clammy, her head light, and her heart beat to a slow, ponderous rhythm that made her wonder if it might stop entirely. "Who?" she asked, forcing the single word past her constricted throat.

"Eddie Sparks."

She stared at Luke blankly.

"Chelsea Sparks's brother."

"Chelsea has a brother?" It was an inane question. Judge Wainright's secretary could have any number of brothers— a whole slew of them, for all Cassie knew. The two women were hardly on a first-name basis.

Luke nodded. "A younger one. In and out of trouble for
years, although he's only had minor charges until now."
Luke moved closer. Putting an arm around Cassie's shoulders, he guided her to the sofa. "Evidently their mother was
at wit's end trying to control him, so Chelsea enlisted Wainright's help. He arranged for a job for the brother and took
a general interest."

Cassie snuggled against Luke's side, drawing warmth from
his body. Absentmindedly she ran her palm over the soft
hairs on his forearm. "That sounds like something he'd do.
Pop said the judge was a real hard-nose about the law, but
he had a soft spot for kids. If he thought Chelsea's brother
was serious about going straight, he'd be the first to help."

"Eddie Sparks is hardly a kid. He's in his midtwenties.
And from what Bradley says, Wainright's actions were far
from philanthropic."

Cassie shot him a puzzled look from under her lashes.

"It was a favor to Chelsea," he explained. "They were…
close, you might say."

Which explained Lydia Wainright's odd reaction to the
mention of the secretary. Cassie sighed. After her years as a
reporter, little shocked her anymore, though sometimes she
was dismayed at the secrets she uncovered.

"Eddie came to see Wainright that afternoon," Luke continued. "His sister left before he was through, assuming the
judge would let him out. Then, when Wainright turned up
dead, she was afraid to mention the visit to the police."

Cassie felt a twinge of pity for the secretary. She knew
what it was like to protect those you loved. How many times
had she done the same thing for her older brothers to save
them from Pop's wrath? Luckily, none of their escapades had
ever been illegal. Except maybe for that time a fifteen-year-
old Henry had hot-wired the Caddie so he could drive it
while Pop was out of town.

But murder? Surely even Chelsea wouldn't lie to cover
such a crime.

Cassie tucked her feet under her and rested her head on Luke's shoulder. She inhaled, thinking she could pick him out in a dark room by his scent alone. "What made Chelsea finally tell?"

"She didn't. Someone called in a tip. They questioned Eddie. He admitted being there, admitted hitting on Wainright for money. But he claims the judge was hale and hearty when he left."

"Then how…"

"They found the murder weapon. At Eddie's apartment."

Cassie jerked upright. "I thought they didn't know exactly what was used."

"They do now. It was a rock—a geode, actually—inlaid with amethyst crystals. The lab's already come up with two different blood samples. One's Wainright's. The other…well, I'll bet when we draw some of your blood, we'll get another match."

Imagining the rock, its lavender crystals dulled by streaks of dried blood, made Cassie wince.

Luke hugged her closer. "It's all right, slugger. It's over."

Funny. It didn't *feel* over.

She forced a wobbly smile and nodded. "I just can't believe someone's younger brother was responsible for everything that happened—the phone calls, the note in the car, the drive-by shooting, the…the mess at my house." She shuddered.

"He was running scared, didn't want any witnesses to identify him."

For a moment she considered his answer, then shook her head. "It doesn't make sense. If he didn't want witnesses, why did he waste time trying to scare me? Wouldn't he just try to get rid of me?"

"Who knows?" Luke shrugged. "Maybe he's not a killer at heart. Maybe Wainright's death was an accident, the result of a disagreement that got out of hand."

What he said made sense. Yet, something still didn't feel

right. "What about the call on my machine? You agreed it had something to do with the judge's death."

"I could have been wrong."

"But are you?" Lips pressed together, she frowned up at him. "I wonder."

Luke pulled away his arm and twisted to face her. "For Pete's sake, let it go, Cassie. Wainright's murderer is behind bars. You're safe."

She stared at him, puzzled by his intensity, until the truth dawned. His job was over. He could get on with his life.

Disappointment burrowed through her, or at least that's how she identified the pocket of emptiness in her chest. It certainly couldn't be more. There hadn't been time for more to develop.

And now they'd go their separate ways.

She unfolded her legs, avoiding his eyes. "It's just hard to believe it's over." Stretching her toes toward the fire, she kept her voice nonchalant. "I guess I can go home now, since they've caught the killer."

"The cleanup crew's not done at your house. Bradley says to give it another half day." He paused. "We could go back to my place..."

"Or stay here," she finished as hope seeped into the empty cavity within her. She stood and placed her hands at the small of her back. Applying steady pressure, she arched and shook her shoulders. "I vote we stay. I don't feel like making the trip back this late. And we've got everything we need."

Peeking from beneath lowered lashes, she caught Luke staring fixedly at the front of her T-shirt. She straightened slowly and arched an eyebrow. "Well, almost everything we need."

Luke acknowledged her quip with a wry smile. Then, before she had a chance to wonder what he was about, his hand snaked out, capturing her wrist. "There's a way around everything," he said.

Off-balanced by a sharp tug, Cassie collapsed against his

chest, giggling. She lifted her gaze, and the sound caught in her throat. Inches from her own, his hooded eyes darkened. Slowly, without a word, he leaned back, pulling her with him until she sprawled across his reclining body. His gaze never left hers. His breath caressed her.

Longing, hot and heavy, filled her. Deliberately she prolonged the sensation, delaying the moment when she'd surrender to the delight of his mouth. And more.

Her body felt liquid, melting, against his muscle and sinew. Straddling him, she felt the solid evidence of his desire. She ran her tongue over suddenly dry lips, and Luke's gaze followed the movement.

"Cassandra Bowers, you're a tease."

Cupping the back of her head with one hand, he shifted slightly, bringing his mouth within inches of hers. His tongue slid over her lips, tasting, then slipped inside.

And Cassie thought she'd die of pleasure.

His fingers glided along her neck, across her shoulders and down her back in a gentle caress before coming to rest at her waist. Cassie moaned against his mouth, wanting more. Wanting it all. But instead of acceding to her unspoken demands, Luke broke off the kiss.

"Duffy needs to go out."

Confused, Cassie looked at the dog, who indeed was standing expectantly by the door. "I'll let him out," she agreed.

"Never mind," Luke said, lifting her from his lap. "I need some fresh air." He gave her a swift peck on the cheek.

"Now who's being a tease?" She gritted her teeth, every nerve in her body screaming in frustration. She wanted to throw herself back into his arms. Instead she let the gap between them widen as he pulled on a jacket and opened the door. Duffy bounded out with Luke on his heels.

Cassie narrowed her eyes. She refused to allow some outmoded sense of chivalry spoil everything. She turned toward the loft, a small smile of determination curving her lips.

* * *

Luke picked his way through the trees, away from the buttery spill of light from the cabin window, away from temptation. Not until the enveloping darkness made it difficult to distinguish shadow from reality, did he come to a stop.

The storm had moved south, sweeping the clouds before it. By tilting his head a bit, he managed to catch the glitter of stars overhead. Strange sounds brushed his ears, mountain sounds. Rustlings, the creak of branches rubbing together. A scrabbling, too clumsy to be caused by a forest dweller, placed Duffy in the undergrowth just ahead—far enough away to feel free, close enough for safety.

A drop of water splattered against Luke's upturned face.

As a cold shower it fell short of the desired effect. But then, even an entire bucket of water couldn't wash away the memory of desire shimmering in Cassie's eyes. Groaning his frustration, he turned and pressed his forehead against rough bark.

It didn't help. Her scent clung to his skin, a faint thread of honeysuckle nearly drowned beneath the aroma of pine needles and damp earth. Nearly...but not quite.

Something bumped his leg. Unclenching one fist, he leaned down, groping until he made contact with Duffy's head. A quick rub, and the dog once again scampered out of reach. Luke straightened and leaned back against the tree, letting the darkness fill him.

Cassie. Why did she have to be so damned perceptive? There was no other explanation for her unease over Bradley's call. Luke certainly had given no indication of his own doubts, yet she'd still managed to sense them. He'd had no choice but to distract her.

His efforts had nearly been his undoing. Once he held her in his arms, felt her eager response, he'd had the Devil's own time not throwing caution to the wind. All his senses had clamored for release. Even now, the mere memory of her softness, her yielding body, resuscitated the ache in his gut.

Hell, Luke realized with sudden clarity, was being stuck in the wilderness an hour from the nearest drugstore.

He would have to keep as far away from Cassie as was humanly possible. Outside was the best bet, if he didn't mind risking frostbite. Summer nights in the mountains were always cool, but in the wake of the storm, temperatures could easily fall to freezing. Even so, he turned the idea over in his mind before rejecting it. The cold he could handle, but the prospect of another sleepless night defeated him. Nope, he'd take his chances back in the cabin. After all, he wasn't an inexperienced teenager. Hopefully, the years had taught him something about control. Cassie might have the power to test a saint, but Luke had no intention of letting his libido get the best of him. Not without protection.

Picking his way through the trees, he directed his thoughts into safer channels. Bradley was convinced they had Wainright's killer. But Bradley wanted things wrapped up, tied in a neat package.

Luke didn't believe for a minute that Chelsea's brother, an inveterate bungler, was Wainright's killer. The kid didn't have the resources or the audacity to carry out the systematic terrorization Cassie had endured. But the fact he was in custody could lull the real killer into feeling safe and leaving Cassie alone. The trouble was, Cassie had to buy it so she'd stay out of things long enough for the police to do their jobs.

Somehow he needed to make a believer of her, persuade her the danger was over. Then he had to convince her he was hanging around for reasons other than protection while he continued his clandestine search for the real killer.

Pine needles crunched beneath Luke's feet, and a finger of wind flicked across his neck. As he turned up the collar of his jacket, he heard a voice from his academy days whisper in his ear. *Proceed with caution.* As if in answer to the admonition, Luke nodded.

He was walking a fine line.

It was increasingly clear that someone wanted to shut Cassie up for good. The same someone who, initially, had misgivings about getting rid of her. Maybe Wainright's death had been an accident—the evidence certainly bore out that possibility. And maybe the killer had only wanted to scare Cassie into silence originally. But today, with the shooting, the killer had crossed an invisible line. He—or she—had chosen personal safety over scruples.

What had started in rage might end in necessity.

Long before Luke discerned any change in light, the odor of smoke told him he was nearing the cabin. The ground beneath his sneakers turned hard as he emerged from the trees. Out of habit he paused to test the locks on the car before crossing to the stoop. He still didn't know who he was looking for, though he'd narrowed the field by one. He doubted Chelsea would frame her own brother, not when she'd gone to such great lengths to protect him.

Hand on the doorknob, he scanned the clearing and listened for changes in the night symphony. Luke might not know who he was looking for, but he sensed he was closing in. It was only a matter of time before the killer made a slip.

And when he did, Luke intended to be there.

He studied the explosion of stars overhead, a spectacle that usually helped put his problems into perspective. Tonight all it did was emphasize his isolation. Cassie's safety, maybe her life, depended on his remaining alert.

Loneliness didn't matter.

His job did.

Satisfied everything was secure, he entered the cabin and peeled off his jacket. The fire had burned down, casting the room in semishadow. A quick glance around assured Luke he was alone downstairs. Cassie must have grown tired of waiting and gone to bed.

Relief warred with an odd sense of disappointment. He told himself it was for the best. He could resist temptation more easily without her in the same room.

He tossed more wood on the fire and poked at the glowing

embers until a log caught, then sat long enough to remove his sneakers and socks. Back on his feet, he pulled his shirttails from his waistband and unbuttoned it while he contemplated the couch. The lumpy, too-short couch. As a bed it left much to be desired, but he'd made do with worse. A blanket from the storage cupboard, his jacket for a pillow, and—

"Luke."

The sound of his name whispered across the room, as enticing as a spring wind off the Rockies. He turned, and his heart slowed to a ponderous beat. She sat at the top of the stairs, clad only in his flannel shirt and a seductive smile.

"Come see what I found." She waggled one hand.

Luke moved closer, lured as much by the tantalizing glimpse of slender legs as by the object she dangled between thumb and forefinger.

"I found it in the nightstand," she announced, then leaned down to place the small, foil package in his upraised palm. Wrapping her arms around her legs, she rested her chin on her drawn-up knees and lowered her voice conspiratorially. "I don't think Mac and Laura will miss it."

Her mischievous grin tugged at his heart, propelling him up the steps until his face was level with hers. Earlier today wisdom had dictated a decision against further entanglement with his ex-wife. And he knew, even if she didn't, that none of the reasons for his decision had changed.

Even so, he couldn't resist playing her game.

"Are you trying to bribe a police officer?" he asked, putting on a stern expression as he slipped the condom into the front pocket of his jeans.

"Can I?" She widened her eyes in feigned innocence before lowering her lashes demurely. "How?"

Luke swallowed hard in an attempt to rein in his galloping imagination.

He was too late.

Nor did Cassie help matters. She reached out and slid her

palm inside the opened front placket of his shirt. Blood pounded in his head.

"Like this?" she murmured, circling his nipple with one fingertip, then tracing the crisp hair downward from his chest to where it disappeared in his waistband. Heat followed in the wake of her touch.

"Or this?" she teased, tangling her fingers in his hair and settling her mouth against his.

She tasted of mint toothpaste, sweet and innocent. Her kiss was anything but. Wild and wanton, it slipped past his carefully erected armor and played havoc with his senses.

Luke gave up all pretense of resistance. Hungrily, without regard for the consequences, he mounted the remaining steps, pulled her to her feet and dragged her close.

Because words were impossible, he let his lips and hands and body declare his desire. Beneath his onslaught, her gurgle of laughter became a moan of passion. He felt her soften in surrender, cling to him, setting loose something dark and primal that didn't care what promises he'd made. He only knew he wanted to bury himself inside her, feel her flame with passion, meet him thrust for thrust.

Sweeping her up, he carried her across the bare pine floor to the double bed where she leaned back on her elbows. His flannel shirt rode high, exposing tanned legs that contrasted sharply with the sun-bleached sheets. Moonlight filtering through the dormer window etched the full curve of her lips. She smiled in seductive invitation. "What took you so long outside?" she asked. "I waited forever."

Forever? She didn't know the first thing about forever, Luke thought, curling his toes into the cotton throw rug beside the bed. Forever was the time he'd spent without her in Texas. It was the eternity that had passed since their lovemaking this morning. It was the ache in his belly and the anticipation in his heart.

And the fear he couldn't walk away a second time.

The loft was distinctly chillier than downstairs, but Luke

scarcely noticed. In the past few minutes, Cassie had managed to stoke a fire that raised beads of sweat on his forehead.

Only with the utmost concentration did he maintain a semblance of his legendary control. Leaning down, he skimmed his palms over the swell of her calves. "I'll try to make it worth the wait," he promised hoarsely.

Delaying long enough to explore the tender skin behind her knees, he crept his hands upward. The hem of his shirt slid higher on her thighs. A finger's breadth away from the scrap of silk guarding her femininity, he paused.

Her sharp intake of air echoed in the breathless night, though he didn't know how he could hear it over the thudding of his pulse.

Their gazes locked.

Luke dragged out the moment. He watched her tension mount, loving the way she trapped her lower lip between her teeth to keep from crying out her frustration.

Slowly he slipped his hand higher, cupping her, feeling her heat. Her fingers convulsed, crushing the sheets within her fists. Air rushed from her lungs in a low moan of ecstasy. She pressed against his palm.

The muscles in his groin tightened.

He slid a knee alongside her on the bed and eased the first button on her shirt from its hole. When she tried to pull him close, he shook his head. "Wait." He kissed the pulse beating in the hollow of her throat. "Let it happen."

She hesitated, studying his expression a moment before she caressed his cheek and dropped her hands to her sides.

Such a small gesture. But what it signified made his heart swell. Not for anything would he betray her trust. He kissed the tip of her nose, then returned his attention to the remaining buttons, until the last one popped free and he could spread the shirt wide. Propping himself on his forearm, he stretched beside her on the bed and admired the view.

Her skin glowed in the moonlight, fresh cream against the darkness of his hand. The contrast was a definite turn-on. If

he wasn't careful, the entire interlude would be over before
it started. But even as he tried to focus elsewhere, his hand
curved around her breast. His thumb brushed her nipple. It
hardened beneath his light touch.

He knew he shouldn't. Every caress to her body, every
soft touch, affected him as much as it did her, but he couldn't
resist. Bending his head, he tongued her nipple, then blew
lightly across the moistened surface just to watch the skin
pucker and the tiny bud stiffen to attention. Cassie's sudden
intake of breath amplified his body's reaction and made him
want to peel away all the barriers between them. Instead he
rolled to his stomach and studied her face.

Her widened eyes, the way her tongue swept her lips, even
the slightly crooked line of her front teeth peeking from beneath her upper lip—all were familiar.

And dear.

His insides froze. Tonight had been a time for confessions,
for guilts and remorse laid to rest. Nothing more. He was
letting fancy—and his libido—take charge of his thinking.

Cassie touched his cheek, smoothed a fingertip across his
lower lip. "What's wrong?" she asked.

Concern threaded her words, but he chose to ignore it.
"Nothing," he soothed. Kissing her long and hard, he shoved
aside his nagging doubt and concentrated on feeding the fire
of their combined passion.

It was no chore. Indeed, he became so immersed in the
process, he nearly neglected to use the protection Cassie had
so graciously provided. At the last possible moment, however, reason reasserted itself long enough to send him groping for the jeans he'd stripped out of. As Cassie drew him
in, spasming around him, release came in an explosion of
sensation that left him shuddering in her arms.

Reality returned in finite degrees of awareness. The feel of
Cassie's fingers smoothing along his spine. Her mouth nuz-
zling the side of his neck. He must be crushing her, but since

she didn't complain, he put off rolling away and savored the lingering aftereffects of their union.

She mumbled something he didn't quite catch.

"Hmmm?" Too wrung out to form anything more than a sound at the back of his throat, he lifted his head to gaze at her. Exertion had kinked her curls into tight corkscrews. Gently, he brushed them away from her damp cheek.

"I want to talk to Eddie."

Her softly spoken words finally penetrated his hazy thoughts, evaporating his euphoria.

"I still don't see his connection to my articles." A slight frown furrowed her brow, and she didn't seem to notice his stillness—or frozen horror, to be more accurate. "I just can't believe a kid engineered all the things that happened to me. I have to see him and get to the bottom of this."

Luke tried to think fast, come up with a reasonable excuse why she shouldn't get involved, but his brain didn't seem to want to cooperate. It was no longer functioning like a steel trap. More like a sodden lump of cheese, if he could believe the queasiness in the pit of his stomach. With a feeling approaching desperation, he forced himself to remain calm, to react like the logical, rational male he was.

"Over my dead body."

He rolled to his side. "Listen carefully," he told her. "Because I won't say this twice." He brought his face within inches of hers, his throat tight at the thought of what could happen to her if she continued to meddle in things she didn't understand. "You are not going anywhere near the jail."

"But—"

"No buts," he said hoarsely, ignoring her startled look. "You're not going. Not with me. Not alone. For once you'll do what you're told and stay out of this. Period."

Cassie stared at him, eyes narrowed, jaw clenched. Then, without a word, she pulled from his grasp, hugged the blanket to her chin and turned away from him.

Luke studied the rigid mound that minutes before had been

a warm, pliant woman, and cursed silently. Settling on his back, he stared at the sprinkling of stars outside the window and sighed.

So much for cool, rational logic.

Chapter 12

"Finishing up your article?"

Cassie nodded without turning from the computer. "I decided it was time, since you have the murderer in custody."

She forced herself to draw a calming breath and commanded her insides to quit quivering. In the early hours of morning, while Luke slept at her side, she'd worked everything out. Last night she'd allowed fantasy to fog her mind. She'd deceived herself that his concern meant he'd changed. But he hadn't. He was the same old Luke—issuing orders, expecting blind obedience.

Luckily she'd found out in time.

Risking a glance over her shoulder, she caught him combing fingers through his sleep-tousled hair, forcing cowlicks to spring away from his head in little boy abandon. The image tugged at her heart. Hastily she looked away and typed some words. "I can still make deadline at the end of the week if I buckle down."

She jumped a little when his hands touched her shoulders, then willed herself to relax. Luke might be intuitive, but he wasn't psychic. He couldn't know she still intended to get in to see Eddie and get the answers to her questions. After all, if the killer had truly been apprehended, there was no reason she shouldn't complete her inquiries. And if, as she suspected, he hadn't, maybe she could uncover something that would encourage the police to continue the investigation.

She tentatively typed another sentence, more aware of the lazy massage he was giving than of the words on the screen. As he worked his way up her backbone, she rested her fingers against the keys and gave up all pretense of typing.

"I'm glad you've seen reason," Luke said. He trailed the pads of his fingers up the sides of her neck, then speared through her curls to knead her scalp. Cassie sighed in contentment.

"After all, now that the authorities have everything under control, you wouldn't want to muddy the waters."

It took several seconds for his words to penetrate the fog of sensation he wove around her. Even longer for their meaning to register and set off a flicker of resentment. Why couldn't he even credit her with enough sense to avoid messing things up? Luckily her stiffening spine coincided with the tickling sensation of his lips across her nape.

"Sorry," he murmured, amusement negating his apology.

Burying her annoyance, Cassie willed herself to relax. Letting her head drop forward, she gave in to the pleasant tingling along her neck.

A costly mistake, she realized, when his tongue traced the curve of her ear. A white-hot flash of heat sizzled through her. Belatedly she tried to squash her reaction beneath righteous indignation, but it was too late.

Luke reached for her hands and urged her from the chair. "When I woke and found you gone, I was afraid you were still angry." He stepped closer, tilting her chin upward so she was forced to gaze into his eyes. What she read there pushed all other thoughts to the back of her mind.

Heat suffused her face. Her temperature soared several degrees. The sweatshirt and pants that earlier had seemed a necessity, suddenly felt heavy and confining. Flustered, she licked her dry lips. Luke retraced her tongue's path, his thumb sliding seductively over the moistened surface.

"You're not, are you?"

Not what? She shook her head, fighting to hold on to her indignation, her sense of purpose, but it grew harder and harder to focus. She tore her gaze away from his, only to find herself staring at his mouth. His full, tempting mouth. Her heart fluttered at the memory of his lips caressing hidden, secret parts of her.

"I think you need a break." His mouth curved in a persuasive smile. His palms moved to her shoulders, lingered briefly, then stroked down her back to cup her buttocks.

Desire pooled low in her belly.

Traitorous thoughts whispered through her. What harm could come from yielding for one little moment?

With a sigh she leaned into him, instinctively seeking fulfillment, savoring the way her body softened against his strength. It was all the invitation he needed. Stooping, he caught her behind the knees and swept her into his arms, banishing her last inhibition.

Lies, she reminded herself as she warmed to the heated look in his eyes—a look that promised passion and something more. She tucked her head under his chin and filled her lungs with his delicious scent while he mounted the stairs.

All illusion, she repeated as he lowered her onto the rumpled sheets and eased her clothes off, then stripped off his own. In seconds he joined her on the bed.

She reached up to brush back the hair that fell across his forehead. Catching her finger between his lips, he sucked, night-dark eyes pinning her to the pillow. Sparks of electricity rippled along her nerves. Her belly tightened.

Daydreams and fantasies...

He dipped his head. His lips burned her. Sanity slipped from her grasp.

But, oh, it felt so good...

* * *

Four hours later, standing on the front porch of her house, her euphoria was nothing but a fading memory. In its place was a growing lump of distress in her midsection. Despite Luke's assurances that all traces of an intruder had been erased by the cleaning crew, she was strangely grateful when he told her to wait on the porch while he checked inside.

Foolishness, she told herself, shaking off a sense of foreboding.

The afternoon sun beat down with an intensity that should have made perspiration pop out on her forehead. Instead, her face felt clammy and her body chilled. She shivered.

"Halloo." Across the lawn, Mrs. Ogalvie bobbed from behind the hedge, her white hair a cotton-candy confection atop her head. "Good to see you and the mister home," she chirped.

Pasting on a smile, Cassie folded her arms across her chest and rubbed at the goose bumps on her skin.

"I kept a watch over things while you were away," the old lady promised. "Didn't see that young man again, but I'm ready if he comes back." She waved a lethal-looking silver-headed cane above her head, the likes of which Cassie had only read about in Sherlock Holmes stories.

Cassie was saved from answering by the sound of Luke's voice in the entry behind her. With a quick nod to her neighbor, she edged through the door. Luke moved silently aside and let her precede him into the living room.

Sunlight glinted off glass and bathed the polished wood furniture in a rosy glow. The astringent odor of household cleanser, mixed with lemon oil and carpet shampoo, lingered in the air, lending a sense of normalcy. Yet tension still tightened across Cassie's skin like a shrunken jersey.

She eyed the rug and couch uneasily, not sure of what she expected—maybe ghostly outlines of Duffy's footprints or minuscule chips of red, permanently embedded in the fibers.

But everything appeared in order. Not a flake of paint marred a single surface. The same was true when she crossed the hallway and checked out the kitchen, bolstered by Luke's arm around her waist. The only thing unusual was the pristine condition of the walls.

Luke released her long enough to point out the new locks on the doors and the window bolts that allowed the windows to open enough to let in summer breezes, but not an intruder. Cassie made appropriate sounds of appreciation, then opened the screen to let Duffy out. She stood in the open doorway, watching him pick up a scent while Luke punched in a number on the phone.

Outside, Duffy had followed the scent to the flowerbed where, nose to the ground, he now dug halfheartedly beneath a bush. A fly buzzed next to Cassie's ear, while a magpie chattered overhead. Luke's low-pitched voice punctuated the lazy afternoon.

"Are you sure?"

There was a long pause during which a car in need of a new muffler chugged down the street.

"I don't agree… Look at the facts… At least four other logical explanations."

Cassie let go of the screen door and crossed to the sink. She filled a glass with water and drank, stopping her ears against the drone of Luke's voice across the room. She didn't want to know what he was saying, didn't want to wonder what the words meant. Since he'd shut the door on the Wainright case, it didn't matter.

It really didn't make sense, though. If she had doubts about the man the police had in custody, shouldn't Luke? She'd always credited her ex-husband with near-superhuman powers of perception. Maybe she'd been wrong about his abilities—blinded by emotion. Maybe his successes were the result of painstaking patience, not flashes of wisdom.

All the better for you, whispered a tiny voice. The last

thing you need right now is some superpsychic anticipating your every move.

Because Cassie was biding her time.

She opened the refrigerator to see if there was anything for dinner. Three cartons of vanilla yogurt and a shriveled-up apple. She swung the door shut.

Duffy's whine drew her to the kitchen door. She let the dog in, releasing the screen as Luke hung up the phone. Frustration was clearly stamped on his face.

"I have to go to the station."

"No problem," she assured him, afraid he'd sense her restlessness.

"I'll be gone less than an hour. Why don't I pick up Chinese for dinner?"

"Sounds good." *An hour should be just enough time to whip over and confront Chelsea Sparks.*

He secured the screen and bolted the back door, brushing aside her comments about being overcautious. "It never hurts," he said as he pulled her close for a quick kiss at the front door. Cassie, who seconds before had been mentally tapping her foot, now found herself reluctant to have him leave.

Obediently she locked the front door behind him, then watched from the living room as he made a call on his car phone. Finally his car pulled from the driveway, and she raced upstairs to change. Slipping outside, she had a twinge of conscience.

Stop it, she told herself sternly. There was no good reason she shouldn't go out if she felt like it. According to Luke, the killer had been caught.

And, if Luke was wrong?

Uneasy, she scanned the cul de sac. Everything looked normal—no unfamiliar cars, no low-lifes lurking in the bushes. If there was a killer still out there, chances were good he didn't know she was back. And—a sudden thought loosened her tight muscles—even if he did, would he risk informing the police they had the wrong person in jail by acting?

Sighing her relief, she slid into the car and started the engine. Straight to the Justice Center, straight home, she promised herself. Surely by now Chelsea had located the other transcripts Judge Wainright had gone through. And who knew, as well as information to fill out her articles, they might contain a clue to the real killer—someone besides a twenty-something-year-old kid with a history of messing up.

Mrs. Ogalvie waved as Cassie backed her car out of the driveway. Cassie nodded but didn't stop. She only had an hour before Luke returned, and she planned to make the most of it.

With her fingers tapping across the keyboard and a small frown between her carefully penciled eyebrows, Chelsea was a picture of focused efficiency. To Cassie, she already appeared to be at home here in Uncle Harry's office, as much as she had in Judge Wainright's.

Then Chelsea saw Cassie in the doorway, and a shutter seemed to fall over her face. "Judge Kimball's in court at the moment, Ms. Bowers."

"I'm here to talk to *you*," Cassie said.

"I'm not giving interviews."

Even though she'd expected a negative reaction, Cassie was taken aback by Chelsea's abrupt dismissal. Knowing charm wouldn't work in this situation, Cassie matched the other woman's icy tone degree for degree. "I don't want one. I'm only checking to see if Judge Wainright read through any other trial transcripts besides those I got last week."

Chelsea unbent enough to deliver a curt reply. "None." She returned her attention to the computer screen, evidently oblivious to the downward turn of Cassie's mouth. "The two batches were all I found."

Confusion collided with a tiny frisson of excitement. "Two?"

"The ones I dug up the day you were here with that detective—" Chelsea reached for the mouse and scrolled back a few lines "—and the ones I found later."

Cassie persisted, feeling rather like a myna bird as she mimicked strategic words. "Later?"

"The ones Judge Kimball said he'd give you." Chelsea glanced up, clearly impatient. Whatever she saw must have convinced her Cassie didn't have the foggiest notion what the older woman was talking about. "You didn't get them?"

Cassie shook her head. "I haven't been home."

"Then they're probably still in his office." Chelsea slipped from behind the desk. "I'll see if I can find them."

Cassie followed her into Harry's office and perched on the corner of the massive desk while Chelsea searched for the transcripts. After the out tray and file cabinets yielded negative results, Chelsea turned to a likely looking stack of folders on the bookshelf.

Shaking her head at the judge's unorthodox method of organization, she handed Cassie the rock that rested atop the folders and slid the stack from the shelf. Her disapproving manner was unfortunately ruined by the eagerness with which she tackled the pile. Cassie suppressed a grin, recalling, from her earlier interview with Chelsea, the pride the woman took in her organizational skills.

Cassie glanced at the rock in her hand. A thunder egg, Uncle Harry had called it. Uneasiness traced the back of her neck like a drop of ice water from a melting icicle. She turned the rock in her hand and light sparked off the violet crystals.

A half-formed memory nudged her. Luke's voice whispered in her ear *...in Eddie Sparks's apartment—a geode, inlaid with amethyst crystals.*

She nearly dropped the rock before reason reasserted itself. Her imagination had gotten the best of her. The police had already recovered the murder weapon from Eddie's apartment. This was just an ordinary rock. She shifted it a bit.

Etched near one edge were some microscopic letters. Squinting, she moved the rock closer.

HK/TW—1994.

Noticing her interest, Chelsea moved closer. "It's from near Estes Park. Judge Wainright had a matching one in his office. He and Kimball found them on a hike they took together." She frowned. "I don't know what happened to the other one. I was going to give it to Judge Kimball since he had its mate, but I couldn't find it when I was packing. Maybe Thomas decided to keep it at home."

Or maybe it was found in Eddie's apartment.

Cassie's stomach lurched. She set down the geode. "Were both engraved?"

Chelsea nodded. "Except Thomas's had the initials the other way around. You know—TW then HK."

She turned her attention back to the pile she was sorting, leaving Cassie to wonder if there was engraving on the murder weapon. She made a mental note to ask Luke when she got back.

A few seconds later Chelsea separated out a manila folder, undistinguishable from the rest to Cassie's eye. "Here they are," she announced triumphantly. She handed it over with a flourish, then glided back to her station, brushing off Cassie's thanks as she settled in front of her computer. "I'll be able to find things a lot quicker in a few weeks. It just takes a little time to train 'em, you know." Turning her attention to the monitor, she signaled the end of the conversation.

Cassie hesitated. Now came the hard part of her visit. Despite what she'd claimed earlier, she *did* want to talk with Chelsea about her brother. A quick glance at her watch told her she'd better think of something fast. "I don't believe your brother's guilty," she blurted out.

One eyebrow arched in disdain, Chelsea swung around. "How original. And now I'm supposed to open up, right?"

Cassie couldn't blame her for being skeptical. Cassie's statement did sound pretty lame, even if it was the truth.

Unfortunately she didn't have time for finesse. Her hour was almost up, and if Luke returned to an empty house...

"Look, I know you think I'm just after information for an article. Well, I am." She paused for effect. "An article on drugs and money laundering. I believe Judge Wainright died because of something he uncovered when he was helping me with my series."

Chelsea's gaze sharpened, and Cassie wanted to squirm. It was evident the woman wanted to believe her. It was written all over her face. For some unfathomable reason, that fact alone made Chelsea seem more vulnerable and sympathetic.

In spite of her attempts to stop it, Cassie felt compassion blur the edges of her resolve.

She gave herself a mental shove. Being kindhearted wouldn't do Chelsea a bit of good. Finding Judge Wainright's killer would.

"These transcripts—" she indicated the folder she held against her chest "—may well hold the key to your brother's freedom."

When Chelsea wavered, Cassie pressed her advantage, appealing to the secretary's pride. "But I need you on my side. I need you to interpret the things I don't understand. And I need to find out everything you remember and your brother remembers."

For long moments, while her brain screamed for her to get moving because Luke was going to beat her home, Cassie held her breath. She was pressing her luck. She knew it. But she needed a break, needed the secretary's cooperation. Waiting for a sign, Cassie saw desperate hope flit across Chelsea's face a split second before she nodded curtly.

Cassie smiled. "Thank you."

Luke's car blocked her driveway.

The bottom fell out of Cassie's stomach as she pulled in behind it and turned off the ignition.

Of all the dumb luck. All the times she'd chafed while

he'd been held up at the station, and now, the one time she'd have given anything for him to be late…

Shaking off her paralysis, she scooped up the folders from the front seat and slid from the car. The car door slammed shut with a bang loud enough to drag Mrs. Ogalvie from her soap operas. Luke, however, didn't appear.

For a moment Cassie remained rooted to the cement of the driveway, eyeing the house for some sign of life. But Luke wasn't a man to pace back and forth across the living room. He was more likely downing a cold beer and cursing her roundly.

Might as well get it over with. Pushing aside her reluctance, she squared her shoulders and marched forward. It was time to beard the lion in his den—her den.

He wasn't in the living room where she dumped Wainright's folder on her desk. Nor was he in the kitchen, although several unopened tubs of Chinese carryout sat on the table. Moo shu and orange chicken—their favorites, she noted as she stooped to retrieve his T-shirt from the linoleum. He'd probably stripped it off, then in typical Luke-fashion, flung it toward the nearest chair.

The back door stood ajar, and Cassie stepped closer to the screen, absentmindedly fingering the soft cotton, the way a toddler might his favorite blanket.

Outside, Duffy dozed in the shade of a cottonwood tree. The scruffy rubber ball between his paws had once been bright blue, but the sun and constant chewing had reduced it to a nondescript gray. At the far end of the yard, Luke crouched beside the flower bed, his bared back to the house. She watched him yank up a weed and add it to the pile at his side and felt a little guilty. Not because she hadn't done the job herself, but because she'd forgotten to call the kid who usually did the yard work.

Luke straightened and swiped sweat from his forehead with one forearm, then moved down a few feet. Stretch, grab, pull, toss. Steadily, methodically, he worked his way along, establishing a rhythm that could have been set to music. From the condition of the flowerbed and the height of the pulled weeds, he'd been working for some time, but he didn't look angry.

Cassie caressed the well-worn cotton of Luke's T-shirt, recalling how, in the past, he had often escaped outside after a particularly harrowing day. Physical labor served as therapy, providing him with a safety valve for pent-up emotions.

Still, she'd better tread lightly.

She hung his T-shirt over the back of a chair and smoothed away an invisible wrinkle before snagging a cold beer from the refrigerator. The screen door barely squeaked as she slipped outside, holding it long enough to prevent it from banging shut.

Duffy sighted her first. He lifted his head and thumped his tail, but otherwise refused to move. Luke didn't seem to notice her presence until she popped the tab on the can and extended it to him. "You look thirsty."

His dark eyes bored into her as he reached for the can.

Self-consciously she wiped her damp fingers on her linen skirt and tried to quell the waves lapping within her stomach. She hadn't done anything to feel guilty about. Sure, she'd made him believe she was staying home…but only to avoid a hassle. So what was the big deal? He claimed the danger was over, didn't he?

Still, his sober stare was unsettling.

Their gazes collided, and Cassie curled her lips into a tentative smile. Luke didn't return it. Instead, his brooding eyes examined her for an uncomfortable span of seconds before he threw back his head and drank deeply.

Just as he'd been aware of her cautious approach, Luke was aware of Cassie's scrutiny. It seared his skin, scorching deeper than the sun on his back. She thought he was angry because she hadn't stayed home, but how could he be when he'd told her everything was fine?

He wasn't angry, but only because he'd second-guessed

her and called Haggerty. The other cop had tailed her and kept Luke informed of her whereabouts the whole time she was away from the house. If danger had threatened, Haggerty would have stepped in and Luke would have arrived minutes later.

Cassie didn't know she was still in danger, and Luke wasn't going to tell her. Not without proof. She'd already dealt with enough terror to last a lifetime.

But damn it all, why couldn't she—just once—do what he asked?

He swallowed the last of the beer and wiped his mouth with the back of his hand. "Thanks. I needed that." He smiled, aware his good humor had her off balance. "Are you ready for some dinner?"

Through the moo shu and orange chicken, Cassie remained uncharacteristically quiet. Luke could tell by the frequent glances she cast that she was trying to guess what he was up to. She'd obviously expected a lot of questions about where she'd gone. Not being asked was driving her crazy. Over fortune cookies she finally cracked.

"Okay, enough of the silent treatment," she said.

Since Luke was in the middle of relaying the story of Mc-Cormack's rafting misadventure, he could be pardoned his surprise, though he was perfectly aware of what she was referring to.

"I know I said I'd stay in the house, but I had an errand to run."

Luke opted for noncommittal. "Must have been important."

"It was." Her expression grew fierce. "And you know you'd have raised all kinds of excuses if I'd told you I planned to leave."

Luke shot one eyebrow skyward and opened his mouth, but Cassie didn't allow him to interject a word.

"You've always thought you could tell me what to do. But I'm not a child."

"Luckily," Luke agreed smoothly, fighting to keep his mouth from curving into a grin.

"You can laugh all you want, Lucas T. Slater, but you know it's true. You always think you know better than everyone else."

"I do know."

"No!"

"Yes," he insisted. "I always know what's best. It's not conceit, slugger. It's fact."

It was all he could do to keep from bursting out laughing at the glare she aimed at him, a glare that would have put a lesser man in his place. He'd forgotten how much fun it had been goading Cassie during their courtship—raising her quick indignation, then watching realization hit.

Her lips twitched as she finally caught on to his banter, though she tried to hide the fact. "You jerk," she said, rising from the chair.

Luke ducked, just missing being hit with his own T-shirt. By the time he straightened, Cassie was busily folding down lids on little cardboard cartons, the picture of innocence. Amused, he awaited her next assault. It came in the form of a question that took him completely by surprise.

"Okay, Mr. Know-It-All, why did Eddie keep the murder weapon instead of dumping it?"

Luke sobered. He'd asked the same thing himself. In fact, it was just one of the inconsistencies that made him doubt Eddie was the killer. But since he was set on not alarming Cassie, he fell back on Bradley's explanation.

"Eddie probably forgot he was holding it, and by the time he noticed, he didn't dare leave it where it could be found."

"So instead, he puts an amethyst-encrusted geode with someone else's initials in plain view in his apartment."

She sounded skeptical, and Luke didn't blame her. From what Burns said, Eddie wasn't the sharpest knife in the drawer, but keeping the rock seemed downright foolish. It was like wearing a flashing neon sign on his chest that proclaimed I Did It. Luke spent an instant considering that image before he realized the significance of Cassie's question.

"How did you know about the engraving?" he demanded.

Cassie looked pleased. "I didn't. I just guessed from something Chelsea Sparks told me."

Which finally solved the mystery of where Cassie had disappeared to. "Did she see it in her brother's apartment?" Luke asked, saving the lecture he wanted to give her for later.

Cassie shook her head. "Chelsea doesn't know it's the murder weapon." She opened the refrigerator and deposited the containers on a shelf. "Did you know it's half of a set?"

Luke bit off an oath that put a grin on Cassie's face. "Okay, okay. I'll come clean," she said, kicking shut the refrigerator door. "But first you have to do something for me. You have to admit you don't always know *everything*."

"The only thing I'll admit is that you have to be the most exasperating woman on the face of the Earth."

Her impish grin convinced him he was right to conceal his reservations from her. This was how she should be all the time—the way she *would* be if he had his way. Never again would fear pinch her expression or worry douse the sparkle in her eyes if he could help it.

Her hip brushed his arm as she leaned close to pour more iced tea into his glass, and he pulled her into his lap. A light scent of wildflowers rose from her skin to tantalize his senses.

This afternoon had been his own fault. If he'd thought about it, he'd have realized she'd see no reason to stay home now that the danger was supposedly over. He'd just have to take care in the future to not let her out of sight.

He nuzzled her neck.

She giggled and wound her arms around him, still clutching the pitcher in one hand. "Do you need something to cool off before I tell you my story?" she asked sweetly.

Chilled glass grazed his nape, and for an instant he flashed on the past. A sultry night and heated whispers...and ice cubes sliding across sweat-slick skin.

The banked fire inside him flared hot and intense.

Smiling, he caught her gaze and held it, pinpointing the moment when she remembered the same interlude by the widening of her eyes. Ice rattled against glass. Tea sloshed onto the tablecloth as she set the pitcher down on the table.

"I don't want to be cooled down," Luke said, his throat tight. He caressed the perspiring pitcher. "Do you?"

Cassie's breath caught in her throat.

He shifted slightly, and his hand hovered over her exposed skin, though neither broke eye contact. A drop fell and she trembled, though surely it was too weightless to be felt.

And then he eased his wet palm up her bare thigh, under her skirt, at the same time lowering his mouth to hers and swallowing her long sigh.

Chapter 13

Luke's arm was asleep. It was too bad *he* wasn't. He flexed a muscle beneath Cassie's head, hoping the subtle movement would encourage her to shift her position a little. His efforts paid off when she murmured incoherently and rolled closer, her cheek against his chest, a possessive arm draped across his waist. Blood rushed back into his hand. His fingers prickled. He wiggled them, trying to hurry the process, then curved his arm around her bare shoulders.

The curtains fluttered at the window in a sinuous dance, while outside, the swaying elm captured a crescent moon within its branches. The ghostly satellite inched its way across the window canvas, a frustrating reminder of Luke's sleepless state.

He'd planned to get up early in the morning for a run, but at the rate he was going it would be morning before he fell asleep.

He tried breathing slowly and deeply the way Cassie had suggested when she first learned of his chronic insomnia. It didn't work any better than it ever had. The more tricks he tried, the more sleep eluded his grasp. Sighing, he gave up and let his mind leapfrog to the afternoon meeting with Bradley.

The chief was no more certain than Luke that Eddie Sparks was their killer. There were too many unanswered questions. Why would Eddie keep the murder weapon in his apartment? Why would he attack Wainright in the Justice Center where any number of people could finger him? Or, for that matter, why kill the goose that laid his golden eggs?

Eddie had been framed. Luke was certain of it. Heck, even Cassie had reached the same conclusion with less to go on than they had. But try convincing the D.A.'s office. Those bozos were so hot to prosecute, they'd have gone after Little Orphan Annie.

Instead, they'd settled for Eddie, hoodlum-in-training.

For the hundredth time, Luke ran over the list of suspects. Evidence pointed to someone Wainright knew, someone who knew Wainright. A guard would have noted a stranger, and there'd been no such entries at Security. That left Luke with a very short list.

True, there could be others he wasn't aware of, but he doubted it. In his experience you didn't have to look far from a dead body to find the culprit. Usually you turned over a few rocks, dug up more secrets than you cared to deal with, aired some dirty laundry and, *voilà,* you had your killer.

Luke's list had only three names. Chelsea Sparks, thwarted mistress. Lydia Wainright, betrayed wife. And Judge Harold Kimball.

Luke's money was on Kimball. Not because he was a man. Luke wasn't chauvinistic enough to discount a woman's anger. No, he just had a feeling. In his gut. Where a good cop's instincts were centered.

Kimball was smooth—too smooth. He reminded Luke of one of those speculators trying to sell you an option on land in the Florida Everglades. The man had shifty eyes, a glib tongue and a smile that didn't reach beyond his lips.

Not much to go on, but enough for Luke. He already had people checking into the judge's background. Soon, Luke would know about every parking ticket Kimball had ever gotten, every indiscretion he'd ever committed.

When his sources got through, Luke would know which pant leg Kimball pulled on first in the morning.

Kimball was Luke's man, all right. His instincts were seldom wrong. He ticked off the events of the last week and a half. Calls, the note—elements in a game of psychological terror.

And the shooting?

He frowned. It had been obvious at their meeting that Kimball considered himself superior to the general population. He was quite capable of playing mind games with someone for the hell of it. The only problem was, Luke couldn't see the man purposely harming Cassie. His attitude toward her had been affectionate, even proprietary. And even the evidence from Wainright's murder pointed to a crime committed in anger, not with premeditation.

Cassie's breath whispered across Luke's collarbone in barely discernible puffs. He closed his eyes and inhaled deeply, drawing in her warm, feminine scent.

No. The shooting didn't fit. Yet. But it was only a matter of time. And his job was to keep this woman safe until the puzzle pieces fell into place.

Glancing down at her, he clenched his teeth in silent promise. He would keep her safe until that moment when he nailed Kimball to the wall. For murder. And for what he'd done to Cassie.

As though picking up his mental tension, Cassie whimpered.

Luke relaxed his jaw and stroked down the curve of her back. A spasm rippled through her. She shifted her head. Her curls brushed his face, but before the tickling sensation fully registered in his brain, her body jerked. A soft, keening sound slipped past her lips.

Luke slid his free hand to her shoulder in a soothing gesture, but Cassie struck at him. "No!" she wailed, shrinking away.

Her eyelids flew open. Luke knew from their glassy stare that she wasn't seeing him, but something from her dreams. "Keep away," she warned, her voice stuttering over the words.

"Cassie, honey, it's me—Luke." He raised on one elbow. As she turned saucer-round eyes on him, he restrained the urge to touch her. Until she truly woke, anything he did would only add to her terror.

She blinked, and he concentrated on gentling his tone, the way he would with a lost child.

"I won't let anything hurt you, slugger," he promised, though he knew the futility of his vow. There were things beyond his control, things that lurked in the dark corners of her mind, beyond even Luke's reach.

But the fib worked.

Her gaze focused. A tremor shook her, and her brave front shattered like fine crystal. As tears welled in her eyes and spilled down her cheeks, Luke sat up and pulled her into the safety of his arms.

When her tears eased, he leaned back against the pillows. "Better?" he asked.

Nodding, she swiped a forearm across her eyes, then hugged his waist. A small hiccup broke the stillness.

Luke realized he'd spent a lot of time like this lately. Letting her cry. Soothing away fear. Feeling needed.

The sensation lapped against him, tranquil and hypnotic. For an instant he struggled against the heady sensation, then gave in.

Caring for others had been ingrained in him since childhood.

Take care of your sister.

He no longer remembered if he'd really heard the words

or had interpreted them from his parents' expressions and glances.

Be there for Mom and Dad.

Had Shelley really said that, or had he read between the lines of her last note?

And in the years that followed...

The faces of countless strangers paraded through his head, each mirroring a silent plea he was unable to ignore—*Help me.*

No, Luke could no more give up caring for people—for *Cassie*—than he could give up being a cop. And what was wrong with that? Could an urge that made him feel so good be bad?

"What were you dreaming about?"

"I'm not sure." She tucked her knees closer and rubbed her cheek against the fur on his chest. "I was alone in a dark room...the sort of dark you want to poke holes in." She shivered.

Luke drew the wash-softened cotton sheet around them and rested his hand on her leg. He knew the kind of darkness she meant. Heavy, inky and ominous, it filled your lungs and pressed against your eyeballs.

And you knew something bad was about to happen.

"There was something in the room with me." She brushed her palm along his arm, from elbow to wrist then back again, as though reassuring herself of his substance.

"I was afraid to move. As long as I stayed still, it wouldn't find me." She gave a tiny, forced laugh. "I sound silly. Like a kid afraid of imaginary monsters."

Her attempt at bravado touched him. "Not silly," he assured her. "Some monsters are real." He wanted to say more—that he would fight her demons for her, keep her safe—but fear of her reaction kept him silent.

Cassie nodded, fingers tracing the tendons on the back of his hand. "I couldn't breathe. And then, just when I thought I'd pass out from lack of air, a light flashed."

From her first words, Luke had sensed this nightmare was different from the one several nights ago. This was a dream of shadows and terror, not one of pain and loss, and it fit with what had probably happened to her the night of the murder. He could feel her tension coiling tighter once more, hear the quaver she struggled to eliminate from her voice. Calling up reassuring tones, he asked, "What did you see?"

"I don't know." Then, as if realizing she'd answered too quickly, she added, "I'm not sure. You woke me."

She'd awakened herself with a scream of terror, but he didn't correct her. If the doctor Chief Bradley had contacted was any authority, she was making good progress to remember this soon. Better than most.

"Thank you," she whispered.

Puzzled, Luke tried to read the expression on her upturned face. "For what?"

"For being here." She traced a finger over his bottom lip, then stretched to kiss him. "I don't think I'm ready yet to face the person in my dream."

Filing away the admission as more proof of her returning memory, Luke was distracted from further speculation by Cassie's movements. She had settled back into his lap, but for some reason, seemed unable to find a comfortable position. He shifted against the pillows and patted the sheet over her legs in an attempt to divert his thoughts from her tempting curves. Although she couldn't yet realize it, her squirming was making him damned uncomfortable.

He performed some mental push-ups, knowing only a lecher took advantage of a woman in distress.

Another wiggle of her derriere, and Luke knew he was on his way to serious trouble. "You need to sleep," he insisted, grasping her waist with the intention of lifting her from his lap.

Cassie, however, thwarted him. With a quick twist, she straddled him, lacing her fingers behind his neck. Her breasts flattened against his chest, and worse, the part of him suffering the most was now in intimate contact with her.

She nibbled his earlobe. "Make love to me."

He wanted to. Lord, how he wanted to. But in her distressed state, was it best for her?

"Please." She rubbed seductively against him.

His body wanted her. *He* wanted her. Restraint at such a time was asking too much of any man.

"I need to forget."

He couldn't ignore her plea, couldn't blind himself to the shadows in her eyes. With a groan he bound her close in a grip of velvet steel, found her mouth and gave up the fight.

Barefoot, Cassie slipped into the bathroom and shut the door behind her. She'd have much rather stayed in bed, but Luke, even asleep, was too tempting. She'd wanted to touch him, snuggle close and draw his scent deep into her lungs. She'd imagined him waking, and even now—a room away from him—she anticipated the lazy invitation in his eyes and the touch of his mouth on her skin.

Heat stirred deep in her belly. Longing for an endless stream of similar mornings teased her.

Abruptly she stepped into the tub and turned on the shower, counting on its rhythmic pulse to cool her imagination. Luke had barged back into her life, and common sense seemed to have taken a vacation. What was it about the man that threw her into such confusion?

Water splattered her skin, and her thoughts veered to last night, when Luke had carried her to the center of a storm so wild she became a part of it, defined only by the sensations rippling through her. No words had passed their lips, no murmured endearments, no promises for tomorrow, just pure, unbridled passion.

So why did it feel like history repeating itself? Why did it feel like falling in love?

Cassie poured shampoo into her palm and scoffed at herself. She was letting her emotions get the best of her. Fairy tales were for children, and no one lived happily ever after anymore. Not even when they had the next best thing to a knight in shining armor.

No, she'd been down *that* road before, and she wasn't going again. It only led to heartache and disillusionment. Head thrown back and arms raised, she lathered her hair, then stood beneath the stinging spray, drawing the scent of mango deep in her lungs while the water sluiced away the suds.

It didn't matter how much Luke was trying to change, how differently he treated her, she couldn't lose her heart again. Because this time, if it all went wrong, she just might not survive.

Dragged from sleep by the shifting of the mattress, Luke opened one eye in time to see Cassie disappear into the bathroom. The door closed behind her with a soft click. He rolled to his back, stretching his arms high above his head. A smile played across his lips, while contentment oozed from every pore.

A few hours' sleep made all the difference in the world, he decided. Sleep, and being able to blot out his preoccupation with the case. He had Cassie to thank on both counts, though granting him respite from his problems had not been her intention.

He sobered as he recalled her night terrors. More than ever he felt certain the key to Wainright's death was locked in her subconscious. And it didn't take a degree in psychology to guess she was scared out of her wits to lift the curtain on those memories. Not so odd, given the circumstances. What *was* amazing was her willingness to admit her fear. Once, she'd have torn off toenails before conceding her terror. And as for asking for comfort...

Thoughtfully, Luke rubbed his whiskered jaw. She'd changed all right. Two years had softened her rough edges. Sure, she was still prickly as a hedgehog, still ready to fight if she thought her judgment was being questioned. But unlike the girl he'd married, she no longer tried to pass herself off as Superwoman.

She changed without me.

Luke threw a forearm across his eyes, blotting out the sunlight as realization jolted through him. Much as it pained him to admit, he doubted her transformation would have occurred if they'd remained together. His own demons wouldn't have allowed it. He hadn't understood that her desire to control her life was as great as his need to protect it. He'd failed to realize they would struggle for superiority, and the battle would destroy their marriage.

Luke had fallen for the sparkling challenge in Cassie's emerald eyes, for the way she tossed her head and took on the world. And then, in his fear of losing what he most valued, he'd tethered her instead of giving her room to soar.

His only excuse was lack of experience. Growing up had taught him to care for those he loved. And when things went wrong—when his sister had run off and his parents had died in a car accident—he'd learned that lesson, too. No matter how hard you tried nothing lasted. After that he'd steered clear of anything resembling a permanent relationship. It was just easier that way.

Until Cassie.

Her crooked smile had beguiled him. The glow in her eyes had cast a spell, and once again he found himself believing he could have it all. It was only after he'd vowed to love, honor and cherish her that doubt set in. He'd sworn to keep her safe. Pledged it in front of her father and brothers and the world. And he, of all people, knew how futile such a promise could be.

Was it any wonder that instead of a loving refuge, he'd constructed a cage?

Two years ago he'd hated her for leaving, hated her for ending their marriage with a note on the kitchen counter. He'd blamed her for the deafening silence of the empty rooms, the cold condemnation of a half-empty bed. Not until he'd run away to Texas did he realize the hollowness that lay deep inside himself.

She'd changed. The woman he'd left had glowed with untapped promise. The one he'd returned to had uncovered it. She was beautiful, warm and responsive. Brave enough to stand on her own, yet strong enough to be vulnerable.

A muffled tattoo from the next room conjured images of Cassie in the shower, and for several moments he considered joining her. He imagined the hard oval of soap in his hands as he worked up a lather. The image was so vivid he could smell the clean scent. In his mind's eye, he coated her with suds. Slid his hands over wet, slippery flesh. Pinned her against the tile wall with his body and filled her...

The phone rang.

Luke snagged the receiver and pulled it to his ear.

"Is Cassie Bowers there?" asked a female voice.

"She's busy right now."

"Oh." The single word caught Luke's attention, for it was edged with more than ordinary disappointment.

"I really need to talk to her. It's important."

The voice was naggingly familiar, but before he could ID it, the caller rushed on, desperation serrating her speech.

"It's a matter of life and death."

The dramatic pronouncement made in breathless tones, tipped the scales. The woman's name flashed in Luke's mind an instant before she identified herself. "Tell her it's Chelsea Sparks."

"Cassie's in the shower," Luke admitted. "But maybe I can help you. This is Luke Slater."

"No!" She was vehement. "The police can't help. They'll only make things worse. I need Cassie."

Since it was obvious Chelsea was in no condition to be reasoned with, Luke gave in. "Hang on and I'll tell her you're on the phone." He set down the receiver, cutting off her incoherent gratitude, and dragged on his jeans.

Water hammered the porcelain tub as Luke let himself into the bathroom. Through the semitransparent curtain he glimpsed Cassie's blurred silhouette, her face raised to the cascade. Before his daydreams returned to tempt him into forgetting his mission, he eased a fluffy towel from the rack and called her name softly. Cassie poked her head out, modestly clutching the border of the vinyl curtain to her chin. Luke decided not to tell her it did little good.

"Chelsea Sparks is on the phone," he said, handing her the towel. "She says it's urgent."

With a worried expression Cassie stepped from the tub, towel draped sarong-style around her body. A drop of water skidded into the dark hollow between her breasts, and Luke was tempted to lean close and trace its path with his tongue.

Desire, hot and sudden, flickered to life.

"What does she want?" Cassie's anxious question prompted him to throw a mental blanket over the flame.

"She wouldn't speak to anyone but you," Luke replied, contenting himself with brushing a bead of moisture from her cheek.

Her expression softened. Rising on the balls of her feet, she feathered a kiss at the corner of his mouth as she swept past. Smiling, Luke leaned against the door frame. He folded his arms across his bare chest and unashamedly eavesdropped when she picked up the phone.

"Of course I don't mind," Cassie said. She settled onto the edge of the bed, blotted at her dripping hair with a second towel from the bathroom, then let it drop to her lap. Her exertions caused the terry cloth to loosen its grip.

Luke watched in fascination as it slid partway down her breasts.

"I said to call if you needed anything. What's the problem?" With one hand Cassie rescued the drooping length of terry cloth, then combed her damp curls back from her face with restless fingers. Midway back, her hand froze. "She what?" Her mouth opened in surprise.

Luke jumped, wrenched from his preoccupation with the slipping sarong by Cassie's sharp tone. What *she* were they talking about?

"I don't care what you did with her husband." Indignation was clearly stamped across Cassie's features. "It's not evidence. The police aren't going to listen to her."

Lydia Wainright, Luke guessed. Which confirmed his earlier suspicions—Chelsea had been having an affair with Lydia's husband. Luke's gaze fixed on the picture of sunflowers on the far wall. Though he was reluctant to set aside his vote for Kimball as killer, Luke had worked too long in homicide not to consider other possibilities. It was quite conceivable Lydia could have lashed out at her husband in a fit of jealousy, but having done so, would she go out of her way to call attention to herself? Luke doubted it. And as for Chelsea—what could have pushed her enough to brain her lover with a rock…and frame a brother she'd always protected?

"Extortion? Why would she claim that?"

Luke straightened, but a warning glance from Cassie halted him before he took a step. Tilting her head to capture the phone between her ear and shoulder, she pulled a pad of paper and a pencil from the nightstand drawer. She wrote something on the top sheet and tore it off. Luke took it from her outstretched hand. It said:

"$10,000 transfer from Wainright account."

"She's just guessing," Cassie insisted. "I don't think banks release that kind of information without a subpoena."

Luke picked up the pad. "What info?" he scribbled and slid it into Cassie's view.

"Where the $ was transferred," she wrote.

Luke leaned closer, knowing Cassie was about to start imparting advice—advice she had no business giving if she was going to stay out of the middle of this mess. He touched her shoulder.

She ignored him. "You didn't admit—" A look of frustration flitted across her face. Her shoulders sagged. "You did," she repeated tonelessly.

Luke held out his hand. Now that Cassie had found out the problem, it was time for a professional to step in. But Cassie refused to relinquish the phone. Instead of giving in to impulse and yanking the instrument from her hand, Luke reached once more for the pencil. "What's $ for?" He shoved the message under her nose. She nodded impatiently.

Rising, she moved to the dresser, leaving Luke with the pad clutched in his hand.

"What was the money for?" she asked, rifling through the top drawer. She flung aside her towel wrap and stepped into a lacy scrap of panties. "There's your proof," she announced triumphantly as she fastened the front clasp of a bra beneath her breasts and pulled the straps into place.

The inviting display couldn't distract Luke. He was too frustrated at not knowing what was being said. He considered racing for the kitchen extension. But with his luck they'd finish talking before he got there. He waggled the note in front of her face again.

Cassie rolled her eyes in exasperation and turned away. "Dig out all your receipts," she advised. "And don't answer any questions without a lawyer present. In the meantime, I'll go talk with Eddie." She pulled a knit top from the bottom drawer of her dresser. "Half an hour... Just sit tight. I'll call you when I get back." Cassie hung up.

"What—"

"Later," Cassie promised, snatching a pair of slacks from the closet and heading for the bathroom.

Mouth open, Luke felt his stomach churn, accompanied by familiar tightening in his chest. Heat rose in his face, like the mercury in a thermometer. Only a few minutes ago he'd convinced himself she'd changed. But leopards didn't change their spots. He stalked into the bathroom. "Not later. Now." He scowled at her in the mirror. "What's going on?"

Her startled gaze flickered to the crumpled note in his

hand, the brush in her hand halting midstroke. "Lydia Wain-right discovered her husband had transferred $10,000 out of his personal account." Looking back at her own reflection, she forced the brush through tangled curls a couple of times before laying it down and turning. "She put two and two together, got eight, and is accusing Chelsea of extorting money from the judge."

Luke followed her back to the bedroom where she dropped to her knees to peer under the bed. "What was the money for?" he asked through gritted teeth.

Disregarding his barely contained irritation, Cassie settled back on her heels, a pair of sandals dangling from her fingers. She smiled in triumph, then perched on the edge of the bed. "Wainright was financing a private drug rehab program for Eddie." She raised her face, a picture of innocence. "You're upset," she guessed. "I suppose you don't want me getting involved."

He stepped closer, keeping a tight rein on his temper. "Would it matter?"

She slipped on one sandal and considered the question thoughtfully. "I guess I'd have to say I'm already involved, and I can't start sitting on the sidelines now. I need to see this thing through to the end." She tugged on the second sandal, then folded her hands primly in her lap. Her eyes, when she raised them were full of speculation. "So. Are you coming with me?"

"Where?"

Her gaze remained steady. "To jail."

"And if I say no?"

"You don't want to come and hear what Eddie has to say?" she asked, deliberately misconstruing his question.

"Oh, I have every intention of coming," he assured her, certain his company was the last thing she wanted. "I wouldn't miss it for the world."

Chapter 14

The slamming of metal doors still echoed in Luke's ears as he and Cassie left the Boulder County Jail. Sunlight singed the apron of grass outside and glinted off something in the sapphire sky. Luke looked up and watched the bright speck grow into a yellow Cessna. It executed a wide turn, lowered its landing gear, and lazily glided earthward. He followed its descent until it disappeared behind the hill across the road. Boulder Airport lay just beyond.

"Now do you believe?" Cassie asked, almost skipping across the tarmac in her excitement. "Eddie seems scared spitless. *I'm* certainly convinced he's not the killer."

"I never thought he was."

"You didn't?" His admission obviously took her by surprise. "Then you believe his story of coming to ask for a job reference?"

"Truthfully? No." His answer seemed to confuse her, as well it should. He'd read Eddie Sparks for a conniving little con artist. But it was equally apparent the kid didn't have the guts to try to kill someone—at least not with a weapon that could have been grabbed from his hands. "I think he came to shake Wainright down for more money. My guess is Eddie threatened to tell Wainright's wife about the affair between Chelsea and the judge, and he laughed in Eddie's face."

"Couldn't that give him a motive?"

Her words were uttered in short, breathless bursts, and Luke realized how fast he was walking. He slowed down to accommodate her shorter stride.

"I mean, what if Eddie got mad because Thomas laughed at him, and he grabbed the paperweight?"

A patrol car rolled to a stop a few yards away. A cop climbed from the driver's seat and, nodding to Luke, circled to open the rear door. Luke acknowledged the greeting with a tip of his head and watched the officer escort a prisoner into the jail.

"Eddie's the type to wait in a dark alley with a borrowed gun. He wouldn't beat a larger man over the head with a rock."

"Luke." Hands on hips, Cassie halted a few paces behind him. She waited to speak until he turned. "If you don't think Eddie is guilty, then why don't you want me to help him?"

"That should be obvious. As long as everyone appears to believe the killer is in custody, the real murderer feels safe. If he feels safe, he lays low and leaves you alone."

She nodded. "That's why I figured it was all right to go to the Justice Center alone yesterday." She started walking again.

Luke fell in beside her. "I'm glad you're thinking before you do things. It makes my job easier."

"Your job," she said, one hand on the door latch. "Guarding me."

He nodded. "Yes. Finding a murderer and keeping you safe while we do."

For a long second she stared at him across the car roof as though trying to figure something out. Luke waited, perplexed, but she apparently changed her mind about speaking.

Then she ducked through the passenger door, her lips twisted in the semblance of a smile. Almost as though she were laughing at some private joke. Luke gazed at the mountains, feeling at a distinct disadvantage. He'd missed something in the exchange, though for the life of him, he couldn't figure out what. He shook his head and climbed behind the wheel.

Cassie remained uncharacteristically quiet for the next several blocks, seeming not to notice his sidelong glances. Something was bothering her, something important. Or else, she was planning something. Luke wasn't sure which alternative he preferred.

"How about some ice cream? I could use a pick-me-up," he suggested, hoping to distract her. When she nodded her agreement, he parked in front of a small ice cream parlor. Several minutes later, at Cassie's insistence, they settled with double cones at a wrought-iron table out front. Luke would have preferred to stay indoors. He surreptitiously watched the passing traffic and tried not to feel like a sitting duck.

"What did you think of Eddie's story?" Cassie asked.

"It's plausible," Luke replied in cautious agreement. "The guard at the Justice Center says Eddie seemed agitated when he left. I suppose being ordered to take a job you didn't want, as a condition for continued financial support, could be reasonable cause to be irritated. He really believed he could get a free ride at his sister's expense."

Cassie's tongue swirled a design across the top scoop of her cone.

"Don't play with your food."

"What would you *like* me to play with?"

She grinned a wicked grin and continued working her tongue across the creamy surface.

Luke smiled. Her response to his thoughtless admonition bridged the gap between past and present. It felt like putting on a comfortable old sweater you'd owned for years, one that fit so well you never noticed the unraveling seam or the baggy elbows.

Their gazes tangled and Luke felt the bottom drop out of his cautious, rational existence.

When had Cassie sneaked back into his life?

All along he'd told himself he was repaying a debt, atoning for the wrong he'd done her. He wanted to alleviate the sense of failure he'd carried like an albatross around his neck, needed to feel competent again. And he'd never planned on sticking around for any longer than it took to accomplish his goals.

Had he lied to himself? Had he been fooling himself when he thought he could make love to her and still remain objective? Could he really walk away when the case was solved? Or was he in too deep?

Cassie's eyes were bright with mischief, the way they'd often been when he first met her. And he'd missed that from his life—the fun, the pure joy of losing himself in the delight she spun around her like a magic spell. She was like the promise of gold at the end of a rainbow, and it would be so easy to throw caution to the wind and follow where she led.

But it never paid to dance on rain-slick rock. One false move could send you tumbling into an abyss. He'd already learned that lesson, and he had no intention of setting his feet on the same path again, no matter how she'd changed.

Memories were sweet, but they were all he dared hang on to. Now and in the future.

Fearful she'd see through his grin to the sudden heaviness in his heart, he bantered with her. "If you're in the mood for play, slugger, we'd better head for home."

Home, Cassie echoed mentally during the short ride. Though why such a simple word should raise her spirits, she wasn't sure. She knew she should concentrate on the little they'd gleaned from the interview with Eddie, but all she could think of was other unfinished business. The promise of passion she'd read this morning in Luke's eyes. The slow burn that seared through her in the wake of his touch. The need building with each passing block.

The sight of a black sedan in the driveway made her want to scream with frustration. Luke stomped on the brake and was halfway out of the car before Cassie could set his mind at ease.

"It's Uncle Harry."

The news didn't seem to reassure him in the slightest. Grimacing, he let Cassie take the lead as they headed for the open gate and followed the sound of Duffy's barking to the backyard. Harry Kimball, looking decidedly awkward, was playing catch with Duffy. The look of relief on the judge's face when he caught sight of them made Cassie want to laugh.

"What a surprise, Uncle Harry."

He dropped the damp Frisbee and gave Duffy a cautious pat on the head. Then he rubbed his hands on his slacks and hugged Cassie. "I was just driving by, sweetpea. Thought I'd stop to see how you were doing. I couldn't get hold of you this week to let you know I'd found the files you were looking for." He stepped away, his gaze flickering to a spot just past Cassie's head, so it came as no surprise to her when Luke draped a possessive arm across her shoulders.

"It's all right, Uncle Harry. I was pretty busy, and then I went out of town..." She trailed off, responding to Luke's warning squeeze.

"*We* went out of town," Luke corrected, his voice intimate, suggestive. His warm breath feathered her neck, just before he kissed her cheek.

Cassie tilted her head sideways in surprise, catching the smug smile he sent Harry Kimball. Public demonstrations of affection had never been Luke's style, yet here he was, boldly staking claim on her.

"It's all right," she repeated. "Chelsea found the files for me."

"I just didn't want you to think I was overlooking my favorite almost-niece."

"We don't want to hold you up," Luke said, his bluntness just short of rude. "Where were you headed?"

Heat flooded Cassie's face. She could guess why he was so anxious to get rid of the other man. Evidently, Uncle Harry could, too, for he cleared his throat, a thin smile signaling his discomfort. Mortified, Cassie stepped out of Luke's embrace and blurted, "Can we offer you some lunch, Uncle Harry?"

"No, no, my dear. I wouldn't want to upset your plans." Harry's gaze wavered between Cassie and Luke. "But, if it's not too much bother, I would appreciate a glass of water."

Throwing Luke a glance that told him he'd better mind his manners, Cassie unlocked the kitchen door and invited Harry inside.

She needn't have worried. As she poured the water, Luke's cellular phone rang, and he stepped into the living room to answer it. She thought she heard the words "Mitchell's," but it was spoken so low she wasn't sure. Had they found the mysterious white van?

"You've done a little redecorating, I see. Quite refreshing." Arms crossed over his chest, a half-empty glass in one hand, Kimball surveyed the kitchen.

Cassie nodded, her mind on Luke's conversation. She wished she could hear better.

Uncle Harry obliged by moving through the doorway. Seeming not to notice Luke's glare, he examined the living room. "Ah-h-h," he said. "I'm glad to see you took my advice...about the rug." He advanced a bit farther, openly taking in every detail.

Luke pointedly turned his back, muttering what sounded like instructions.

"Are your articles almost done?" the judge asked, nodding toward the desk in the corner.

"Nearly," Cassie replied. "Just a few things left to pull together."

She hated to admit she still hadn't discovered what Judge Wainright might have been trying to tell her. If the final transcripts Chelsea had given her didn't provide any leads, Cassie would have to throw in the towel. Eckhart would run Smitty's stuff in place of hers.

"Good, good," Harry murmured, sidling closer to the desk. He touched the manila folder on the top of the pile. "In that case, why don't I return this and save you a trip."

She hadn't yet had a chance to go through its contents, but before she could say so, Luke ended his phone call and crossed the room. "No need," he told Kimball, sliding the folder from beneath the judge's hand. "We're not quite done with it. I'll return it later."

A look of irritation crossed Harry's face. Cassie couldn't say that she blamed him. Luke was acting as prickly as a mother bear with newborn cubs. "Actually," she admitted in an attempt to relieve the tension between the two men, "I haven't had a chance to go through it yet. But I promise we'll get it back tomorrow."

Harry nodded understanding. Returning to the kitchen, he downed the last of his water and set the glass in the sink. He checked his watch. "I'd better be going. I told the mayor I'd meet him for a round of golf."

Cassie hugged him goodbye and was surprised when, instead of returning the hug, he clasped her shoulders and pinned her with his best judicial stare. "Are you sure you're all right?"

Touched by his concern, she opened her mouth to reassure him. She never got the chance.

"She's fine." Luke's voice rumbled with barely concealed impatience. "And I intend to make sure she stays that way."

Cassie wanted to sink through the floor. Luke couldn't have made his animosity clearer if he'd taken out an ad in the *Denver Tattler*.

Uncle Harry, on the other hand, gave no sign of taking offense. Years on the bench had evidently taught him to deal with petty annoyances by ignoring them. Without sparing Luke a glance, he continued talking to Cassie. "I'm sure you realize your father's beside himself. It's all I can do to keep him from charging up here to your rescue…your three brothers in tow."

Cassie grimaced at the thought.

Kimball dropped his hands and regarded her sternly. "You must admit he deserves some reassurance that everything is well with you."

"You're right," she admitted with a sigh. Her father just couldn't handle the idea that his baby girl had grown up and could take care of herself. What had happened to her just added fuel to his theory.

"What can I say to him?" Harry asked. "Has your memory come back? Do you remember…anything?"

Maybe some of Luke's mistrust had rubbed off, but for the first time, Uncle Harry's concern seemed…well, intrusive.

Immediately after the thought popped into her head, Cassie felt a wave of guilt. How could she be so disloyal? Uncle Harry only wanted the best for her. She opened her mouth to mention last night's dream, but was stopped by a nearly imperceptible shake of Luke's head.

"No," she said quickly. "Nothing."

Uncle Harry didn't believe her—she could tell by the way his gaze lingered on Luke—but he was too polite to expose her lie. Clasping her hands between his, he smiled benignly. "Well, I guess I'll have to make do with an account of your glowing appearance. Maybe that will be enough."

Though she held still while he pecked her cheek, she was relieved when he turned to go. "Don't forget, sweetpea. If you need me—day or night—just call."

"She won't," Luke said, holding open the front door. "I'm taking care of her."

His tone was perfectly polite, yet Cassie sensed a challenge behind the words. Heat rose in her neck and she held her breath, feeling like a bone caught between two growling dogs. Fortunately Uncle Harry refused to pick up the gauntlet. Shooting one brow skyward in scornful disdain, he left the house.

Luke closed the door behind him, putting a period to the visit with a decisive click. "I don't like that man. And I certainly don't trust him."

Cassie slapped down the transcript and pushed away from the desk. It was the record of one of Uncle Harry's trials, dealing with money laundering, the process where illegal gains were disguised as legitimate investments. It seemed to have as little bearing on her article as all the others she'd waded through over the last few weeks. She was no closer to knowing what Judge Wainright had been so anxious to tell her than she'd been the day after his murder, and without that information, her article had nothing to lift it above the ordinary.

Stretching to relieve the ache in her shoulders, she stared glumly at her computer screen. Somehow, with nothing but bare statistics and a few anecdotes, she was going to have to deliver a dynamite beginning to her series. Or give up the lead position to one of the most obnoxious male chauvinists it had ever been her misfortune to work with.

Duffy must have decided she was taking a break. He padded to the kitchen door and looked expectantly at her over his shoulder. Preoccupied with her dilemma, Cassie let him out, then stared, unseeing, at the backyard.

She could play up Judge Wainright's murder, hint that his death was orchestrated by drug lords. Too bad she had an aversion to exploiting tragedies, especially when a major reason was to beat out Smitty. But darn, she hated the thought of the man lording it over her. He had few scruples, and

Cassie could just imagine how he'd sneer if he knew of her qualms.

Duffy seemed to be having too much fun running loose to want back in any time soon. Closing the door, Cassie wandered back to the living room where the curtains trembled from a small breeze. Sighing, she stared at the computer and rubbed at the crick in her neck. She didn't have the slightest urge to get back to work.

If she had any sense, she'd have laid down for a nap with Luke. But since she'd planned to finish her article, she'd sent him upstairs alone.

The sound of steps on the stairs made her glance at her watch. It was nearly five o'clock. From the foot of the stairs, she watched Luke descend. How did he manage to look so deliciously sexy in all this heat?

"What's the matter, slugger?" he asked, rubbing a thumb across the frown lines on her forehead and kissing the tip of her nose. "Tough going?"

"Tough *not* going," she admitted, leaning her head against his chest while he massaged her shoulders and neck. His skillful fingers loosened the kinks there, then moved down her spine.

"Mmmm." How was it he always knew just what would help her relax the most? Of course, he was also good at pushing the exact buttons to set off her temper, but that seemed to be happening less and less lately. Either Luke was learning diplomacy, or Cassie was letting things roll off her back more than she used to. Indeed, things were going so well between them, she almost wished...

Beneath her ear, Cassie felt his heart pump. Strong. Steady. Reassuring. Like this man. Her man.

Who would leave when his job was over.

Dismay fluttered in her throat. She didn't want to lose what she'd so recently refound. Didn't want to contemplate lonely days stretching into the future. But she harbored no illusions. When the danger was past, Luke would disappear from her life, this time for good. He'd said so. And Luke always did what he said.

Inhaling, she filled her lungs with his scent, imagined it skimming through her bloodstream like a drug, imprinting itself on every cell. It conjured up their first kiss, the first time they'd made love, the nights they'd slept in each other's arms. It was why no man before or since had come even remotely close to winning her heart.

Hooking a finger beneath her chin, Luke tilted her face, covered her lips with his clever mouth. His kiss left her breathless, craving more. Hours, days, weeks more. A lifetime more.

"I missed you." He pulled back to rest his forehead against hers. "I want you."

Shivers crawled along her back at his words. He'd missed her. Would he miss her in the years to come? Or was his need transitory, fleeting—a product of proximity?

"I haven't been able to get you out of my head all day," he confessed. His fingers traced her breasts through her flimsy T-shirt, then brushed her nipples, making first one then the other tighten into hard nubs.

He pressed closer, and she felt his arousal against her thigh. It made her wet with longing, wobbly kneed in anticipation. She sagged back against the wall, her heart beating a mile a minute.

"All day I've wanted to touch you here…" He cupped her breasts, then traced the curve of her rib cage.

"And here…" His hand slid inside the elastic of her waistband, pushed slacks and panties over her hips, then returned to rest, palm atop her belly. The aching in her core grew and spread, like the ever-widening circles that disturb a pond's surface when a stone is dropped in its depths.

"And here." His fingers moved lower, parted her curls and slipped between the folds, finding her damp, pulsing core.

Gasping, Cassie arched against his hand, clutching his

shoulders to keep from falling. Inside, a fever built, searing away all rational thought. With each stroke of his fingers, he pushed her closer and closer to the edge of a precipice.

"Not...alone..."

For an instant he pulled back. Not far, just enough to read the plea in her eyes. "All day," he repeated. Then his mouth covered hers in possession so consuming she wanted to cry out. But even more, she wanted—no, *needed*—to feel him, too. Needed to feel him surge in her hands. Needed him inside her.

Clumsy with desire, she fumbled at his jeans, finally freeing him. Her fingers closed around him, glided his length. A groan, raw and fierce, tore from his throat. With little wasted effort he pulled protection from his pocket and slipped it on. Then he gripped her buttocks, lifted her, and nested between her thighs. Supported against the wall, Cassie wrapped her arms and legs around him as he thrust deep within.

She rode him like the wind. Wild and unrestrained. The tempo increased, keeping pace with the thundering beat of her heart. She felt him strain to make the final leap, and she hung on tight, her entire being focused on following. For long seconds they teetered on the edge, then fell, spinning in a wide, golden arc through space.

Afterward they settled on the couch, lying close in each other's arms. Dust motes drifted down a fading shaft of sunlight. Shadows stretched across the rug as afternoon slid into evening.

Cassie nuzzled his neck, adrift in a sea of contentment, where the future stretched beyond the horizon and nothing seemed impossible.

She could make him stay. It would always be like this. All she had to do was change. Just a little. Become the kind of woman he thought he wanted—sweet and even tempered, with no ambitions beyond home and family. If she tried, she could tangle herself so tightly around his heart, he'd never break free.

A chip of diamond-hard laughter spiked in her chest. Who was she kidding? She couldn't be what he wanted, not in a million years. In bed they were two pieces of the same puzzle, snugly fitting together into a unified whole. In the real world she was flint to his steel.

"What's wrong, slugger?" Luke asked in response to the whimper of distress that slipped from her throat. "A cramp?"

Cassie shook her head. Never in a million years could she be anything different, and if she tried, she'd end up hating him for what she'd become.

Curving his wrist around her back, he checked his watch. "Hunger pangs, then. Guess we ought to eat before we start gnawing on each other in earnest." He swatted her bare bottom and eased to a sitting position. "And you'd better get some clothes on if you don't want breakfast to be our next meal."

Cassie hugged him fiercely, before scooping up her things. If only it could always be this easy between them. She hopped into her slacks and headed for the kitchen, detouring to straighten the top of her desk.

"Let it be," Luke insisted, slipping behind her. His arms encircled her waist and he nipped her earlobe, sending heat sizzling down her neck. "I'll straighten up." He pulled the most recent folder from the pile and began stuffing papers back in it. "I think there's some leftover Chinese..."

What had halted him midsentence? Halfway to the other room, Cassie cast a curious glance back. Luke was studying the top sheet of paper from the manila file.

"I've already gone through that one," she assured him. "Set it by the door and I'll return it tomorrow."

He didn't answer. Instead, he pulled out another page, a frown creasing his forehead.

"What's the matter?" Cassie edged closer.

"I don't know," he replied. He closed the folder and bookmarked his place with one finger. "Probably nothing."

His response might have been more convincing if he didn't

sound so evasive, Cassie thought as she crossed the kitchen, but she couldn't very well call him a liar. Not if she wanted to give their relationship a chance.

Opening the back door, she called for Duffy.

What had Luke found in the transcript that was so interesting? All she'd seen was a dry account of a trial, recorded without inflection on the pristine pages.

Realizing the terrier hadn't responded to her first call, she tried again. "Here, boy."

Still no answering bark, no heavy panting to signal Duffy's approach.

Cassie stepped into the gathering dusk, letting the screen bang closed behind her.

The silence wrapped around her, punctuated only by the chirp of unseen crickets. Where was that dog, anyway? If he'd managed to dig his way under the gate again...

Exasperation sent her hustling around the corner of the house. She followed the familiar path, needing no light to find her way. If Duffy *had* managed to get out, it would be hours before he returned home, frisky and unrepentant.

Already guessing the effort was futile, she called again. "Duffy, come!"

A tiny sound, separate from the rustling of leaves on the trees, different from the rush of bat wings, whispered across the breathless night.

Cassie stopped, strained to hear.

There it was again...and again. Little more than a vibration of air, it made the hairs rise on her neck.

"Duffy?"

The sound quavered back. A low, wounded call of distress. *Duffy*.

A band wound around her chest, tightening until she thought her lungs would collapse from the pressure.

She couldn't see him in the dark. She needed a flashlight. But there was no time. She had to find him now.

Trying not to think about what could have happened to

him, Cassie stepped from the path and edged toward the spot the sound had come from.

There. In the lilac bushes along the fence.

She stooped, reached out blindly with one hand.

And touched fur.

Crouching, she ran a questing palm over the small body, searching for injury. "What's the matter, baby?" she crooned.

Duffy whimpered but didn't move, not even to lift his head.

Cassie cursed the inky darkness. Without knowing what was wrong, she didn't dare move him.

She must.

Breathing a silent prayer, she slipped her hands beneath him, pulled him closer so she could lift him. He whined but didn't fight her.

He felt so small, so vulnerable, in her arms. Like a floppy, beanbag toy. Her eyes stung.

"Luke! Luke!" she screamed. Clutching Duffy against her chest, she ran for the house.

Chapter 15

Gun drawn, Luke met her halfway.

"Call the vet. Call 911." She knew hysteria edged her words, although she fought to remain calm. It would do Duffy no good if she fell apart.

Luke holstered his weapon, his grim expression softening as he took in her drawn face and the bundle of fur in her arms. "Is he bleeding?" He reached out to relieve her of the burden.

"No." Cassie tightened her grip on the terrier, shaking her head from side to side. Duffy whimpered in protest. "No blood. But he's...he's..." Her voice cracked.

As if sensing her tenuous control, Luke lightly touched Duffy's head. "It'll be all right. What happened?"

Cassie wanted to scream at him. What difference did it make what had happened? Duffy was hurt, and they had to get help. That's all that mattered.

She bit her lip, knowing she was thinking irrationally. If they were going to help the little dog, they needed information. Trying to imitate his calm, Cassie took a shaky breath. "I don't know. I found him under the bushes..."

Before she could finish, Luke had retraced her earlier steps. "Here?" he called.

"A little to your right."

Duffy breathed in shallow pants. Cassie's chest ached in sympathy. She murmured soothing syllables while Luke dropped to his knees and felt around, reaching far back beneath the shadowy shrubbery. When he rose, something dangled from his hand. "I'll need a bag," he said in clipped tones.

Rather than comforting her, Luke's matter-of-fact manner pushed all her alarms. This was how he acted in emergencies—cool, rational, deliberate.

It was how he'd acted when he'd pulled her from the wreckage of Durrell's car two years ago.

Her vision blurred. She followed Luke into the kitchen, widening her eyes to keep the tears from falling. She refused to let panic gain the upper hand. Duffy would be all right.

"We can go to the all-night animal hospital next to Crossroads," Luke decided, dropping what looked like a chunk of steak into a plastic sack.

Cassie stared. *Poison.*

Why else would Luke save a piece of spoiled meat? Someone had tried to poison Duffy. *Had* poisoned Duffy, she corrected. Horror curdled her stomach, making her feel as though she'd been poisoned herself.

"I'll drive. You keep him calm."

Luke's voice seemed to come from a great distance. Cassie concentrated on it, narrowing all her focus to the rumbling sound. Setting one foot carefully in front of the other, she shuffled past the living room, where Luke scooped a folder from the couch, and out the front door.

Seated in the car's passenger seat, she curled around the terrier, sheltering him with her body. "You're going to get better. I won't let anything bad happen," she whispered.

This time she'd fight death with every weapon at her disposal. This time she'd win.

It seemed an eternity before they reached the animal hospital, though when she checked the clock on the dashboard, less than ten minutes had passed. Inside the building Cassie finally relinquished Duffy at the vet's insistence. She'd be in the way while they pumped the dog's stomach.

After carrying him for so long, her arms felt empty, and she wrapped them around her waist. Shoulders hunched, she tried to ignore the astringent, pine scent that failed to disguise the smell of pet urine and animal fear.

Luke touched her. She shook off his hand, but he didn't take the hint, only moved closer.

Determined not to give in to her fears, Cassie remained stiff and unyielding when he pulled her against his chest and tried to comfort her. He seemed not to notice.

"He'll be okay," Luke said in a low voice.

She tried not to be seduced by his quiet words, by his gentle hands on her back. She dared not accept the solace he offered. She had to remain strong until Duffy was out of the woods. If she didn't... She pushed the thought away.

Fighting back tears, she stared at her polished toenails poking from the fronts of her sandals. "It's my fault."

"No!" Luke grasped her shoulders, forcing her to look up.

"It is," she insisted. "I shouldn't have let him out alone. If I'd been more careful, this wouldn't have happened."

"You tell me how being careful would have prevented some sick son of a—" Luke stopped himself midsentence, realizing she wasn't hearing him.

"You don't understand. Duffy doesn't know any better. He's just a little dog. I'm the one who should have taken charge and made sure he was safe."

Worry etched dark shadows across her features, and Luke wanted to hold her and tell her everything would be all right.

He couldn't. He wasn't God, although he'd spent a lifetime

trying out for the role. He knew what she meant about being the one in charge, the one who should be in control. Better than most.

And who, better than he, knew the task was impossible?

He touched her cheek, shaking his head with sad regret. "All the care in the world doesn't stop bad things from happening."

"It should," she persisted soberly.

Aching for her hurt, he wrapped his arms around her rigid body. Gently he stroked her hair, knowing her need for denial and the bitter struggle going on inside her. He'd fought the same battle, denied the same truth—that no matter how hard you tried, you couldn't create a world free of pain and sorrow and suffering. Hell, it had taken him thirty-six years to face facts. How could he expect her to do it in the blink of an eye?

She relaxed. In the circle of his arms, he suddenly felt a loosening of muscles and the infinitesimal shift in her center of gravity. Satisfied, he hugged her, then tipped her face up. "He'll be all right. I promise."

Cassie smiled and nodded, though they both knew how hollow such a promise was. If Luke could guarantee such things, Danny would be alive today.

Over the next half hour, Cassie read every animal care pamphlet in the waiting room while Luke paced, trying to make sense of the transcript he'd brought with him. As far as he could tell, two sleazebags, accused of laundering drug money, had elected to appear before a judge rather than a jury. That information alone, didn't bother him. He knew enough of judicial procedure to be aware that individuals often preferred to rely on the court's expertise rather than trust the vagaries of assorted peers, who might or might not be sympathetic.

No, what had roused his suspicion was Kimball's keen interest in reclaiming the transcript. Luke didn't believe that Harry had planned to turn it over to Cassie. If Chelsea hadn't searched the judge's office, Luke was convinced it would never have seen the light of day.

Reading through the single-spaced pages, Luke was struck by the number of blunders. Missing witnesses. Botched investigations. Lack of sufficient evidence. Rarely had he seen such a conglomeration of errors in one trial. Either the prosecution had been incompetent or the defendants had had an exceptional attorney. Or...

An idea began to form—an idea that might provide Kimball with a reason for keeping things quiet. At this point, Luke didn't dare share his opinion with Cassie for fear some misguided sense of loyalty to Kimball would drive her to act carelessly.

When they got home, he would contact Haggerty and Burns to authorize a search of court records for any other money laundering cases Kimball had ruled on without a jury. Tomorrow he hoped to have proof for his theory that Kimball had probably been involved in taking bribes to let drug dealers go free.

In the middle of Luke's plans, the veterinarian emerged from the back of the clinic.

"Duffy's going to be fine. We were able to extract most of the poisoned food from his stomach, and I've given him something to counteract the little that may have made it into his bloodstream."

Cassie's face, which had drained of color when the vet came into the waiting room, now flushed with relief. "Thank you, Doctor," Cassie said. "He wasn't outside more than half an hour."

The vet nodded. "It's lucky you found him so quickly. He barely had time to digest anything."

Now that the danger was past, her mind turned to the question that had plagued Luke since they'd found the tainted meat. "I just don't understand why anyone would poison him. He isn't a barker, and all the neighbors know to call me if he digs his way out of the yard."

Luke's cellular phone interrupted her speculation. Excusing himself, he moved to a quiet corner.

"Slater, we're down one suspect."

"What do you mean?"

"We've got an accident up Boulder Canyon. A car crash."

A premonition clawed its way up Luke's back. "Who?" he snapped.

"We're not absolutely sure—the car's still in the creek. Highway Patrol's been down and report the driver's burned pretty bad, but we think it's Judge Kimball."

Luke muttered an expletive. "Are you sure?"

"Well, they'll need dental records for a positive ID, but it's his car. Who else would it be?"

Who else? Luke echoed silently. It was too bad Kimball had to go and die just when they were about to pin Wainright's death on him. Now they might never know all the whys.

From across the room, he studied Cassie's face, noting the lines of worry etched around her mouth and eyes. Concern for Duffy had strung her tighter than a cop on bomb-squad duty. How was he going to tell her that her honorary uncle was dead?

"How long before we have an official report?" he asked, shifting his gaze to a chart on dog breeds.

"The body's already on its way to the morgue. Shouldn't be more than a couple of hours."

He would wait, he decided. Time enough to break the news to her when the ID came back.

"Luke, they're getting ready to raise the car. Bradley wants you out there to take a look inside."

Luke glanced back at Cassie, who was arguing with the veterinarian about taking Duffy home. At the moment, the vet looked like he was winning. Good. That suited Luke fine. Until he made certain Kimball was the killer, he didn't want to leave Cassie alone. She'd be safe here while Luke went to the accident scene.

"Luke, you still there?" The voice in his ear brought him back from his speculations.

"Yeah—just making plans." He checked his watch. "I'll be there in twenty minutes." Pushing the off button on the phone, he crossed the room.

"He should stay the night," the doctor was saying.

"You told me the anesthesia would wear off shortly," Cassie argued. "He'll be under stress in a strange place."

"Ms. Bowers, I assure you the staff is trained to deal with sick animals. We'll do everything possible to relieve your dog's anxiety."

Knowing the vet's objections would only stiffen Cassie's resolve, Luke stepped in. "You're absolutely right, Doctor. Duffy shouldn't be moved right now. But what if Ms. Bowers stays with him until he is fully awake?"

Cassie's mouth set into stubborn lines, but before she could object, Luke explained about the call, carefully avoiding specifics.

"But why do they need *you* on a car accident?"

"Some odd circumstances," he said. "The chief wants homicide involved to play it safe."

Since Cassie still didn't look convinced, Luke threw in the clincher. "It shouldn't take me longer than an hour. I promise when I finish I'll pick you *and* Duffy up."

Minutes later, Luke backed his car from the clinic and headed down the street. The summer night wrapped around him, ruffling his hair and cooling his skin. The temperature had dropped several degrees, and the air felt charged and expectant. Ozone charged. Luke flipped on the radio, and the newscaster confirmed his guess.

Thunderstorms likely.

Cassie poured herself a cup of black coffee from the carafe. She'd propped open the kitchen door when the rain had started, and now she moved to stand by the screen, inhaling the scent of moisture and wet earth. Lightning flashed, followed almost immediately by a long roll of thunder.

Not far off.

Raindrops swirled in a gust of wind and splattered against the screen, spraying her with a fine mist. The moisture felt good, a soothing balm on her heated skin, but she'd soon be soaked if she wasn't careful.

Stepping back a few paces, she blew on her coffee, then took a cautious sip before closing and locking the door and returning to the living room. Duffy opened his eyes at her approach, then let them slide closed again. She ruffled his coat. Tired, but alert enough. Tick off one of the vet's concerns.

An hour and a half after Luke left the clinic, Cassie had taken Duffy home in a taxi. It wasn't so much that Luke was late—she knew how easily an hour turned into three or four on an investigation. But she really didn't want to spend half the night sitting in a sterile clinic with a steadily improving dog who would be more comfortable at home. Besides, Luke couldn't say she'd been careless. She'd paid the taxi driver extra to walk through the house with her before locking herself in. She passed the desk where the glowing screen of her laptop waited. She felt no urgency to sit down. The article was nearly done, and knowing how long even the simplest investigation took, she knew she'd finish before Luke returned.

Pushing aside the living room drapes, she looked out over the street. From front porches along both sides, light wove shimmering ribbons through the onslaught while trees dipped and swayed. Rain skipped across the sidewalks and danced in glittering pools of water in the street.

Not a soul was about. All cars were tucked into their garages. Even Mrs. Ogalvie was probably snug inside, drinking tea from a china cup and listening to the rain on her roof.

Cassie grinned. Definitely not a night to stand sentinel.

Sliding into the waiting chair, she set down her mug and

studied the computer. Not her best work, but competent. It wouldn't win prizes, but neither would it put her to shame. She scrolled through the last page she'd written and checked it against the trial transcript Luke had shown so much interest in. As far as she'd been able to tell, there was little to catch anyone's attention in the dry pages. She suspected Luke was grasping at straws. He hadn't liked Uncle Harry from the start, but that was no reason to suspect him of murder.

Staring into space, Cassie thought about the man she'd known since she was a teenager. A gentle, sweet man who wouldn't hurt a fly—well, maybe a fly—but never a human being. How could someone like that kill anyone, let alone his best friend?

He couldn't, she answered herself. She set down the transcript and shoved it to the corner of the desk.

Most murders are committed by someone the victim knows. Luke had told her that once, years ago. Was that why he was so suspicious of Uncle Harry, or was there something more?

She thought back to this afternoon, to the strangeness that had crackled in the air. Uncle Harry had been alone in the backyard with Duffy, playing Frisbee—a game he obviously found distasteful. Why had he chosen to wait there for them instead of in his air-conditioned car?

The memory of Luke, rising from the bushes with a piece of meat in his hand, insinuated itself in her head.

No! Uncle Harry wouldn't hurt a little dog. And he had no motive for killing a friend.

Don't trust anyone.

Luke's voice again. Angry, she squashed it like a bug and turned to her computer screen. She refused to let Luke's suspicious nature turn her against a man who was almost a part of her family.

She'd just started her concluding paragraph when Duffy lifted his head and whined. A few seconds later there was a knock at the kitchen door.

Frowning, she pushed aside the drapes. Her driveway was

empty. A neighbor, then, she decided, rising from her chair. Probably Mrs. Ogalvie, though why the poor woman would venture out in a rainstorm instead of calling was beyond Cassie.

Remembering Luke's warnings this afternoon, she peered through the peephole before opening the door. Harry Kimball stood on the stoop.

Dismay snaked through her, making her hesitate. Then, a dozen memories flashed across her brain, all involving this man who'd served as a sounding board for her hopes and dreams and who'd never wished her anything but the best. Luke mistrusted Harry Kimball, but then Luke didn't know him like she did.

Mortified that she had let Luke's suspicions cloud her judgment even for a minute, she fumbled the door open. "What are you doing out on a night like this, Uncle Harry? You're soaking wet." She shoved the door shut and slid the bolt into place. "Here, let's get that jacket off, and I'll get you a towel."

Together they managed to peel off the sodden windbreaker. Cassie laid it over the back of a chair and urged him into the next room.

"I didn't feel comfortable with the way we left things this afternoon." His voice followed her up the stairs.

What had bothered him? As she opened the linen closet door, Cassie replayed the afternoon's conversation, and finally concluded Luke's behavior had put Uncle Harry off. Maybe he thought she hadn't felt free to talk openly. His next words confirmed her assumption.

"I decided to come back when that ex-husband of yours was gone."

Grabbing a towel, she hurried down the stairs and handed it to him. "You ought to know I always speak my mind, no matter who's around." She smiled wryly.

He scrubbed at his hair, his voice muffled by the absorbent

material. "Well, Slater's a pretty overwhelming individual. Isn't that why you divorced him?"

The question made her uncomfortable. Cassie hadn't believed in forcing friends and family to take sides during a divorce, and she wasn't going to start laying blame now. "There were other problems."

Uncle Harry's face appeared from beneath the tented terry cloth. She knew he expected more of an explanation. She wasn't going to give one, not even to him. What had happened between her and Luke was just that—between her and Luke.

In the ensuing silence, she crouched in front of the tile-framed fireplace. "It's a good thing I had this converted to gas last winter." She turned the handle, and flames licked the ceramic logs. It was nearly as good as the real thing, if you didn't look too closely, but more important, it gave off heat. She was still watching the fire's erratic dance when another thought struck her. "How did you know Luke wasn't here?"

The pause that followed was brief, but long enough to make her lift her head.

Uncle Harry stared at her, firelight reflecting in his eyes. His hands gripped the ends of the towel he'd draped around his neck. "No car in the driveway."

But unless he'd purposely driven onto the cul de sac, he wouldn't have known Luke's car was missing.

Pulling her gaze away, Cassie tried to shake off her disquiet. She put her palms on her thighs and straightened. "How about some coffee? I have a pot going."

"Wonderful."

His tone was unnaturally jovial, jarring even, and unbidden, Luke's accusations resurfaced in her mind. She tried to ignore them, but they refused to go away. Irritated with herself, she strode toward the kitchen.

A lightning flash partnered by an ear-shattering clap of thunder accompanied her exit.

Duffy yelped.

The lights went out, halting her mid-stride.

Anger overflowed. "Damn!"

"Do you have any candles?" Uncle Harry's calm voice echoed eerily from the next room.

Ashamed at her outburst, she edged toward the counter where she kept emergency supplies. "It'll just be a minute," she assured him, groping in the drawer. Her fingers found a waxy column. Striking a match, she lit the wick, then used the light to locate a holder for the candle. Picking up the glowing taper, she returned to the living room where Uncle Harry stood, looking at her computer screen.

She set the flickering candle on the coffee table, pausing to give Duffy a pat.

"It's better to light one little candle..." Harry quipped.

"Than to curse the darkness," she finished. She tried to return his smile, but the muscles involved felt stiff and clumsy. What was wrong with her that even familiar rituals rang false? Where was the easy camaraderie they'd once shared?

She joined her uncle in front of the computer. Thank goodness she'd switched to battery power when the storm started. All her work was still there, marching across the screen. Intent on what he was reading, Harry scrolled through the article without acknowledging her presence.

Cassie moved to the window and lifted the drapes. Everyone seemed to have lost power. There were no lights anywhere.

No lights, no people, no cars.

The street was a ghost town. Trying to shake off a growing sense of unreality, she let the material fall back into place. She should probably check to see if Mrs. Ogalvie was all right. Lord only knew what could happen to an elderly lady in the dark. Cassie reached for the phone. It was dead.

"You haven't finished your article."

"Nearly." She tapped the phone's button several times. Nothing happened.

"Is the phone dead?"

Nodding, she replaced the receiver. Should she run next door? She hesitated, reluctant to brave the downpour.

"Storms create myriad problems." He fingered one of the folders containing trial transcripts, then lifted it from the desk. "Who were you trying to call?"

"My neighbor. She lives alone. I thought she might be concerned by the power outage."

"Next door? I wouldn't worry about her, my dear. She has company. I saw them through the window when I went by."

Relieved to have one less worry, Cassie sighed. "How about that coffee I promised?" she asked.

His steps oddly heavy, Uncle Harry moved to the fireplace without answering. Shoulders slumped, he gazed into the flames, a lonely scout standing vigil by the campfire.

The image brushed a memory, one Cassie couldn't quite catch, but it made a shiver climb her spine. "Uncle Harry?"

"What? Oh, coffee." He shook his head, apparently clearing cobwebs of his own. "That would be fine."

When Cassie picked up the candle, Duffy whimpered and tried to get off the couch. "Oh, no you don't. You stay here," she insisted. "Stay."

He must have been weaker than he expected because, to Cassie's surprise, he obeyed. When she reached to pat him, he licked her hand, then dropped his head atop his paws. "Good boy," she soothed. Turning to go, she met Harry's inquisitive gaze. "He's a little under the weather," she explained, reluctant to go into detail.

Uncle Harry didn't pry. Instead, he returned his attention to the fire as Cassie moved toward the kitchen. "You were always my favorite pretend niece."

The odd remark, distorted by rain pounding against the house, stopped her halfway to the door. She grinned, not sure she'd heard correctly. "I'm your *only* pretend niece."

He didn't respond.

Her grin faded in the uncomfortable silence. An unseen draft caught her candle flame, and she cupped her hand around it. "I'll be right back with that coffee."

In the kitchen she braced herself against the counter and closed her eyes, baffled by the strangeness that permeated her house. Something was wrong—terribly wrong—with Uncle Harry, and she didn't know if she could deal with him alone much longer. She wished Luke would come home. He'd know what to do.

She tested the carafe with her palm. It hadn't cooled off yet. She poured Harry's coffee. Then, since the cup she'd poured herself earlier was undoubtedly cold, she reached in the cupboard for another mug.

"It's not going to work."

The solemn pronouncement from the kitchen doorway made her scalp tingle. Her hand jerked, and coffee sloshed onto the counter. Setting down the carafe, she grabbed a sponge and mopped at the spill.

"What isn't going to work, Uncle Harry?" She tried to speak calmly, tried to hide her alarm at his bizarre behavior. But she feared he could discern the quaver in her voice and sense the apprehension building deep inside her.

He didn't seem to hear her question. Or maybe he just refused to answer. "I should have known you wouldn't give up. And now you're remembering, aren't you?"

"Remembering?" Panic jostled her rib cage.

"Oh, not everything," Harry said. "Just bits and pieces, odds and ends. Little things that seem of no import. You see, I understand how it works. I've done my homework."

Rain splattered the window like pellets from a shotgun. Overhead it beat a discordant rhythm, muffled by the second floor and the attic above.

Her insides turned to ice, Cassie picked up the coffee carafe and her mug before turning to face this stranger she'd thought she knew.

In the glow of the single candle, he was a dark shape backlit by the fire in the other room. She couldn't read his expression, but his eyes glittered twin flames.

Too late a warning whispered in her head as all the inconsistencies clamored to be heard.

No cars. There'd been no cars parked on the street. Not his, not Mrs. Ogalvie's company.

Why had he come to the back door?

A chill started in her toes and began a swift climb through her body.

Lightning flashed, illuminating Harry Kimball for one brief instant. The following roll of thunder seemed to go on forever.

Cassie's heart caught in her throat.

He held a gun.

For once the weather forecasters were right on target. By the time Dispatch patched Mrs. Ogalvie's call through, the promise of rain had become reality. Water slicked across Luke's hastily donned Gore-Tex jacket and splattered in the mud at his feet, blurring the prints left by a dozen or more people.

Mrs. Ogalvie's message sent Luke scrambling up the slippery slope, shouting instructions over his shoulder to the team at the water's edge. "I'll be there in less than ten minutes," he promised the old lady. "You stay put."

Radioing for backup, he slammed the car into gear and maneuvered away from the tow truck ahead of him. His tires spat gravel as he whipped the wheel hard left and pulled off the shoulder onto the asphalt.

His fingers tightened around the steering wheel as he considered Mrs. Ogalvie's message. Cassie was home and the old lady had spotted a prowler.

Maybe the man Mrs. Ogalvie had seen sneaking into Cassie's backyard wasn't a threat. Maybe it was some teenager taking a shortcut. Maybe—

There were no maybes. Teenagers didn't cut through fenced yards unless they were running from the police.

Cassie was in danger, and Luke had only himself to blame. If he'd told her his suspicions, he wouldn't be racing across town in an attempt to outrun a madman. She'd ignored Luke's instructions, but only because he hadn't trusted her with the truth.

Luke leaned harder on the gas pedal, sending the car careening around a curve, but the added speed didn't ease the foreboding that coiled through him.

Whoever Mrs. Ogalvie had seen lurking in Cassie's yard was no ordinary prowler. It was someone pushed by fear to take the steps necessary to ensure his survival.

He rounded yet another curve, and the rock walls fell away. The car shot from the canyon mouth onto Canyon Boulevard. Rain spun in his headlights, sparkling like splintered glass against the inky black of the street. Half a block ahead, taillights glowed red, like two Satanic eyes.

Luke couldn't recall an exact moment he'd sensed something wrong at the accident scene. It was more a series of impressions that didn't quite add up. It had seemed too easy. The car, a gun, an empty can of paint...and Wainright's missing cellular phone. All tossed into a not-so-pretty package and tied with a damp ribbon.

The coroner's call had come as no surprise—the charred remains from the car weren't Kimball's. Dental records didn't match.

They still didn't know who had died in the crash, but unless Luke missed his guess, they'd found the driver of the white van and the guy who'd taken a shot at Cassie. At the moment, however, identifying him mattered less than finding Harry Kimball. Before he reached Cassie.

Coming up fast on the bumper of a slow-moving VW, Luke swung into the left lane, ignoring the way the rear wheels shimmied on the rain-slick street. Once again he punched in Cassie's number and listened to it ring. On and on and on. Something was wrong with her phone line, otherwise the answering machine would have picked up. With a curse he thumbed off the phone and sped through a yellow light.

A band of steel wound around his heart, squeezing tighter and tighter. He slammed his fist against the steering wheel, trying to cut through the pain.

She's safe. She's fine.

His assurances rang hollow because he knew there was one person from whom she wasn't safe—the one person she refused to doubt—her Uncle Harry.

Luke didn't believe in coincidence. It was no accident that the crashed car belonged to Kimball, no accident police had assumed the dead man to be the judge. He'd planned it all to lure Luke away, leaving Cassie exposed and vulnerable.

Lightning flashed, followed by thunder loud enough to wake the dead. The downpour increased, forcing Luke to turn the wiper blades to high. Even then he found himself leaning forward, straining to see through the water sluicing across the windshield. As he neared the downtown area, he refused to let up on the gas, silently breathing thanks that most people were inside their snug houses tonight.

A right turn, nearly too fast. His rear wheels slewed, and he fought to straighten the car. On up the hill. Another Keystone Kops turn and he screeched to a halt two doors down from Cassie's, jumping from the car almost before it quit rolling. He had outrun the backup he'd called for.

Drawing his gun, he ran, slipping on the wet grass, toward Cassie's house.

Hang in there, slugger. I'm coming.

Chapter 16

"Luke was right." Horror dried Cassie's mouth, making it difficult to wrap her tongue around the words.

"To be suspicious? Most assuredly." Harry Kimball inclined his head. "But to believe me a cold-blooded murderer?" He raised one eyebrow reflectively. "I think not."

His response might have reassured her, but for two things—the gun in his hand and the direction in which he pointed it. Fear tingled across her scalp, followed closely by a cautionary voice. Given the right circumstances, almost anyone could kill, but only a mad man—or a desperate one—killed again to cover his crime.

Cassie's fingers cramped around the handle of the carafe she still held in one shaking hand. Coffee sloshed inside the glass container, but she didn't dare set it down. She didn't dare move. She hardly dared speak.

But speak she must.

If she'd learned anything as a crime reporter, it was to keep the suspect talking. As long as Harry Kimball talked, he wouldn't pull the trigger.

Praying for strength, she kept her tone calm and unthreatening. "It was an accident, wasn't it?"

"A terrible tragedy," he agreed. "Thomas was a fool, but you don't kill people for being fools."

A fool would not have been how Cassie would have described the deceased judge, but she wasn't about to argue the point. "You had a fight," she guessed.

"A disagreement," he corrected. "Although I have to concede I lost my temper."

"A disagreement...about...?"

Harry's expression grew secretive. "If I tell, then everyone will know."

"Only me, Uncle Harry." She forced herself to address him by the familiar name. "And I agree Wainright must have been at fault. It was obvious he considered himself superior to everyone. You can trust me not to tell."

He smirked. "I think not. You were going to write about it in your articles."

"That's only because I didn't know you were involved. Now that I know, I'll keep your secret." Desperation added sincerity to her words.

Head cocked to one side, Kimball thought about what she'd said. "Yes, I believe you would, but that husband—excuse me, *ex*-husband—of yours would get it out of you."

"Luke and I had a fight. That's why he's gone."

"He's gone because *I* planned it that way."

His smug satisfaction rasped against her nerves, although she'd heard him use the same superior tone dozens of times in the past. "Of course you did," she assured him. "But we had a fight over his leaving. He won't be back."

"He was never right for you, anyway," Harry said. "Rather rough around the edges."

Cassie nodded, thinking she could really use some of Luke's rough edges right now. Silently she sent a prayer skyward. "What did you and Wainright argue about?"

Kimball frowned. "Ethics." When Cassie raised her eyebrows, he explained further. "Thomas was always too damned straight for his own good. He had a nasty habit of sitting in judgment on the rest of us mortals, even off the bench."

Judge Wainright had died because he was ethical?

"He didn't approve of some of the favors I'd done, or the gratitude shown me by certain acquaintances." A sneer twisted his lips. "Of course, Mr. High-and-Mighty never had to worry about money or social standing. He *married* his."

If her knees hadn't been knocking with fright, Cassie might have taken time to unravel the twisted skein Harry Kimball had tossed her way. As it was, she concentrated on maintaining a sympathetic expression on her face.

"And *he* had the nerve to look down his nose at *me*."

His words were muttered, but Cassie had no trouble catching the resentment and envy. "That *was* rather small of him," she agreed.

"I wasn't doing anything he hadn't done. But not everyone has a gullible debutante fall into his lap."

It was obvious jealously had eaten away at Harry Kimball for a long time. As a reporter she would have liked to explore the emotion further. Unfortunately, as a woman being held at gunpoint, she knew time was running out.

"Judge Wainright accused you of doing something illegal?"

"It's not like I let hardened criminals go free. Investing money isn't against the law, and people can hardly be blamed if they don't check where that money comes from, now, can they?"

The trial transcripts. Suddenly it all made sense. Cassie's articles weren't the threat. Uncle Harry had been afraid of what she might uncover in the transcripts. He'd been afraid of exposure—not for dealing drugs, not for money laundering, but for his part in getting such cases dismissed.

Theoretically, what he'd done wasn't illegal. Anyone could request a trial by judge instead of a jury trial. Then, if the judge were favorably inclined, if his palm was suitably greased... Cassie felt sick to her stomach. Harry Kimball had taken bribes, apparently more than once. That was what Judge Wainright had discovered when he went through the transcripts. That was what Harry had tried to keep Cassie from learning.

"The sanctimonious bastard." Warming to his topic, Harry glared into the shadows. "He had the nerve to threaten to turn me in. *Me*—the man he'd called his best friend. He wouldn't listen. He wouldn't give me a chance to explain. Just kept spouting drivel about the sanctity of the law."

Cassie shrank against the counter, forgotten for the moment as Harry ranted. If only he would forget her long enough for her to escape. But she knew such hopes were useless. Any minute he would refocus his attention.

Her mind scrambled to formulate a logical plan, to figure a way out of this mess, but every avenue she explored dead-ended against the reality of a gun and a bullet.

The plain, bald truth was she was going to die. Here. Soon. Without ever seeing Luke again.

Regret sliced her heart. She couldn't die. Not without telling him how she really felt. Not until she'd apologized for doubting him, not before she'd spoken the words *I love you*.

Abruptly Kimball stopped his tirade. "What was that?"

Cassie listened. Rain still fell, and the old house protested the indignity with its usual array of creaks and moans. Wind rattled the screen door. Water splashed in the gutters.

Darkness amplified every sound, yet she detected nothing that might have caught his attention, and certainly nothing to give her hope. As much as she wished the cavalry would arrive and save her, it wasn't going to happen. The only one she had to depend on was herself.

Another long moment crept past before Kimball came to

the same conclusion. "We're wasting time. As much as I'd like to continue our little chat, I'm afraid I can't afford it. Our convenient rainstorm seems to be waning."

He was right. In the past few minutes there'd been a gradual reduction in the storm's intensity. Instead of resembling the sound of water rushing over Barker Dam, the rain now struck a new rhythm—softer, steadier. Except for a faint undercurrent of barely perceptible taps.

Was this what Kimball had heard? She shot him a glance from beneath her lashes, but he didn't seem to be listening anymore. Was she imagining things? No, there it was again—faint and erratic, like someone signaling at the back door.

Luke? Her heart leaped, then plummeted. There was no way for him to rescue her. She'd thrown the bolt.

Keep Kimball talking.

Banking on his not being able to resist bragging about his superior intelligence, Cassie blurted, "I don't understand how you managed to get the murder weapon into Eddie's apartment."

"Simple, my dear."

Inwardly cringing at his smug tone, she maintained an air of interest. If she could buy time, she might come up with a plan to help Luke get in.

"I merely called in a few favors," Kimball explained. "And it turns out it's actually quite easy to break into an apartment with the right tools and experienced help. I must admit, though, if I weren't so good at seizing opportunity when it presents itself, I would have been in a bit of a fix."

"Opportunity?" She tightened her fingers around the handle of the carafe, praying the coffee hadn't cooled. As it was, she was going to need a lot of luck herself. Her plan was a long shot, but it was all she had.

"The young hooligan appeared quite out of sorts when I

passed him outside Thomas's office," Kimball said. "It was obvious he hadn't had a successful meeting."

Without taking her eyes off Kimball, she eased back the carafe lid. Tension coiled through her body. From head to toe, each muscle and nerve grew taut with purpose. Then, as her honorary uncle continued with his self-congratulatory speech, she acted.

Lunging sideways, she flung the contents of the carafe. The coffee was hot, but not hot enough to scald him, so she attributed his shout to shock.

One chance. She only had one chance. Blindly she reached out, touched cold metal and shoved.

The bolt didn't budge.

Behind her, Kimball staggered a few steps, the gun wavering in one hand while he swiped at his face with his forearm. His finger jerked on the trigger. An explosion split the air. A bullet struck the kitchen window, shattering the glass.

Cassie pressed against the door, a scream welling in her throat, but she couldn't suck in enough air to get it out.

Run! Hide!

Something struck the locked door from outside, rattling it in its frame. The blow vibrated through her.

Luke. He was trying to get in. She had to help.

Kimball shuffled closer. She heard his rasping breath, felt the movement of air at her back. With one last desperate effort, she threw her weight against the bolt. It gave.

She jumped out of the way just in time. The door crashed open, hitting with enough force to send the handle through the drywall.

Kimball's fingers clamped around her upper arm. He yanked her back against his chest.

"Let her go." Luke stood silhouetted in the doorway.

Luke. Her protector. Her friend. Her love.

Time slowed to the bore of Kimball's gun pressing against her skull. To the last of the rain dripping from the eaves.

To the click of toenails against the linoleum.

Toenails? In the next instant time went into overdrive. Things happened so quickly she caught only scraps and flashes of events, like a dance viewed through a strobe.

The gun swung toward Luke. Duffy sank his teeth into Kimball's ankle and he yelped in pain. Trying to shake off the dog, he loosened his grip. Cassie jerked free. And the electricity came back on.

Shots rang out.

Cassie launched herself forward, knowing even before she reached Luke she was too late.

His chest burned as if someone had stabbed him with a hot poker. Whoever had said being shot wasn't as painful as being sliced was a damn liar. It hurt like the Devil.

He tried to move his head, wanting to see where he'd been hit, but his head felt heavy. Too heavy to lift. Besides, he didn't have to see the damage to assess it. Cassie's blanched face and the way she avoided meeting his gaze told him everything he needed to know.

It was bad.

He tried to reach for her hand and tell her not to worry. He would get through this. After all, he'd survived lots worse.

''Don't move,'' she commanded. Grabbing a towel from the counter, she pressed it against his left shoulder.

Pain seared in a crazy, jagged path to his spine and climbed upward, lodging at the base of his skull. He clenched his teeth together, determined not to give in to the agony. While the room tilted and blurred around them, he focused on Cassie. On her sweet mouth. On her stormy eyes, filled with tears.

Why was she crying? She was safe. Kimball had taken a direct hit. Luke had made sure before releasing himself to the pain. Cassie had nothing to fear anymore. He should tell her. It would reassure her. But his vocal cords refused to cooperate, and to make matters worse, his lids felt weighted with cement.

Darkness washed over him, accompanied by regret. Regret for not telling her he still loved her.

For the second time in two weeks Cassie found herself in the hospital, staring at the ceiling, counting holes.

It was a lot harder, she decided, being the visitor instead of the patient. They didn't give visitors anything to help them rest, not even when they spent the night curled on an empty bed, listening to muted breathing across the room.

She'd been here three days now. Three days of watching Luke slip in and out of consciousness. Three days of praying while they waited for his fever to break. Three days of hell.

He was better now. The endless tossing and thrashing had subsided to an occasional restless movement. The nurse had said he might regain consciousness at any time.

Weighed down by fatigue, Cassie tried for the umpteenth time to fall asleep. Instead the events of that horrible night in her house played across the backs of her lids as they had every time she'd closed her eyes. Blood oozing from Luke's chest. Using Luke's cellular phone to call an unruffled 911 operator. Mrs. Ogalvie's arrival at the door, followed by Luke's backup.

And try as she might, Cassie couldn't blot out her last sight as she trailed Luke's stretcher to the ambulance, of Harry Kimball's lifeless body sprawled across her white linoleum.

Cassie opened her burning eyes, shivering in the chilled air. Why did they always keep hospitals so cold at night? She thought about getting up to find another blanket, but decided it wasn't worth the effort. Instead she tugged the one she had higher and curled onto her side.

Would the night never end?

She checked her watch. Five o'clock. Wasn't it about time

for morning rounds to start? Propping herself on one elbow, she peered at the next bed. Through the shadows she made out the almost imperceptible rise and fall of Luke's chest.

Reassured, she sat up and slid to the floor. The tile against her soles felt like ice, and she pulled the blanket from the bed. Draping it around her shoulders, she crossed to the window, pausing on the way to brush a kiss on Luke's cheek. She parted the curtains with one hand. A sprinkling of stars hung over the city, floating in the last, dark hollow of night.

Luke would be all right—the doctor had said so. His wound would heal. He'd leave the hospital. And then?

Her throat tightened. Then he'd walk out of her life forever. Unless she did something.

But could she? And would it do any good?

All her insecurities joined hands, clamoring for her attention. *Too many differences.* Luke was cautious—she took chances. He planned for the future—she lived in the present. Maybe they couldn't overcome their differences. Maybe they both were too set in their ways to work things out.

It would take courage to confront him, maybe more than she had. But could she let him go without telling him what she'd suspected ever since he'd reentered her life? Did she dare reveal the truth she'd discovered in the hushed hours between darkness and dawn—that she loved him, had always loved him?

Two years ago she'd allowed grief and insecurity to override her heart. She'd rejected him before he could do the same to her. Now she had another chance—a chance to stand and fight for their happiness. How could she face herself if she took the coward's way out again?

A faint groan nudged the silence, pulling her from the window. Her bare feet carried her noiselessly to the side of his bed. Luke tossed restlessly, his muscles jerking against the straps holding his sling immobile. To calm him Cassie stroked his other arm. "Be still."

Eyes closed, he quieted. She would have assumed he'd fallen back asleep if not for the muscles, still tensed beneath her palm. And then he spoke, his voice hoarse from the anesthetic they'd given him.

"It's too cold for Hell, so it must be Heaven. But what are you doing here, slugger? You weren't killed."

Cassie stifled a grin of relief. "Brace yourself for a disappointment, love. You're still in this realm. In the hospital, to be exact."

"I was positive…" He opened his eyes and squinted. "Damn. Do they have to keep it so dark?"

Cassie reached to the wall above his head and flicked on the nightlight. "Better?"

"Much." His free hand found hers. "Are they afraid I'll hit someone?" he asked, indicating with a slight dip of his head the sling strapped to his body.

"You had a fever. It's to keep you from reinjuring the wound."

Wearily he closed his eyes. "How long have I been here?"

"It's been three days since you were shot." Then, when he didn't respond, she added, "It's Thursday morning— nearly dawn."

"And you've been here all this time." He opened his eyes and focused on her face. "Why?"

He'd provided the perfect opening for her to confess her feelings, but doubt stayed her tongue. What if he didn't return her love? She dodged the question. "The newspapers are having a heyday. You're everyone's hero. They'll probably give you a medal and the keys to the city. After all, you were injured in the line of duty by a madman who'd already killed two people."

"Two?" Luke frowned.

"Wainright…and the dead man in Kimball's car."

Seeing his gaze slide to his bandaged chest, Cassie rattled on. "The bullet lodged in your shoulder. There was some tendon-and-muscle damage to repair, but it missed your lung and heart.''

''Duffy.''

''Yes. If Duffy hadn't spoiled Kimball's aim…'' Remembered terror cut off the rest of the sentence.

''You'd be making my funeral arrangements,'' he finished, closing his eyes.

Her heart somersaulted. She forced what she imagined to be a sickly smile to her lips. ''I guess I was right all along to call him a guard dog.'' Then, before Luke could voice the next question, she hastened to add, ''He's fine. Mrs. Ogalvie took him home with her.''

''Mrs. Ogalvie?'' He opened his eyes, confusion evident in his gaze.

''Yes—it helped her overcome her disappointment.'' Cassie pulled a sober face. ''She'd intended to attack the prowler with her cane.''

Luke started to laugh, then winced at the movement.

Cassie bent closer. ''Do you need a painkiller?''

He shook his head. His fingers tightened around her wrist. ''Just you.''

Their gazes locked. For several seconds neither moved. Cassie was first to look away. Telling herself not to read too much into his words, she drew a shaky breath. ''I'm here.'' When she glanced back, Luke's attention was fixed on their intertwined fingers.

''Have they identified the crash victim?'' he asked without looking up.

She nodded. ''An ex-con Kimball must have hired to do his dirty work. A paint store clerk recognized a picture of him as the customer who'd purchased several buckets of red paint, and the slug they dug out of your apartment door matches the gun from Kimball's car.''

''And Kimball?'' The flatness of his tone told her he already guessed the answer.

"Dead."

"I'm sorry."

His expression of regret startled her. "I'm not," she said, pulling her hand free. "Before you got there, he admitted most everything. The rest the police have pieced together."

Cassie clutched her blanket cloak closer. She stared at the panel of buttons on the wall above Luke's head, determined not to feel sympathy for the man who'd betrayed her trust. "The note, my kitchen—even the shooting at your apartment building—were all designed to scare me off."

"Desperation makes dangerous men."

The words, uttered in the near darkness, sent a shiver skittering up her spine. "Very dangerous," she said tonelessly. "He was willing to do anything to save his reputation and his comfortable life."

Knowing how Kimball's betrayal must hurt her, Luke nodded in understanding. "He was afraid you'd eventually regain your memory and identify—"

Cassie gave a strangled laugh. "What a waste."

Startled, Luke sharpened his focus. "A waste?"

"Exactly. Uncle Harry had nothing to fear on that count."

"You remember?" he asked, not needing her nod to confirm it. Corroboration resided in the bitter twist of her mouth and the bleak look in her eyes. Acid licked at Luke's stomach in counterpoint to the throbbing in his head. "When?"

"When the lights came back on in the kitchen—when you both fired your guns." She looked past Luke, recalling the details. "It was raining that night, too. Raining and thundering, and Judge Wainright's chambers were as dark as my kitchen. Darker." She took a shuddering breath.

Luke would have taken her hand, offered solace, but she held herself just out of reach. Sensing her need to finish the journey through the past by herself, he stifled his instinct to ease the way and let her continue.

"I remember hitting the wall switch, but it didn't help.

The sudden glare blinded me...and then I got clobbered." She turned a shaky smile on him. "Poor Uncle Harry. He should have left well enough alone. I couldn't expose him as a murderer—he had to do that himself."

She pinched her lips together and stared at Luke for a long moment. "You warned me. Told me not to trust anyone. Why couldn't I listen?"

"When it counted, you did."

He'd intended to reassure her, but his words seemed to have the opposite effect.

"I nearly got you killed," she said. In the muted glow of the nightlight, he caught the shimmer of tears in her eyes before she abruptly turned away and strode to the door.

She peered into the hall. "Has everyone taken a break?" she grumbled. "Someone should have checked on you by now."

"Don't worry about it," Luke said quietly, suspecting her gruffness was a cover to give herself time to pull fragile emotions back under control. "I'm all right. Are you?"

She nodded, not turning. "Do you know he poisoned Duffy?"

"I suspected." Luke studied the rigid set of her back, guessing there was more to come. He was right.

Easing the door shut, she swung around. "He apologized before he died and said it was nothing personal." Bitterness dripped from her words. "He only needed us out of the way so he could get back the trial transcript before we figured things out."

Luke remained silent, but his lack of response seemed to add to her self-blame.

"I nearly got you killed," she repeated.

Pain bled through her words, piercing his heart. Ignoring his tender muscles, he groped for the control box on the rail. "Come here," he insisted as the bed propelled him to a sitting position. Amazingly, she obeyed. Her hand, when he took it, lay icy cold in his. Fighting off a wave of dizziness, he rubbed it between his palms. ''You're blaming the wrong person, slugger. You weren't holding the gun.''

''But—''

Before she could accuse herself of more crimes, he laced his fingers through hers. ''Sit,'' he said, then croaked out a raspy ''please'' for good measure. It was taking unfair advantage, he acknowledged, but desperate times called for desperate measures.

''Cassie...love.'' How to begin? What to say? Once she'd called him a poet. Now he knew himself for a tongue-tied fool who couldn't proceed for fear of saying the wrong thing. How could he make her understand that being shot was nothing next to the fear of losing her, and that if Kimball had succeeded in killing her, Luke would have died, also.

Tracing a finger down her cheek, he tried to explain. ''It doesn't matter that Kimball shot me. What matters is that you're alive.''

Shaking her head, she opened her mouth to reply, but before she could contradict him, he curved his palm at the back of her head and drew it down. It would have been less awkward if he'd had two good arms, but he wasn't about to complain. Against his, her lips parted, and a soft sigh escaped from her throat.

So sweet, so beloved. He deepened the kiss, urging her closer—

Pain shot through his chest, making him flinch.

Cassie jerked back, smothering a gasp of horror behind her hands. ''I've hurt you.''

The burning sensation faded. Luke shook his head in denial, but it was too late—the tenuous thread binding them together was severed. Uncertainty flickered in Cassie's eyes, and she looked away. Luke's heart dropped. Did she think he'd kissed her just to comfort her?

Apparently so, for while he contemplated the best way to

erase the last few seconds of awkwardness, she spoke. "I suppose now that you've caught your killer, you'll be moving out."

Speechless, he could only stare. What was she saying? He didn't want to discuss leaving. He wanted to talk about the two of them, about new beginnings and second chances. "That depends," he ventured, made cautious by her averted gaze and deliberate tone.

"On?"

Luke shifted uneasily, wondering why it felt as though Cassie were miles away instead of mere inches. "It depends on what you want."

"I want…"

Something twisted in his gut. Maybe he'd been deluding himself all along. Maybe he'd misinterpreted her reactions. What if she felt only gratitude and a lingering physical attraction? What if she wanted him gone so she could pick up the pieces of her life—a life that didn't include him. Suddenly he didn't want to know what she wanted. Not yet. Not until he'd had his say.

"I'm trying to change," he blurted out, feeling control slipping from his grasp. "It's not easy for someone who's made a life of caring for others to let the person closest to him handle things herself. But I'm willing to try."

"I don't want you to," she said, staring at her hands.

The words detonated inside him, hurling shrapnel through his heart. He'd tried his best. Now he knew the truth—his best wasn't good enough. She didn't want him.

They said knowing was better than uncertainty. Whoever *they* were, they were wrong.

Luke settled his head against the wrinkled pillow and closed his eyes. It had been a long week—too long. He'd been to Heaven and Hell and back, but nothing had been so hard as what he now faced. Losing Cassie.

Again.

Silent, he let the room's darkness fill him, let it settle into the empty corners of his heart where someday it might block out the memories. When he'd begged Bradley to let him take the case, he hadn't planned on falling in love again. It had just happened. And now…

He'd survived without her, without anyone, the last two years. He could do it again.

Cassie realized the instant Luke's face went blank that he'd misunderstood her. She'd fouled things up already. She swallowed around a lump in her throat, one that tried to expand and cut off her words. "I don't want you to try and change," she explained, stumbling in her rush to set things straight. "It's not you—it's me. I'm the one who's been reckless and stubborn…and stupid. I'm the one who ran away two years ago instead of working things out."

Her admission seemed to have no effect on him. His face still wore a closed, wary expression. "It's my fault you're lying here," she choked out. "If I didn't always insist on being so damned independent, none of this would have happened." Her fingers, working in tandem to her thoughts, plucked at the sheet beneath her. "What I'm trying to say is I've learned my lesson. Finally. And I'm through running." She looked away, pushing herself to finish before she lost courage. "I won't leave you again, unless you ask me to. I love you."

The seconds ticked by in silence, and with each one that passed, her heart shriveled a little more. If she could have cried, she would have, but her tears had dried into a salty lump in her throat.

She'd waited too long to set things right.

Abruptly she slid from the bed, unable to meet the disdain she knew she'd find in Luke's eyes. Halting in front of the window, she forced a composure she was far from feeling. "It's all right, you know," she insisted with only a trace of a quaver in her voice. "I wouldn't want you to stay out of pity." She yanked on the cord, and the curtains slid open. Beyond the window a ghostly, misty gray heralded the approaching dawn. It matched her mood. Dismal.

Then, as she watched, the sky outside changed from charcoal to indigo to a heart-aching Wedgwood blue. In the distance the stark slabs of the Flatirons were tinged with pink, then orange, before finally unveiling their true granite hues.

"Your independence was one of the first things I loved about you."

His quiet statement took her by surprise. Dumbfounded, she turned to search his face.

"I just forgot it for a while." Luke smiled wryly. "I guess the things we love most in another person are often the same things that scare the living daylights out of us." Without warning, he glared at her. "Damn it, woman," he growled. "What good is being in a weakened condition if you're not going to take advantage of me?"

Her jaw dropped.

"Come here," he insisted, impatience edging his words.

Surprise held her immobile. "Why?"

"Because I don't want you to go…"

She took a hesitant step as hope quickened within her.

"Because you're the one thing in life keeping me sane."

Warmth flooded her veins and lifted the corners of her mouth. She took another step.

"Because you make me happy…"

Reaching the bed, she caught the glitter of humor in his gaze. His uninjured arm snaked out, and he captured her wrist.

"And because without you, I'll end my life a bitter old man."

Amused by his histrionics, Cassie grinned. "I don't think I could live with the guilt."

"Could you live with the love?"

Sobered by the serious expression on his face, Cassie held her breath. Was he saying what she thought?

"I'm asking you to marry me…again. I want a second chance."

"For better instead of worse?"

He nodded, and she sat next to him, drawn as much by the promise in his eyes as the fingers on her wrist. She brushed her mouth across his, then kissed his throat. Beneath her lips she felt the familiar cadence of his pulse, strong and steady—and right.

"Yes," she breathed. "I'll marry you."

He must have heard, for his arm slid around her shoulders, snuggling her to his side—where she wanted to be, where she belonged.

Always.

* * * * *

If you enjoyed what you just read,
then we've got an offer you can't resist!

Take 2 bestselling love stories FREE!

Plus get a FREE surprise gift!

MONTANA MAVERICKS
Big Sky Brides

Legendary love comes to Whitehorn, Montana,
once more as beloved authors

Christine Rimmer, Jennifer Greene and Cheryl St.John

present three brand-new stories in this exciting anthology!

Meet the Brennan women:

SUZANNA, DIANA and ISABELLE

Strong-willed beauties who find unexpected
love in these irresistible marriage of
covnenience stories.

Don't miss
MONTANA MAVERICKS: BIG SKY BRIDES
On sale in February 2000,
only from Silhouette Books!

Available at your favorite retail outlet.

™

ENTER FOR A CHANCE TO WIN*

Silhouette's 20th Anniversary Contest

Tell Us Where in the World You Would Like *Your* Love To Come Alive... And We'll Send the Lucky Winner There!

Silhouette wants to take you wherever your happy ending can come true.

Here's how to enter: Tell us, in 100 words or less, where you want to go to make your love come alive!

In addition to the grand prize, there will be 200 runner-up prizes, collector's-edition book sets autographed by one of the Silhouette anniversary authors: **Nora Roberts, Diana Palmer, Linda Howard** or **Annette Broadrick**.

DON'T MISS YOUR CHANCE TO WIN! ENTER NOW! No Purchase Necessary

Silhouette®

Where love comes alive™

Name: _____

Address: _____

City: _____ State/Province: _____

Zip/Postal Code: _____

Mail to Harlequin Books: **In the U.S.:** P.O. Box 9069, Buffalo, NY 14269-9069; **In Canada:** P.O. Box 637, Fort Erie, Ontario, L4A 5X3

*No purchase necessary—for contest details send a self-addressed stamped envelope to: Silhouette's 20th Anniversary Contest, P.O. Box 9069, Buffalo, NY, 14269-9069 (include contest name on self-addressed envelope). Residents of Washington and Vermont may omit postage. Open to Cdn. (excluding Quebec) and U.S. residents who are 18 or over. Void where prohibited. Contest ends August 31, 2000.

PS20CON_R

SILHOUETTE'S 20TH ANNIVERSARY CONTEST
OFFICIAL RULES
NO PURCHASE NECESSARY TO ENTER

1. To enter, follow directions published in the offer to which you are responding. Contest begins 1/1/00 and ends on 8/24/00 (the "Promotion Period"). Method of entry may vary. Mailed entries must be postmarked by 8/24/00, and received by 8/31/00.

2. During the Promotion Period, the Contest may be presented via the Internet. Entry via the Internet may be restricted to residents of certain geographic areas that are disclosed on the Web site. To enter via the Internet, if you are a resident of a geographic area in which Internet entry is permissible, follow the directions displayed on-line, including typing your essay of 100 words or fewer telling us "Where In The World Your Love Will Come Alive." On-line entries must be received by 11:59 p.m. Eastern Standard time on 8/24/00. Limit one e-mail entry per person, household and e-mail address per day, per participant. If you are a resident of a geographic area in which entry via the Internet is permissible, you may, in lieu of submitting an entry on-line, enter by mail, by hand-printing your name, address, telephone number and contest number/name on an 8"x 11" plain piece of paper and telling us in 100 words or fewer "Where In The World Your Love Will Come Alive," and mailing via first-class mail to: Silhouette 20th Anniversary Contest, (in the U.S.) P.O. Box 9069, Buffalo, NY 14269-9069; (In Canada) P.O. Box 637, Fort Erie, Ontario, Canada L2A 5X3. Limit one 8"x 11" mailed entry per person, household and e-mail address per day. On-line and/or 8"x 11" mailed entries received from persons residing in geographic areas in which Internet entry is not permissible will be disqualified. No liability is assumed for lost, late, incomplete, inaccurate, nondelivered or misdirected mail, or misdirected e-mail, for technical, hardware or software failures of any kind, lost or unavailable network connection, or failed, incomplete, garbled or delayed computer transmission or any human error which may occur in the receipt or processing of the entries in the contest.

3. Essays will be judged by a panel of members of the Silhouette editorial and marketing staff based on the following criteria:

   Sincerity (believability, credibility)—50%
   Originality (freshness, creativity)—30%
   Aptness (appropriateness to contest ideas)—20%

   Purchase or acceptance of a product offer does not improve your chances of winning. In the event of a tie, duplicate prizes will be awarded.

4. All entries become the property of Harlequin Enterprises Ltd., and will not be returned. Winner will be determined no later than 10/31/00 and will be notified by mail. Grand Prize winner will be required to sign and return Affidavit of Eligibility within 15 days of receipt of notification. Noncompliance within the time period may result in disqualification and an alternative winner may be selected. All municipal, provincial, federal, state and local laws and regulations apply. Contest open only to residents of the U.S. and Canada who are 18 years of age or older, and is void wherever prohibited by law. Internet entry is restricted solely to residents of those geographical areas in which Internet entry is permissible. Employees of Torstar Corp., their affiliates, agents and members of their immediate families are not eligible. Taxes on the prizes are the sole responsibility of winners. Entry and acceptance of any prize offered constitutes permission to use winner's name, photograph or other likeness for the purposes of advertising, trade and promotion on behalf of Torstar Corp. without further compensation to the winner, unless prohibited by law. Torstar Corp and D.L. Blair, Inc., their parents, affiliates and subsidiaries, are not responsible for errors in printing or electronic presentation of contest or entries. In the event of printing or other errors which may result in unintended prize values or duplication of prizes, all affected contest materials or entries shall be null and void. If for any reason the Internet portion of the contest is not capable of running as planned, including infection by computer virus, bugs, tampering, unauthorized intervention, fraud, technical failures, or any other causes beyond the control of Torstar Corp. which corrupt or affect the administration, secrecy, fairness, integrity or proper conduct of the contest, Torstar Corp. reserves the right, at its sole discretion, to disqualify any individual who tampers with the entry process and to cancel, terminate, modify or suspend the contest or the Internet portion thereof. In the event of a dispute regarding an on-line entry, the entry will be deemed submitted by the authorized holder of the e-mail account submitted at the time of entry. Authorized account holder is defined as the natural person who is assigned to an e-mail address by an Internet access provider, on-line service provider or other organization that is responsible for arranging e-mail address for the domain associated with the submitted e-mail address.

5. Prizes: Grand Prize—a $10,000 vacation to anywhere in the world. Travelers (at least one must be 18 years of age or older) or parent or guardian if one traveler is a minor, must sign and return a Release of Liability prior to departure. Travel must be completed by December 31, 2001, and is subject to space and accommodations availability. Two hundred (200) Second Prizes—a two-book limited edition autographed collector set from one of the Silhouette Anniversary authors: Nora Roberts, Diana Palmer, Linda Howard or Annette Broadrick (value $10.00 each set). All prizes are valued in U.S. dollars.

6. For a list of winners (available after 10/31/00), send a self-addressed, stamped envelope to: Harlequin Silhouette 20th Anniversary Winners, P.O. Box 4200, Blair, NE 68009-4200.

Contest sponsored by Torstar Corp., P.O. Box 9042, Buffalo, NY 14269-9042.

PS20RULES